I0780560

# The
# BAREFOOT
# SERENADE

## M _for_ MELE

### -Book 1-

## BRANDON OSWALD

Publish Authority

Copyright © 2025 by Brandon Oswald

All rights reserved.

No part of this book may be reproduced in any form or by any electronic or mechanical means, including information storage and retrieval systems, without written permission from the author, except for the use of brief quotations in a book review.

Editor: Janie Mills
Cover design lead: Raeghan Rebstock
Interior Design: Teresa Evans

ISBN 978-1-967213–06-1 (Paperback)
ISBN 978-1–967213-07-8 (eBook)

Published 2025 by Publish Authority,
300 Colonial Center Parkway, Suite 100
Roswell, GA, USA
PublishAuthority.com

Printed in the United States of America

*For Devin*

Always remember that you are absolutely unique.
Just like everyone else.

— MARGARET MEAD

1

*This isn't just a room. It's the Stern Auditorium at Carnegie Hall,* Ronin Blue thought while his recently broken nose throbbed. He looked like he had just walked away from a car crash. The nose was broken badly enough that it created a black and blue shiner in his right eye, which looked more gruesomely worse than it felt. The bones in two fingers of his right hand, too, were busted and wrapped tightly in gauze. Blue's side hurt as well, possibly a cracked rib. He wondered if he even deserved to be sitting in such an esteemed auditorium in his condition.

Nevertheless, the room dazzled the senses and heightened one's anticipation. Indeed, the venerable space was reserved for the most special occasions and performances. The place will eventually be packed with people. It's always full of people. It's Carnegie Hall—The Theater of Dreams. Blue smirked. He thought about what the great violinist, Isaac Stern, once said, "Everywhere in the world music enhances a hall, with one exception: Carnegie Hall enhances the music."

Blue loved that idea and repeated it in his mind. If there was one goal he had in life, it was to be known for a quirky, irreverent, or intelligent quote. He believed that all the great people that were living and ever lived thought of great quotes. Blue took a moment and tried to cite something about the hall himself. After a minute or so, he couldn't do it. Nothing clever came to his mind.

*Damn me.*

Blue understood, however, that if he were to produce a profound proverb about the hall, he would have to play and become an important, yet momentary, appendage of the stage. For a brief moment in time, fifteen minutes, or a half hour, or perhaps an hour, the performer has to be indispensable to the hall. The hall has to want to hold you and hug you.

*The hall wants to chew on its performers like a piece of gum; the taste of the great ones lasts the longest.*

Blue shook his head and rolled his eyes.

*That was lame.*

One of the first ones to take his seat, he looked at the closeness of the stage, then looked behind him, and smiled. The Parquet. Row M, Seat 112.

*It's a perfect seat to watch a perfect performance.*

Blue smiled again. It didn't take long for his happy thought to turn a little sour. Now, in his early thirties, he felt like he had nothing to show for it. No career. Not even a job. He wondered if he was even worthy enough to sit in Row M, Seat 112 of the Parquet.

*What the hell is a guy like me doing in a place like this?*

More and more guests began to take their seats, and the place started to reek of perfume and cologne.

A lady in front of Blue approached her seat and took off her small jacket before sitting down. Blue noticed instantly that she was doused in a flowery perfume.

*Oh, crap!*

He felt a sneeze coming on.

*The sneeze is going to hurt like hell. Must hold it in.*

Because of his sore ribs, even a half sneeze would be excruciating to endure. Blue made a muffled, snarling sound and winced. His eyes watered. He tried to wipe the tears with his right hand and remembered that it was also broken and bandaged. He quickly used his left hand to wipe the dripping tears.

*Damn me.*

Blue noticed the lady in front of him turned to look at him. His fat lip quivered, and he thought that he must look like a gargoyle. Nevertheless, he pretended to not notice her and prayed that he wouldn't get a whiff of her perfume again.

Looking up at the ornate ceiling, Blue became dizzied by the blurry circle of lights that seemed to dance and radiate throughout the room. Through his watery eyes, it cast a certain inviting glow, illuminating the four rows of balcony seating and creating this illusion that there is no bad seat in the house. There's also something about sitting in a balcony that's so cool. High off the ground and looking down at people and the stage gives one a certain arrogant feeling that you're floating and observing something from an unusual position.

He smirked and looked back at the stage.

*I'm sitting in the Parquet. Row M, Seat 112.*

He did wish he could relax. But he could never relax during a performance, especially during *her* performance. He wondered again about his placement in the audience.

*How the hell did a guy like me get a seat like this?*

He barely noticed when an elderly couple took their seats to his left. He quickly glanced at them. The couple was dressed to the hilt, and Blue felt a little underdressed in jeans and a long-sleeved, solid color shirt. But he didn't really care. He wasn't there for them. He thought the couple were regulars, probably season ticket holders, and had been coming to Carnegie for the past forty years. They've seen it all. The woman was nose-deep in the program and her husband was already half-asleep in his seat.

Blue turned his attention back to the stage. His left knee started shaking up and down—a nervous twitch he had all his life.

The buzz of more guests taking their seats and anticipating the performance began to rise like bees returning to their hive. This only heightened Blue's reality of what was to come. All of a sudden and out of nowhere, Blue got nervous. The butterflies in his stomach felt like they were gnawing themselves free. He tried to calm himself. It was excitement, not nerves.

*Row M, Seat 112.*

A few orchestra members from the esteemed and well-respected Mannes School of Music Orchestra took their place on stage to get in a last-minute practice before the performance. They were wearing leis of brightly colored flowers. Blue watched them with some fascination. He knew the Perelman Stage was reserved for only the best the prodigies, the protégés, the gifted, and the finest. Tchaikovsky christened it in 1891, and since then the stage had been graced by notable performers such as Mahler, Saint-Saens, Rachmanioff, Prokofiev, Gershwin, Stravinsky, Duke Ellington, Ella Fitzgerald, Louis Armstrong, the Beatles, Bob Dylan, and Isaac Stern, to name a few. The list of non-musical greats speaking on stage was also impressive with the likes of Booker T. Washington, Winston Churchill, Albert Einstein, Ernest Hemingway, Dr. Martin Luther King Jr., and Groucho Marx. *Great people do great things.* The thought of tonight's performer stepping on the stage and adding her name to the long list of distinguished artists and dignitaries made him queasy.

Blue felt that he should use the toilet, but before he got up, the old lady next to him leaned closer and whispered, "I'm sorry, sir, but your barn door is wide open." But it wasn't a whisper. The old lady never whispered anything in her entire life.

Horrified, Blue quickly looked down at his crotch and frantically grabbed it with his bandaged hand and tried to pull the zipper with his good hand. He wasn't nervous anymore.

*Damn me.*

The lady in front turned around and looked at Blue.

Blue struggled to pull his zipper up and had to stop when three young ladies in their late twenties had to scoot by to the seats to his right. They were taking a break from the usual girls night out at a Broadway show, and this time decided to try a different sort of entertainment. They were a little tipsy and each one of them stepped on his feet as they got to their seat. Even when he moved his feet, the ladies' three-inch heels inevitably stomped him.

Blue wasn't sure if they saw his unzipped pants or not.

"A whole lot of cows were getting out of there," the old lady announced.

*What the eff does that even mean?*

Attracted by the old lady's announcement, the young lady sitting on the other side of Blue looked, giggled, and then turned to the others. Laughter among the three of them erupted.

With one last tug of the pants, Blue successfully pulled his zipper up. He sighed and turned to the old lady and reluctantly acknowledged her. "Thanks."

"Ooh, dear, that's a nasty looking shiner you got there," she noticed, forgetting about the zipper.

"Yeah, I know."

"You need a hunk of steak. Go to Schumman's on 86th Street. He's got the best meats in the city."

Blue didn't really want to get into old wives' tales with the old lady... although he had no doubts that Schumman's had the best meats in the city. He just wanted to get up and go to the toilet. Better yet, he wished he had the auditorium to himself. No people, just him and only him in Row M, Seat 112.

But it wouldn't be fair. It wouldn't be fair to *her*.

He wasn't even sure if she wanted him there.

The butterflies had broken free and were now gnawing on Blue's spleen. He didn't know what a spleen was or even its purpose. He smiled at the thought of the quote from the character Ishmael in *Moby Dick* who said, "I thought I would sail about a little and see the watery part of the world. It is a way I have of driving off the spleen, and regulating the circulation." Blue had used this quote before and always wished he had thought of it first.

On stage, the entire orchestra members had now reached their seats and were ready to start the performance. They stopped practicing, adjusted their music on the music stand, and patiently waited for their conductor. However, first, the concertmaster stepped on stage and went to the chair closest to the conductor's stand. The murmur of the crowd, which reached its crescendo ceased, and everyone clapped for the lead of the orchestra.

As the orchestra tuned their instruments to, first the principal oboist, and to the concertmaster, Blue felt that the performance was nigh. The butterflies reached his lungs. He couldn't breathe. The bathroom was calling him. He wanted to leave Row M, Seat 112. He tried to stand but quickly sat back down when the conductor, a tall European man resembling the great Paavo Jarvi, walked out on stage holding the hand of a twelve-year-old Samoan girl in bare feet carrying a violin. "Oohs" and "awls" filled the auditorium as the crowd cheered the arrival of the star performer.

Blue's nerves waned a bit as he became transfixed on the Samoan girl. She wore a purple flower-printed Samoan dress. Her long black hair with a white hibiscus flower behind her right ear and black eyes shined and sparkled under the lights of the stage. She curtsied the crowd, which reciprocated with louder claps and "awls." The Samoan girl smiled with an air of arrogant confidence, just like all the great artists who performed on this stage before her.

The old lady leaned to Blue. "The girl's name is Mele Blue. Ever heard of her?"

"She's my daughter," Blue said, blushing.

The old lady quizzically looked at him, "Adopted?" Blue didn't think the question was rude. He had become used to it over the past twelve years.

"No."

The three young ladies clapped louder, laughed, and one even whistled. Blue can hear their comments about Mele performing in her bare feet. It just doesn't happen on stage, especially in Carnegie Hall. But he's heard it all before during recitals, competitions, and performances. As much as Mele was a Samoan-American, she was an island girl, and she would always remind everyone of this.

Blue could also hear the loud, Caribbean accented voice of Mele's private violin teacher, Donna Ledante, coming from a few rows behind him. He turned and could barely see the top of the head of the five-foot violin mentor with intricately braided hair. Donna was the one who personally picked the plucky Mele from a music competition and brought her to New York. Although Blue never truly got along with Donna, he respected her experience, wisdom, and obstinacy. He knew that she was solely responsible for preparing his daughter, her protégé, for the prestigious Carnegie debut.

The crowd's invigorating support softened to a silence as the conductor raised his arms to ready the orchestra. The lights of auditorium dimmed to darkness. Mele positioned her violin under her chin, eager to hit the first note of Max Bruch's devilishly rich and attractive Violin Concerto No.1 in G Minor, Op.26.

The butterflies settled in Blue's throat. He proudly choked and settled into his seat—Seat 112, Row M. M for Mele.

He couldn't leave now. The bathroom must wait. He studied his daughter on stage.

*She's almost a teenager and looking more like her mother every day.*

Blue wished Mele's mother was there and sitting next to him, but she had stayed in Samoa, and they hadn't seen each other in seven years. He imagined them holding hands while watching their daughter perform her heart out on stage as she always did from the very first day she picked up the violin and bow.

Time seemed to stand still on stage. Blue was transfixed on his daughter and her patience to begin playing. He couldn't help but think of *Island Time. Samoa Time.* Nothing is done in a hurry. In this instant, he realized that his whole life wasn't truly a waste. It wasn't always Samoa Time. His mind wandered down a forest path jumbled with branches and leaves.

Blue then wondered if his daughter could see his shiner in the darkness of the audience. Did it glow from the stage? There are two kinds of people: *Great people do great things. But the non-great people help great people do great things.* His existence wasn't about himself. He was always peeved with himself for constantly trying to justify his life. It was exhausting. But it was about Mele. It was all for Mele. Blue understood this now. *It was to help Mele be great.* He became proud of himself at this notion. This is the Parquet in Carnegie Hall—Seat 112, Row M. M for Mele.

The orchestra played the short opening. Samoa Time

broke. Then Mele shifted her violin under chin, closed her eyes, and passionately played those first notes that have haunted her throughout countless hours of practice. It sounded sublime. Blue wondered if he would even hear a note as he thought about the last twelve years that were all for Mele. He would stare at his daughter's Samoan flower-printed dress and become lost in the *Fa'a Samoa*, the Samoan Way of Life. For the moment, he can hear the distant repetitive rumble of the surf crashing against a reef that sounded like a metronome and invariably became louder, drowning out the melodies of the orchestra and Mele. For the moment, it was Samoa Time.

2

---

onin Blue never had dreams or aspirations of a career. He was, however, a very good musician, especially playing the piano, but never thought that he would make a career out of it. Blue enjoyed all genres of music. When asked what he liked playing the most, he simply said, "I play anything from Bach to Bernstein to Blake to Beatles to Bow Wow Wow to Blink-182." From time to time throughout his later high school days and most of his college years at San Diego State University, he would take piano-playing jobs at various North San Diego County resorts where he performed mostly Broadway and Disney tunes. Blue's downfall at the resorts was that he only showed up for work when he felt like it, much to the chagrin of his employers, thus jobs never seemed to last more than a couple of months. Sometime during his third year in college, he suddenly decided to quit playing the piano altogether.

Blue decided to apply for a two-year volunteer service called Helping Hands Volunteers and left for Samoa shortly after his twenty-first birthday. He had just graduated from college and had never been out of California. He felt that the time was right to see something of the world. His drive to seek worldly adventures was heavily influenced from what he learned in literature classes at San Diego State: Ishmael's quote in *Moby Dick*, "It is a way I have of driving off the spleen, and regulating the circulation," and Pacific Islands' author Robert Dean Frisbie's search for the perfect, secluded island to solely concentrate on writing his masterpiece. Ronin Blue wanted to go to Samoa to write a novel. He never wrote anything in his life before, but he found the notion of creating something strange in a strange land very romantic and *cool*.

The sixteen-hour travel to Samoa throughout the night was uneventful.He tried to watch a movie here and there, but he would inevitably doze off for a short spell and miss important scenes. He finally gave up watching anything all together and popped in his headphones to listen to music. He thought to himself, *we share the same damn ocean—how far is this place?* Blue mostly amused himself by watching how the other passengers created little habitations within their crowded seats to help them better endure the long flight. He thought their small areas looked like a rat's nest strewn with blankets, pillows, clothes, and carry-on luggage.

By the time he landed at the Faleolo International Airport on the main Samoan island of Upolu in Western Samoa he was tired, weary, and hungry. He wasn't sure what to expect next or where to go. As he got through customs, he went straight to get his luggage in the baggage area where a string band awaited visitors. Blue couldn't help but stop and listen to them. He wasn't in a hurry. *Island time*, he thought. He wished he could've pulled up a chair to sit in and fall asleep to the melodious sounds of the guitars and ukuleles. If he knew any Samoan songs, he would've requested one. Blue's bag was the last one spinning on the luggage carousel.

It was a skinny Samoan man in his forties wearing a tank top and a black *lavalava* that approached Blue. The Samoan was holding a sign with the handwritten words, "Helping Hands Volunteers." He held it up to Blue's face and inquired in English, "You Ronin Blue?"

"Yeah, how'd you know?"

"You only *palagi* here."

Blue never heard of the word *"palagi,"* but had an idea that it meant white boy.

"I grab your bag and take you to office. I drive," the Samoan said. Before Blue could react, the driver grabbed Blue's carry-on bag, and speedily went to the carousel to get the volunteer's luggage. It was heavy, and in fact, had a sticker on it that read, "Heavy Baggage." The poor driver struggled to lift and maneuver it, but it was impressive how he managed to carry it to his car and load it as if he had done it a million times before.

On the drive to Apia, the lack of sleep, accompanied by the heat and humidity of the day made Blue drowsy and sweaty. He wanted to have a conversation with the driver, but the driver was already singing Samoa's favorite pop songs on the radio.

The Helping Hands Volunteer office was on the second floor of a colonial building in the middle of Apia. It was a single room, oppressed by the heat, and only cooled by a ceiling fan that wasn't even turned on. By the time Blue entered the office, his shirt was drenched with sweat. An Australian woman in her early thirties enthusiastically greeted him.

"G'day, Ronin. How was your trip?"

"Long," Blue answered, wiping sweat from his forehead. He noticed the woman was wearing a light pink sweater and showed no signs of perspiration while she sat in her chair. What fascinated him the most about her, however, was her hairstyle, which was puffy and curly and resembled a style worn in the eighties. He was compelled to tell her his favorite joke—*the _ is calling and it wants its _ back.*

"Yeah, I bet," she agreed, but quickly moved on. "I'm Lola, and I'm your volunteer representative. I'm the one who'll make sure your time here will be successful."

Blue smiled, and then blurted out, "Hey, the eighties are calling and Madonna wants her hairstyle back!" Blue laughed. The joke was still funny to him.

Lola looked at him quizzically. "Pardon?"

Blue quickly sensed she didn't get the joke. He cleared his throat. "Sorry, I, uh, was just... you know... it was a long flight." He sighed.

Lola smiled, looked at the time on her watch, and quickly moved on, handing Blue a piece of paper.

"Ever been to Samoa before?" Blue shook his head. "Right. You've been assigned to the village of Vaimasina to help school children with their reading. Brilliant. We haven't had a volunteer there in a couple years." She handed Blue a contract that included a few pieces of papers stapled together.

Blue glanced at the contract, and he tried to read it. But it was long and wordy, and the words began to blur.

"The last volunteer went batty," Lola continued. "Miles Coach was his name—from Adelaide. Never forgot him. Shoulda never sent him there."

Blue shot Lola a concerned look.

"What happened?"

"He stripped off all his clothes and ran into the bush. The authorities never found him. Poor fella. Once you get lost in the interior, you'll never find your way out. Insects probably devoured him."

"Good Lord," Blue exclaimed. He signed the contract and handed it back to Lola.

"Brilliant. You're now officially part of the Helping Hands family," Lola said with an air of ownership. "Right. Grab your stuff. We got a bus to catch."

"Now?" Blue was wishfully thinking of crashing on a bed in a hotel room at least for a night.

"Yeah. Come on," Lola beckoned as she stood up from her desk. Blue noticed that she was quite pregnant. Moving quickly to the door, the extra weight wasn't going to slow her down. As she exited the office, she grabbed a tote bag that was hanging on coatrack.

Blue peeled his sweaty back off the chair, sighed, and followed.

The bus station adjacent to the Fugalei market bustled with people either loitering outside a bus or sitting in one and listening to Samoan pop music that blasted from the driver's area. None of the buses seemed to be in a hurry to go anywhere. Nevertheless, the buses were, indeed, colorful and artistically painted with unique colors, pictures, and slogans. No two buses were alike. The rows of picturesque buses looked like something out of a coffee table book about Samoa, and Blue was mesmerized by the myriad of immobile majestic machinery.

"Tourists come from all over the world just to ride a bus in Samoa," Lola proudly said, moving from one bus to the next.

"How do you know which bus is ours?" Blue asked, trying to keep up with her.

"Well, all buses prominently display the name of the destination in the front window. But most people just know by the colors and pictures."

Lola quickly moved to another row of buses. These didn't give the impression that they were going anywhere or anytime soon. Blue tried to keep up with her, but she moved like a cheetah on the hunt in a savanna of buses.

*How does a pregnant woman move so fast in this heat?*

A recent rainstorm created puddles here and there, and he tried his best to keep his rolling luggage out of them.

"Ah, there!" Lola exclaimed, pointing to a black and dark purple bus with a picture of the phases of the moon painted on one side. The other side had the English words, "Sweet Dreams."

Lola swiftly hopped on the bus as if she was late and was eventually followed by Blue. But there was no reason to be in a hurry. The bus driver was eating taro and reading a newspaper. He didn't appear to be ready to go anywhere.

"*Talofa,*" greeted Lola, and handed the driver some change. The driver took it without even looking up.

The bus was quite full as Lola and Blue looked for available seats. The thought of hauling his luggage down a narrow aisle seemed taxing for Blue. Sweat poured down the sides of his head.

Then a young couple got up from their seat and headed towards the back of the bus. Lola pushed Blue to take the seat and made him shuffle next to the window. It was a tight fit. Blue was about five feet ten inches or so tall, and the seat seemed squished to him. Lola sat next to him, and together, the two positioned his luggage as best they could so that it wasn't sticking too far in the aisle.

"Foreigners are usually given a seat up front," Lola said. "It's an unspoken rule among the Samoans."

Blue nodded, but he didn't want to be given any special treatment.

After fifteen minutes had passed, the heat in the crowded bus became intolerable for Blue even with most of the windows down. It felt like sitting in a sardine can.

"When do we go?" asked Blue wiping the sweat off his face with the bottom of his shirt.

"I'm afraid there are no timetables," Lola answered with a tone of defeat. "We go when the driver's ready to go." She then reached into her tote bag, pulled out a small towel, and handed it to Blue. "For your sweats."

"Uh... thanks." Blue wiped the sweat off his face, but it didn't take long for the watery beads to reappear and dot his forehead. He thought that his long, brown and curly hair that almost reached his shoulders was, perhaps, not suited for this kind of climate. He wondered if anyone would be disgusted if he were to put his hair in a ponytail like a girl.

At last, as a few more people jumped on the bus, the driver turned on the ignition. Blue got excited and anticipated a breeze smashing against his sweaty, hot face.

It didn't take long for Blue to become drowsy as the bus made its way outside Apia and along the Samoan road with an azure ocean to the left and a dense verdant jungle to the right.

"It'll take about an hour to get to Vaimasina," Lola said.

She thought that this was the right time to hand Blue some more paperwork explaining what to expect while living in a village. She started to speak about the "*dos* and *don'ts*" while interacting with Samoan villagers.

Blue tried hard to listen to her. He didn't want to be rude by nodding off mid-sentence. However, he wished she would just let him sleep. But the warm breeze on his face and the hum of the bus was too much to overcome.

He fell asleep instantly and dreamt of colorful buses flying on a warm current of air and dancing around thunderhead clouds to a reggae beat of the John Denver song, "Sunshine." Feeling groovy, he then leaned to his left to kiss his girlfriend, or fiancé, Harper, who he left unceremoniously behind in San Diego.

But a kiss is a kiss—live or in a dream. Blue hadn't kissed many girls in life thus far, so it felt good to him. It always felt good.

He kissed Harper hard on the lips. He could feel the sweat trickling down both sides of his face and colliding under his chin. Even as he dreamt, Blue began to feel uncomfortable about exhibiting this kind of affection in front of the audience on the bus.

The music pulsated. The sweat poured. The eyes burned. People stared.

Harper bit his lip, which bled.

When Blue woke up, the last image of his dream was

Harper sucking the blood from his lip like a vampire. Groggily, he looked out the window and noticed that the bus was stopped. He turned to Lola, but she wasn't in the seat. She was gone. His large luggage was simply sitting in the aisle of the bus, and even the bus driver was missing. Blue then looked behind him and saw that at least half of the bus was empty of people.

He stuck his head out of the window of the bus to see if Lola or the bus driver was close. He didn't see anyone. The bus was parked on the side of the road resting against the forest. The wind pushed a leaf of a banana plant into his face, which he swatted away as if it were a fly.

And that's when he saw them.

Tucked in the jungle and wearing white Samoan *puletasi* dresses, were six or seven young females aged twenty to forty. The tropical foliage covered their heads and faces. He thought they were waiting to get on the bus, but they didn't move. They just stood there about five feet apart from each other.

"Hello?" Blue called out. He felt like a moron for using English, but he didn't know any Samoan words yet. The females didn't answer. They only stood there like white Polynesian statues. The wind pushed the foliage around the females, teasing Blue that at least one face would be revealed. He leaned further out of the window.

Blue was just about to call out again when Lola returned and plopped herself down on the seat next to him. He straightened himself in the seat.

"Whew. Nature called," she said, trying to get comfortable in the seat. "I think my little stinka's sitting on my bladder. I always have to pee like a puppy."

Blue smirked. He had spent many hours in the bathroom for one reason or another in his short life. In fact, he felt that most of the flight across the Pacific Ocean was spent in the bathroom.

*Did she just use the bush?*

He remembered the odd females and quickly looked back out of the window. They were gone. He leaned out further and saw nobody. They were simply gone as if the jungle consumed them. He then turned to look at the door of the bus, anticipating that the females would board. Only the driver entered, sat in his seat, and revved the engine. The door closed and the bus moved on down the road.

*Damn me.*

Blue leaned back in his seat listening to a strange, Pacific version of the Bob Marley song, "Three Little Birds."

"We're only about twenty minutes from the village," Lola said and then quickly changed the subject. "You were really sawin' logs. I hope you dreamt of something nice."

Blue looked at her and wondered if he wasn't still dreaming.

3

<hr>

When the bus made its final stop on a dirt road in front of the church of Vaimasina, a half of dozen people disembarked into what seemed to Blue to be a sleepy village. Lola and Blue were the last ones off the bus and started to make their way across a long grassy field towards a large traditional *fale tele,* or the chief's meeting house that was also used for special occasions. Instantly, the two were struck with the smell of food cooking in an *umu,* or underground oven.

Once again, Blue struggled to keep up with Lola. The uneven terrain made it difficult for him to roll his luggage. Eventually, he had to give up the ease that the wheels were meant to create and carry the heavy bag, which slowed him down even more under the oppressive, late afternoon sun.

After a few yards, the out-of-shape volunteer had to stop and take a rest.

To Blue, the village seemed to be devoid of people except

for a group of boys playing rugby on the field, and a group of girls sitting together in a circle eating papaya and playing a board game. At times the rugby players' game would lead them through the girls' circle, which ended with the girls throwing papaya at the boys as they ran by. This amused Blue. But what really intrigued him most of all was the fact that none of the children were wearing any shoes. He wished that he could go sockless and shoeless and let the air cool the spaces between his *piggies*.

"Here—wrap yourself in this," Lola demanded, breaking Blue's breezy daydream. She then pulled out a black *lavalava* from her tote bag and handed it to him. Blue took the wrap but had no idea how to fix it to his waist.

"I've no clue," he said defeated.

"Like this," Lola instructed and showed him how she fixed hers around her own waist. "See?"

Blue tried again, but it was futile.

Impatiently, Lola took the *lavalava* from him and began to place it around his waist.

Blue became a little embarrassed, especially when the rugby players nearby stopped playing and laughed at the couple, who looked to be in a compromising position. Their amusement, however, was short-lived after one of the boys got hit in the head by the ball and the game resumed.

As Lola fussed with tying the *lavalava* around Blue's waist, Blue got a chance to purview the village. The Samoan lush forest and the interior of the island were to his left. A giant mango tree towered over the bush at one end, and a large banyan tree was at the other end. A couple of trails led into the forest towards a tall hill. Between the fringe of the bush and the hill was a moon-shaped freshwater pool fed by a stream that came from the hill, which he couldn't see at the moment. The pool was the source of the village's name. Blue tried to look over the fringe of the bush and got the impression that beyond the hill, one would easily get lost in an endless series of valleys and mountains.

To Blue's right was the village, which consisted of square Western-style buildings in different colors with tin roofs and oval traditional *fales* with either tin or thatched roofs. They were scattered throughout in no conformity. Giant birds of paradise plants, banana plants, pandanus plants and coconut trees danced around the structures in the wind. Roosters, chickens, dogs, and *veavao* birds roamed aimlessly from building to building looking for a bite to eat or to rest in a shady, cool spot. A couple of dirt paths led down to the beach, and Blue could see the waves smashing against the reef. The blues of the lagoon within the reef changed colors from dark to light depending on the whims of the clouds playing hide-and-seek with the sun.

"The blue is arrogant," said Blue, marveling at the inviting lagoon. "Somerset Mom, or Mag-ham," he added. "I don't know how to say his name. I've never heard it. I've only read it."

"There," Lola answered after finishing wrapping the *sulu* around his waist. "Now I got to pee."

Lola continued her journey towards the *fale tele*, pulling out a flowery printed *lavalava* from her tote bag and wrapping it around her waist. Blue followed, wondering what else she had in her bag.

Then with a pep in his step, a tall, muscular young

Samoan man, about twenty years of age, quickly approached the two. He was wearing shorts and a Kobe Bryant LA Lakers basketball jersey. His right arm from his neck to just below his elbow was tattooed with a very intricate Samoan design. Smaller tattoo patterns could also be found on the back of his neck, and on his left leg.

"*Talofa*! I'm Togi!" he yelled exuberantly.

Togi came upon the two and shook Lola's hand first. "*Talofa*, I'm Togi," he repeated. He then turned to Blue and took his hand. "Hi-ya, I'm Togi."

"He's Togi," Blue sarcastically stated to Lola.

"So, I've heard," she answered.

Togi grabbed Blue's luggage and swung the large, heavy bag upon his shoulder as if it was a stalk of bananas. "You American? I love America. I want to go there. Meet Keanu Reeves," Togi genuinely said and smiled.

"Don't we all," Blue responded.

Togi then spoke Samoan to Lola, gesticulating and pointing with one hand. His enthusiasm was infectious. Blue watched the two converse and tried to understand, even pretended to understand what they were discussing. Togi laughed. He was one of those people who one likes instantly.

Lola turned to Blue. "Just as I suspected," she said. "Everyone's waiting for you in the *fale tele*. They want to honor your arrival."

"I take bags to your *fale*," Togi said. "I take you fishing later. Bonito. Good bonito."

Blue watched Togi gallop off towards the village buildings. The weight of the bags didn't faze him. In fact, he even stopped to talk to another villager without placing the bags on the ground.

Lola stopped Blue just short of the *paepae* of the *fale tele*.

"Did you bring a gift?" Lola asked.

"A what?"

"A gift. To give to the *Ali'i*."

"The who?"

Without questioning Blue any further, she reached into her tote bag and pulled out a woven mat rolled up and tied with a string. Blue watched in amazement, wondering again what else she had in her bag.

*She's like Felix the Cat.*

Blue and Lola went up the steps of the *paepae* and into the *fale tele*. Most of the village was inside sitting on the ground waiting for the two, and as they entered, all heads turned to look at them. Immediately, Blue felt intimidated. The sight of everyone's eyes seemed to expel an incantation towards him. A drumbeat was made by a couple of drummers. Blue froze like a wooden tiki. Lola had to reach back, grab him by the hand, and lead him to a mat that was placed specially for the two. Blue was relieved when they sat down. The late afternoon breeze disappeared, and the heat intensified within the *fale*. Blue folded his sweaty legs, knowing that when the time came to stand up again, they would stick together. The thought of having sticky legs made him grimace.

Two little girls holding *'ulas* made of flowers apprehensively approached Blue and Lola. The girls placed flower necklaces around each of their necks and smiled.

"*Faafetai*," Lola said, adjusting her lei.

Blue nodded his head at the girls, but the scent of the

flowers made him instantly sneeze. The girls laughed and skipped away.

As more villagers made their way into the *fale tele*, Blue noticed six distinguished adults sitting in the middle. Three of them were leaning against poles. They seemed regal, stoic, like royalty. None of them even looked in the direction of Blue and Lola. They sat perfectly still, looking forward, and waited patiently for the latecomers to take a seat.

"They look serious," Blue whispered while elbowing Lola.

"They're the *matai* of the village. Chiefs," Lola shared. "This village is unique because they have a female *matai*, Fiame Lafau. Very rare. But she's awesome."

Before Lola finished her sentence, Fiame looked at Blue and studied him. Her glasses fell to the bottom of her nose to get a better look at the volunteer. Fiame was the youngest *matai* of the group. In her early forties, she had risen steadily to this prominent position in this patriarchal society. She didn't smile or acknowledge Blue in any way.

Blue saw that Fiame was staring at him and became nervous. His legs fidgeted, and he wondered if he was sitting correctly.

Blue would later learn that the *matai* were, indeed, part of a complex hierarchal system known as the *'fa'a Matai*. They were the leaders of their extended family, or *aiga*, and their titles were connected to certain districts, villages and plots of family land. The *matai* were responsible for administrative duties, maintaining traditions and customs of the village, and were the spiritual caretakers of all those who fell under their authority. The three leaders leaning against poles were a special *matai* known as the *Ali'i*, who were generally the decision makers and were responsible for the most important aspects of Samoan culture within the village. The three leaders not sitting against a pole were a second type of *matai* called the *Tulafale*, or talking chiefs. They were skilled orators and mostly keen on keeping the many oral traditions and duties within the *Fa'a Samoa* of the village.

Lola leaned into Blue and said, "The big man in the middle with the *tuiga* on his head is Chief Joseph Tuputala. He's like the top *Ali'i*. He's been around forever."

Blue looked at Joseph and thought he was *the sprinkles on top of the donut...* he then quickly thought about what he had just thought, and it didn't make sense to him. Joseph was anything but sprinkles. The main chief was in his early eighties, yet he had very few gray hairs in his silky black head of hair. The man was truly ageless. He had seen it all and had lived it all. He even fought the Japanese in World War II.

The village respected and adored Joseph. His legs were as thick as tree trunks, and his arms were large enough to wrestle a grizzly bear. Joseph was immense, impressive, and his overall disposition gave off an ice-cold feeling even within the steamy tropics. Blue would eventually love hearing the stories about how Joseph drowned a twelve-foot shark, made love to a siren, caught and cooked a sea serpent, and repelled a curse from a sorcerer in Papua New Guinea. He was a man of few words, but when he did talk, everyone listened. Joseph was the stuff of legends. Whenever someone asked him if the stories were true, he would smile and simply say, "It is spoken."

When one of the *Tulafale* began a chant, it marked the

beginning of the ceremony. Everyone took their seat on the ground, and there would be no more latecomers allowed in the *fale tele*. The chant then turned to story. The *Tulafale* told the story of how the village of Vaimasina began and grew over the centuries, how the people had always lived in harmony, and how privileged they were that God had sent them another volunteer to help their community grow. It was a long, perfunctory performance. One could easily tell that this particular *Tulafale* has told the story a million times without much change. Blue would have fallen asleep if wasn't for the swarm of flies that fiercely descended upon him, forcing him to swat at them every two seconds.

The sound of the slit drums that marked the end of the speech was a welcome sound to Blue. He tried to slap a fly on his leg and missed. Lola grabbed his arm, signifying that she would like him to stop making a commotion.

Next, a group of villagers consisting of five women and three men within the ages of late teens to early thirties quickly entered the *fale*. The males were wearing yellow *lavalavas,* and *'ulas* made of shell hung down their bare chests. The women were dressed in purple *puletasis,* and large yellow flowers were attached to their hair behind their right ears.

As the group sat down and crossed their legs, the crowd in the *fale* began to cheer. In this community of around 275 people, performers were always met with genuine affection and enthusiasm. Even the boys playing rugby had to stop their game and rush over to the *fale* to watch the performance.

The drummers changed the rhythm and at times added a chant.

The group began a dance in a seated position known as the *sasa*. Their hand movements energetically reflected the chants that were about activities from their daily life such as climbing coconut trees, paddling a canoe, and making food. The clapping and smacking of the ground with their hands in between arm movements only heightened the dance. At times, they would gracefully change sitting positions by shifting or rolling their body to show a different daily activity.

Blue was enthralled by the performance. He had never seen anything like it. The sitting dance made him forget about the pesky flies. As Blue watched the dancers, he was particularly smitten by a young female performer in the front. He would later learn that her name was Aumua and that she was the youngest child of Chief Joseph.

Aumua wasn't the stereotypical beautiful, helpless South Seas Polynesian girl that attracted white Europeans found in books. On the contrary, even at the age of seventeen, she was more independent and confident. Although she was big boned, she was not fat. Her delightful disposition displayed a certain coyness charm, much like that of a Southern belle in the southeastern part of the United States. Blue also recognized how athletic her movements were. He admired this trait most of all because it was the complete opposite of him. He never felt that he was much of a sporty person. Nevertheless, perhaps it was Aumua's smile and sincere love to perform that instantly attracted him.

Aumua's best friend of the same age and height, Maeva, was next to her. The two had been inseparable since birth, and most visitors often believed that the two were sisters.

They had grown up learning all the traditional dances, songs, and customs together. They also never missed an opportunity to pull out a karaoke machine to sing all the latest hits from Taylor Swift and Katy Perry. Although the two were closing in on the end of their secondary school years, they hoped to remain friends despite the different paths that would most likely force them apart during their young adult years.

The group stood and eventually ended the *sasa* on their feet. The crowd cheered.

Blue, who was taught from an early age by his mother to be a passionate and devoted patron of the arts, got up on his knees and clapped and cheered the loudest. Named after the Shakespearean character, Juliet, Blue's mother followed in her father's footsteps and became an actress. She worked at a plethora of theaters and playhouses from Los Angeles to San Diego. She had a wide range of acting disciplines and could easily work shows that were dramas, comedies, and even had a wonderful voice to star in musicals. She was a versatile actress and always jumped from one job to the next.

In her midthirties, Juliet was performing in a production of Anton Chekhov's, "Uncle Vanya," at a San Diego theater. She became infatuated with a charming visiting director from New York. The two hit it off during rehearsals, and during the six-week run of the play, her crush evolved into a quick and rash affair with the dashing director. It was an impassioned, yet frivolous few months, which she mostly spent with her lover in a downtown San Diego hotel. Eventually, the play came to an end, and with it, so did the relationship between them, as the director returned to New

York. He didn't even bother to ask her to come to New York with him, which was just as well for her since it didn't feel right to leave, as well as she truly believed that it wasn't her destiny. Besides, the dynamic director could recite Shakespeare, Eugene O'Neill, and Tom Stoppard, but he couldn't sing a note from "West Side Story" or "Les Misérables" which turned her off. Thus, the two amicably split. Juliet often wondered how many other actresses he charmed and seduced across the country while in the position as a visiting director.

A month or so later, Juliet would find out that the director had left a surprise inside of her, which she reasoned wasn't really a surprise at all after the short and sizzling affair they had. She would never speak to the fashionable director for the rest of her life. In fact, as far as she knew until the day she died, the director had no idea that he was the father of her child. Juliet also wondered how many other surprises he left inside actresses across the country.

Juliet welcomed baby Blue into the family. Only she and her sister, Ophelia, knew who the father was. When Blue was older and started wondering who his father was, Juliet wouldn't share much information except that Blue's father was a traveling thespian. She wouldn't even divulge his name except that he was the visiting director. It would be years later, after the death of his mother that Ophelia would tell Blue about the affair at that theater between his mother and the director. And like her sister, Ophelia never revealed to Blue his father's name, pretending that she couldn't remember it and also simply referred to him as the visiting director.

On those occasions when Juliet wasn't working, she

never wasted the opportunity to take her little Ronin to the movies, children's theater, story time at the library, concerts in the park, international dancing festivals, and the circus. When Blue was six years old, Juliet tried to get him started in children's theater, hoping that he would carry on the acting lineage of the family, but he was too shy and didn't like to participate. This disappointed her greatly, and every week she would try to take him back to the theater, hoping that the new week would be better than the previous one and that he would come to enjoy it. He didn't and withdrew deeper and deeper from socializing. Fortunately, Juliet noticed when he showed a proclivity towards music by banging away at the ivory keys of the family piano and quickly got him lessons. She was relieved when he stuck with it year after year.

When Blue was in the ninth grade, Juliet suddenly passed away from a short and intense bout with cancer. It took some time before he could attend another movie or live performance. But when he did, he always thought of his mother. Even here in Samoa, eight years later, he wondered what his mother would've thought of the group performing a *sasa*. He had no doubt in his mind that she would've have loved it.

As the dancers exited the *fale tele*, a new group of villagers made their way to the forefront and positioned themselves within the circular seating pattern. This group was part of the *'ava* ceremony. Blue had seen his fair share of speeches and international dances, but the making, distribution and drinking of *'ava*, or kava as it known throughout the rest of the Pacific, was quite foreign to him. The drink was made by mixing dried roots of a kava plant

(*Piper mythesticum*) and water, and then strained for drinking.Blue watched them with amazement while a million questions went through his mind.

"They're making the *'ava* now," Lola said, leaning into Blue.

"What's that?"

"It's muddy water with a hint of peppermint. You'll love it," Lola snorted. "Just be grateful that it isn't as strong as the Vanuatu kind."

Blue watched the *'aumaga,* or makers, sit behind a large wooden bowl called the *tanoa.* Another *Tulafale* began speaking in Samoan. Not that this mattered to Blue who was too engrossed at watching the event unfold in front of him. The *palu'ava* was seated right behind the bowl. His job was to mix the pepper root and the water, and to his right was the *sui'ava,* whose job it was to pour the water into the bowl. Behind them was the *tāfau,* who caught the strainer that was tossed over the *palu'ava's* right shoulder. The *tāfau* then shakes out the excess root fiber and tosses it back to the *palu'ava's* waiting hand.

Once the *'ava* was made, a *tufa'ava,* or distributor, began calling out names in the order of those who would be served with the beverage. The *matais* of the village would naturally be served first. Then, a half shell of a ripe coconut was used as a cup and dipped into the swampy water of the bowl. It was then passed to Chief Joseph whose name was called first, and he downed the shell with one big gulp. Then, Fiame's name was announced second.

"Wait. We have to drink it?" Blue anxiously asked Lola.

"Of course," she answered with a bit of a supercilious tone.

Blue felt the air within the *fale* stagnate again. The temperature rose. The flies buzzed all around him.

Blue was a frail child. When he was a baby, he had jaundice and colic. As he got a little older, he often suffered from sore throats and fevers. Of course, it didn't help that his mother mollycoddled him. Being asthmatic was the hardest on him. If his mother didn't nix a physical activity, she certainly reduced the time he was allowed to enjoy it. He was often embarrassed whenever he got caught into an uncontrollable coughing bout. His classmates said he wheezed like a dog toy. If he went swimming, he would inevitably get an earache. If he swung upside down on a jungle gym, he would get a nosebleed. He had it all: from sties in the eyes to crummy in the tummy. Blue was a picky eater and drinker. He had to be. His body would easily reject any unwanted substance through one or more orifices of his anatomy.

Lola's name was called next, and a coconut shell was first washed in a bucket of water, and second, dipped in the *tanoa*, and brought to Lola. Blue was taught to be germ phobic and grimaced a little at the sight of her downing the 'ava in one long swig. As she handed the shell back to the server, she wiped her mouth with the back of her hand.

"Mr. Ronin Blue," the *tufa'ava* announced.

A shell came to Blue and he looked at the earthy water apprehensively. Everyone in the *fale* was waiting for him. Lola nudged him with her elbow. Blue brought the edge of the shell up to his mouth. He could already feel his lips turning numb. Perspiration poured down the sides of his face. He could feel one teardrop of sweat slowly trail down the center of his back like a raindrop rolling down a car window.

"Go on, mate," whispered Lola.

It took Blue longer than the others to gulp down the murky beverage. He closed his eyes the entire time. It tasted like it looked. When he finished, he gagged, and then coughed. Some of the audience laughed.

"Good on ya," Lola proudly said, patting his back.

It wasn't long before the *tufa'ava* called out Blue's name again and a second shell came his way. He brazenly drank it a little quicker, and his tongue and lips were numb. He became a little woozy.

By the time the third coconut shell reached Blue, he could feel his stomach begin to grumble. He gulped the shell quickly and knew instantly he was going to pay for this bravery.

Short bursts of pain shot up from his stomach to his throat and down to his anus. A waterfall of sweat cascaded down his back. He positioned himself on his knees.

"I... I don't feel so good."

Lola looked at him and tried to sit him down.

"We're almost done. Then we feast," she said.

"I don't think I can... I can eat. The place's... spinning."

Blue gagged and stood up. Everyone's eyes turned to him. He gagged again and held his mouth. His eyes began to water. The flies, sensing his discomfort, relentlessly taunted him.

Blue couldn't stand it. His stomach was going to explode. He hurriedly wobbled through the *fale* like a drunken sailor in a bar, knocking into people on his way out. Once outside, he fell to the grass and vomited.

Lola caught up to him as Blue vomited again.

"Are you alright?" she asked.

Blue heard the question and had a million snarky and sarcastic comments for her, but he let the latest retch answer for him.

Dozens of people were leaning out of the *fale* watching the event. It was Togi who pushed people aside and leapt onto the ground to Blue's aid.

"Togi will help you, bro," Togi said with confidence.

Blue retched again and again.

"Sorry for... for ruining the... the party," Blue apologetically said.

"No worries, bro. Togi will help."

Togi then helped Blue to his feet. But Blue could barely stand. He keeled over and retched again.

Togi then picked Blue up and carried him like a husband carries a bride over their first threshold beyond the *fale tele*, down a dirt road, and to a small *fale* with a tin roof painted green. The *fale* was surrounded by a couple of large bird of paradise plants and a fat panadanus tree. Togi laid Blue down on a mat on the floor and closed some of the blinds. He then sat down next to Blue and crossed his legs.

Moments later, Lola and a middle-aged (but looked much older) village woman named Taatiti, carrying food wrapped in a banana leaf and a coconut shell, entered the *fale*.

"Ronin, are you doing alright?" asked Lola.

Blue rolled onto side and moaned.

"My stomach's on fire." Blue retched again. The village woman placed the shell next to his face. "Oh God, no." He rolled on his other side away from the shell.

"It's not *'ava*. It's medicinal. It'll help your stomach," Lola explained.

"Nooo," Blue answered.

"Taatiti will fix you up, bro. She heals everyone's injuries with her mixes," Togi interjected.

Taatiti placed the shell in front of Blue's face and said a quick chant in Samoan. "Drink. Drink," Taatiti said in English. Blue turned his head away, but she calmly placed a hand on Blue's neck and held the shell to his lips. "It's okay. Drink."

Blue reluctantly drank the liquid from the shell. When he finished, Taatiti helped him lie down on his back. His pain began to wane, and his moaning became less frequent.

"All good," Taatiti said with a smile, stroking Blue's head.

After a few minutes, Blue's body calmed. Everything was at peace. He fell asleep, but his own snoring abruptly woke him.

"Uh, Ronin. I'm gonna leave this paperwork with you," Lola said while digging into her tote bag. "I'm gonna go, and then head back to Apia." She placed the packet near his head. "You'll feel better in the mornin'."

Blue raised his thumb up. Lola leaned into him to get closer to his ear.

"Just don't turn native. It'll kill you just like it killed Miles," she whispered.

Blue's eyes opened wide. Before he could say anything, Lola stood up.

"I'll check on you in a few months," Lola continued. "I know you'll do a great job here and will make us all proud at Helping Hands. But, if you need anything, just call me, okay?

Well, gotta pee!" And with that she left the *fale* in a hurry without saying goodbye to the others.

Taatiti patted the top of Blue's head and pulled down the mosquito net over him. The last image that Blue saw that day was the smile and the black teeth of Taatiti. His favorite joke came to mind: *Some witches just called, and they want their teeth back.* Blue smirked and then fell asleep.

4

Perhaps it was the sound of a heavy rain that was like a million nails hammering upon the tin roof that awoke Blue. He groggily lifted himself from the mat into a sitting position and wiped the sleep from his eyes. Although he was parched, the sound of the rain helped him to mentally quench his thirst for the moment. However, through the mosquito net he saw a bottle of water and a large banana leaf that was folded over, the flies flickering around frustrated that they couldn't free the contents of the leaf.

Blue reached out from the net and quickly grabbed the bottle of water. He downed it in a gulp, then pulled the banana leaf inside the net to open it in peace from the flies. The content of the leaf was quite modest and consisted of a piece of cooked chicken, fish, taro, papaya, and a banana. He wondered if the food was from the celebration—his celebration from yesterday. But he only wondered for a second; sometimes hunger doesn't care where food comes from.

As he ate, Blue tried to look around his small *fale* through the mosquito net. Besides his mat, mosquito net, and luggage, the space only had one piece of furniture. It was a nightstand with a lamp on it. The electric cord of the lamp simply dangled uselessly in a place without electricity. Blue squinted his eyes, looking for a spot to plug in the lamp.

Lightning snapped and was followed by a burst of thunder. The rain lost its mind and carelessly smashed to earth.

Togi then crashed into the *fale* dripping wet and approached Blue. He raised the mosquito net, exposing Blue smacking on the piece of chicken.

"Bro, you late for school," Togi said wiping his wet forehead.

"What day is it?" Blue asked.

Togi shrugged his shoulders. "I don't know. Tuesday?"

"How long have I been sleeping?"

"A couple of days, I think."

Blue spat out the chicken that was in his mouth. "Days?!"

*Shit.*

"No worries. I watch you when you sleep. You dream heavy," Togi said.

Blue stumbled towards his luggage, opened the large suitcase, and pulled out a new shirt. He then quickly pulled off the shirt he was wearing and replaced it.

Togi continued. "You kick like a daydreaming dog, and you get stiffy."

Blue was digging into his suitcase looking for sandals when the word, "stiffy," made him stop and look at Togi.

"What?" Blue asked.

"You get stiffy," Togi said with a chuckle. "See? Your zipper down."

Blue looked down at the crotch of his pants, and quickly zipped his pants.

*Damn me.*

"You must have lots of ladies in dreams, Mr. Ronin," Togi said. "But we find you real women who like stiffy, no?"

Blue didn't answer. He found his sandals and slipped his feet into them. He then quickly picked up his backpack, grabbed some food, and stuffed it in the front pocket before he left the *fale* into the pouring rain. After about five yards, he stopped and turned to Togi.

"Togi, where's the school?"

"Behind church," Togi answered.

Blue looked around, not knowing which direction the church was. He raised his arms to Togi as if asking, *help, which way?*

"Go up the road a bit. Pass the *fale tele.* Can't miss it, bro."

Togi watched Blue disappear behind a curtain of rain. He then sat on the mat and wrestled the rest of the remaining food away from the flies and ate it.

Blue tried to quickly make his way up the road, but the driving rain and wind hugged him and held his progress. Water and mud engulfed his sandals and oozed through his toes. He rarely wore sandals back home, and each step he took created a squishy feeling that he wasn't used to. He cringed when mud squirted out from the side of his sandals.

*At least the flies aren't bugging me.*

It wasn't long before he passed a large *fale* that was attached to a Western-style house. Some of the blinds were pulled up, and he glanced in and noticed several mats, mattresses, mosquito nets, and small furnishings. Blue didn't want anyone from the *fale* to see him walking in the rain like a dumb tourist and turned his concentration on continuing up the road to the school.

"*palagi,*" a booming voice from the *fale* called out.

Blue stopped. He thought he heard something, but it was hard to tell from the loud sound that the rain made hitting the tin roofs in the area.

"*palagi,*" the voice said again.

Blue squinted his eyes towards the *fale* and tried to adjust his sight to see who was in the darkness of the house.

"Come to me," the voice said again.

Blue walked closer to the *fale* and stopped at the *paepae*. From the shadow, Chief Joseph leaned forward.

"Come," the *matai* commanded.

Blue went up the steps and entered the *fale*. Although it was nice to escape the grip of the rain, he knew he was late and really wanted to get to the school.

Joseph was sitting on a mat and having his breakfast. A mound of food was piled in front of him, which to Blue seemed only fitting for the leader of the village. The man mountain ate a whole banana in one bite and tossed the peel on another mound of inedible discards.

"*Le malaga faiaga e timula,*" said Joseph.

Blue looked at him quizzically, not sure how to respond.

"You have to learn Samoan, my friend," Joseph stated. "It means 'the delayed journey is rained upon.'"

"I'm more than delayed. I'm late," Blue rebutted.

"Hmmm," the chief grunted with a quick smile.

Blue watched the big man eat a square loaf of *fa'apapa*. He then licked his fingers one by one after he finished the bread. Blue had always been a tidy eater who used napkins, and the sight of someone licking his fingers had always made him turn away with a bit of disgust. However, he didn't turn away from the chief who sucked on his fingers as if they were sausages.

"What is your name? Joseph asked.

"Ronin. Ronin Blue."

"Blue. From California," Joseph vaguely remembered what someone else told him about the volunteer.

"Yeah. San Diego County."

"San Diego. Hmm. We share the same *moana*."

"Uh, yeah. Our ocean's cold though."

"Hmm." A slight, awkward pause ensued. "But you use the ocean nonetheless."

"I don't go in the water."

"Fish?"

"No. I don't go on the water either."

"Hmm."

Joseph Tuputala came from a long line of *Ali'is*. His father, grandfather, and great-grandfather all served as *matais* of the village. In his youth, Joseph had no interest in becoming a *matai*. He mostly enjoyed looking for trouble, chasing girls, and having fun in Apia with his best friend and older brother. He never thought that he would ever be mature enough to handle such responsibilities and always believed that his older brother showed more proclivities in leadership. But it all changed after the war, and he was thrust into continuing the lineage and became the biggest advocate of ensuring that the village of Vaimasina continued to thrive and prosper. He would have two wives and eight children—Togi and Aumua being the two youngest. Although most of his children had left for bigger opportunities in Apia, New Zealand, or the USA, he knew it was his duty to serve the village until his death.

"What is it you do? he asked Blue directly.

"I'm... well... I'm writing a book," Blue answered with uncertainty.

"Here. What do you do here?"

"Oh, here. I... uh... teaching school kids to read."

With his black eyes, Joseph examined Blue, perhaps piercing the cognitive and physical aspects of his guest and wondering if there was more he could do.

"What's your story about?" Joseph asked, not sure if he should really care to know.

"It's about forsaken lovers who unexpectedly meet amid a disaster," Blue proudly answered. He'd practiced answering the question before.

"Like *Titanic*," Joseph said.

*Damn me!*

Blue has heard this critique before. He heard from his girlfriend, or fiancé, Harper, and then again from an airline passenger who was sitting next to him on the journey to Samoa and asked what he was writing.

"No. It's partially on a boat," Blue defended himself. "It has..."

Joseph interrupted him by looking towards the house behind the *fale* and shouting in Samoan. It was more than a call; it was a command. Blue thought that this was a good time to take advantage of the slight pause and move on to the school.

"I guess I should let you finish your breakfast," Blue said, backing up to the exit.

"I learned English from American G.I.s during the war," Joseph commented without a care in the world if Blue was late or not. "Swear words first." The chief let out a snort.

"You speak it pretty well."

"It was either English or Japanese. I liked the Americans better."

*If the man wants to learn English, who the hell's gonna stand in his way*, Blue thought.

Despite speaking to the most influential and venerable man of the village, Blue was getting antsy. He really wanted to leave, but he also didn't want to be rude, especially to the *matai*. Aumua and her older sister, Lupesina, then hurriedly entered with a plate of taro and a jug of lemon water. They placed it in front of Joseph. Blue got the feeling that the two attended to their father's needs throughout the entire day.

Joseph then made an order in Samoan to Lupesina, and she quickly returned to the house. Aumua straightened herself and smiled at Blue. He instantly lost all track of time.

"You danced really well," Blue complimented her.

She smiled and bowed. "Th-thank you."

"What kind of dance was that?"

Aumua looked at her father and asked him a question in Samoan. The chief shrugged his shoulders and answered her after eating some taro. She then turned her attention to the volunteer and smiled. Blue was impressed with how much she looked like her father. They both had high cheekbones and black eyes that can look deep into someone's soul and release shivers of calm and understanding. Blue felt at ease in their presence.

"Not sure how to say in English. In Samoan, it's called *sasa*," she answered.

"It was pretty cool."

"You want and learn it?"

Blue knew that he was never much of a dancer. He tried to learn how to tango, break dance, hip-hop, salsa, and the dozens of other dances that his mother knew for the stage, but he was only truly good at swaying to a beat. He would tell people that he blamed his dancing inadequacies by being born with two left feet and it explained why he believed that he was never truly athletically coordinated.

But today was different. This was Samoa. This was a new girl. He was, perhaps, a new man. He can be a better dancer as a new man in a new place.

"Sure... if you're teaching," Blue flirted.

Chief Joseph grew bored with the two. He ate the last piece of taro and spoke to his daughter in Samoan.

"Father wants me to teach you Samoan first," Aumua said to Blue.

"Of course. Any time." Blue felt a little relieved. One doesn't have to be coordinated to learn a language.

Joseph spoke again to Aumua in Samoan. She picked up her *lavalava* so that she could hurry to the other side of the *fale*. The *matai* looked at Blue and said something in Samoan that Blue didn't understand.

"I'm sorry. I didn't..."

"Women, like rain, can also delay you," Joseph said in English.

Amuau quickly returned to Blue and handed him an umbrella.

"Thank- *faafafeti*," Blue botched trying to say thank you in their tongue. Aumua couldn't help but giggle, trying hard not to laugh.

Lupesina then returned to the *fale* with her seven-year-old daughter. Both of them were carrying plates of fruit, bread slices, sausages, and a cup of tea that they prepared for the guest.

However, Blue didn't stay for breakfast. He tried to make a stoic exit out of the *fale* but slipped and stumbled on the steps. The wind then grabbed his umbrella, turned it inside out, and stole it like a street thief.

As Aumua, Lupesina and her daughter watched Blue chase the umbrella up the road, Joseph took the plates of food from his daughter and grandchild and began eating it.

"The *palagi* needs to learn how to not fight with the rain," the chief said.

Lupesina and her daughter stopped watching Blue and headed back to the house. Aumua couldn't help but keep her eyes on the volunteer.

## 5

At last, Blue made it to the front of the church and much to his relief, the rain eased a little. The scent from wet grass and dripping leaves of a large Polynesian chestnut tree near the church swirled around him. He sneezed, hoping that the wetness had only kicked up his allergies instead of a cold coming on.

*Nothing worse than getting sick in a foreign country.*

Momentarily, the sun pulled aside the black belly clouds and streamed down upon the village, causing steam to rise off the tin roofs. It wasn't long before the clouds muscled their way back in front of the sun, shutting out its rays. Throughout the rest of the day, the sun and the clouds would wrestle for world dominance.

As the tallest structure of the village, St. Cecilia Catholic Church was by far the most prominent building and most respected by the villagers. Although there were a couple of other denominations in the village, the majority of villagers were Catholic and devoted most of their time to the church as it became a major focal point in their lives. St. Cecilia was the patron saint of music, and indeed, music played an important role during Mass every Sunday.

Built in 1910, it had recently celebrated its 100th Anniversary, and remnants of the celebration remained intact, such as a bow of ribbon across the top of the front doorway. Blue marveled at the whitewashed walls of the church that was constructed with coral and limestone. In the hidden exterior corners of the church where the sun wasn't found, a black mold surreptitiously flourished like a creeper in the night. One bell tower rose from the front right side of the door, and the bell was only rung on Sundays at Mass times, every day for 6 p.m. evening prayer curfew, called *Sa*, and on the Feast of St. Cecilia in November.

The narrow, rectangle interior of the church was quite modest and looked as if it hadn't changed since the day it opened. The small sanctuary consisted mostly of an altar table and a wood pulpit with a small, spiral stairs that led to a microphone for readers and cantors. At the back of the altar was a gold tabernacle on the wall, and above it, was a statue of the crucified Christ that most Catholic altars around the world were known for. The original pews with wood kneelers remained and showed years of wear and graffiti of people's names, dates, and small pictures. The cement floor had been tiled over and was probably the latest remodeled effort in the last couple of decades. Ceiling fans, too, had been recently added. However, many churchgoers brought their own personal, homemade fans constructed of colorful dyed coconut leaves and feathers to provide additional coolness, especially on those extremely hot days. At the back of the church in each corner, a spiral staircase led to a balcony, while another narrow staircase led to bell tower. Between the two staircases in the middle of the church was the front door.

Stained glass windows lined the sides of the church, three on each side. Perhaps one of the earliest forms of storytelling using light and color, these particular windows told the glorious, yet sad story of the martyrdom of St. Cecilia. Living in Rome during the third century, the first window showed her vow of virginity as an angel watched over her. Cecilia's husband could be seen in the corner getting baptized so that he could see his wife's guardian angel. The story turned morbid in the second window when Cecilia's husband was executed after refusing to make a sacrifice to the Roman gods. Cecilia and her angel could be seen mournfully leaning over her husband's grave. Despite losing her husband, Cecilia defiantly and steadfastly devoted her time converting hundreds of people to Christianity in the third window. The angel watches proudly as people are being baptized.

The fourth window examined how Cecilia's life turned even more sorrowful as she was tortured and condemned to suffocate in a bathhouse. Although her angel showed pity and sympathy, it did nothing to help the future saint. Miraculously, Cecilia survived the bathhouse in the fifth windowpane, only to meet an executioner's blade. Unbelievably, she survived three blows from the ax and was left to bleed to death. Cecilia continued to preach the message of the Lord until her death three days later. Her angel holds her until her last breath. Finally, the sixth window portrayed how Cecilia was joyously received in heaven, and her angel could be seen standing right behind her as it did throughout her life. Below, on earth, Christians adored her through music, poetry, and art.

For stained glass windows of a church in the middle of a small village of a small island, and in the middle of an ocean, the story was quite gripping. For decades, the church attracted many tourists, religious or not, who came to watch in the early morning as the sun rose from the ocean in the east and gently, slowly told the splendid and sublime story of Saint Cecilia.

By the time Blue reached the front of the church, the rain had abruptly stopped. it seemed the rain never lingered in the tropics. It was either full on, or not at all. Blue felt a little relieved from the relentless downpour. He looked to the heavens. The sun was still losing the fight, and he wondered how long he had before the clouds would proudly open up. Not that it mattered now. He was soaked through to the skin. He only hoped that the contents of his backpack were dry.

Before he took another step, three dogs swooped forward from the side of the church and sat down. Although they were less than a year old, they were medium-size island dogs. None of them looked the same, yet their active disposition, and perhaps their eyes and snouts, suggested they were from the same litter. They were mutts born in paradise. Island dogs are the epitome of living the carefree life: frolicking, foraging, and fornicating. The dogs lived fast, and in many cases, died young. Blue would eventually compare their lives to that of rock stars. Instinctively, they knew their boundary from the sea to the village to just beyond the forest at the edge of the grassy field. In the heat of the afternoon, nothing was better for an island dog to do than to find some shade, sleep, and dream of making their village rounds for scraps, which was the first thing they did when they awoke.

The dogs began scratching and licking themselves and then turned on each other by first chewing on each other's chins and then licking each other's heads. They made ungodly growls and whines like sunbathing seals on a crowded buoy.

Blue didn't trust dogs, or any pet for that matter. He never had pets while growing up, mostly because his mother and aunt traveled for work and would be gone for long periods at a time. And so, as Blue continued his journey to the school, he tried not to look at the dogs and kept his head down as he made his way.

The hounds on the other hand, had Blue in their sights and instantly took note of him and growled. They began to bark. Blue kept moving. Ironically, they reminded him of Cerberus protecting the front of the church.

"Stephen King just called and said that Cujo wants his puppies back," he said out load.

Blue smirked. He liked his joke.

*Too bad there wasn't anyone around to hear that one.*

The dogs finally got off their hind legs and began trotting towards Blue who temporarily froze, wondering if he should simply run or if he should remain still. He chose the former and began moving at a swift pace towards the back of the church. The dogs picked up their trot, growling, and were quickly on top of Blue, forcing him to stop again. He pulled his backpack up to his chest to protect himself, but he was also ready to swing it in defense, as it was the only weapon he had. However, the hellhounds were anything but hell and instead of making Blue a quick snack, they lunged lovingly up and down his chest.

Reassured that the dogs only wanted to be friendly, Blue reached into his backpack and pulled out a squished protein bar that he had packed before his trip to Samoa, broke it in three parts, and gave a piece to each dog. The hounds swallowed their tasty morsels and then sniffed each other's mouth and the ground around them hoping to find even the smallest crumb.

Blue continued on his way behind the church. The dogs followed him, but not in a straight line, as they tried to pick up a scent from the ground or got in a wrestling match with each other. Once they all got to the schoolyard, the dogs got even more distracted by a couple of chickens. Blue watched the hounds gallop towards the chickens, enthusiastically barking all the way.

St. Cecilia Primary School was a small, simple one-story building in the shape of an "L," and was constructed of large concrete bricks painted light blue. Murals depicting tropical and religious scenes such as angels flying over a taro plants, or Jesus blessing coconut trees were painted on the walls. Trees towered above and behind the school and constantly dropped leaves and moisture on the rusted tin roof.

There were six classrooms and an office, and at the end was a small, attached *fale* with a few wooden tables for the children to eat. Each room had glass window louvers and a ceiling fan to help cool the students and teachers during the day's lesson, which, however, never seemed to be enough on those extremely hot days. The classrooms had a chalkboard, a teacher's desk, and were overcrowded by wooden student desks. Artwork, maps of Samoa, and a crucifix could be found on the walls. Hooks to hang backpacks and lunch sacks were strewn along the back wall. To Blue, it looked as if the classrooms were lost in the past. In fact, every time he looked into one of the rooms, he smiled thinking about the joke that started, *The 1950s called...*

Finally, Blue caught the attention of a young teacher in her early thirties who stopped her lesson and said something to him in Samoan. She was dressed in a flowery blouse and a black skirt. Every child in the classroom turned his or her head to look at the volunteer, excited about the distraction from the lesson. The boys looked smart in their white-collared shirts and purple *lavalavas*, while the girls appeared even more fashionable in their white-collared shirts and purple jumpers, their skirts modestly hanging below their knees.

"Hi... uh... *Talofa*," Blue softly said. He was proud that he used a Samoan word. The children giggled. "Uh... I'm here to teach reading. Do you know which room?"

As the teacher walked towards Blue, the students took advantage of the break and jumped out of their seats. She quickly turned around and barked orders to her class to return to their seats. All of them complied, however none of them sat down again. They clung to and around the desk as if it were a jungle gym.

"Down the way. Last room," the teacher said in English, pointing towards the end of the building.

"Thanks," Blue replied.

"I'm Vaveao Suisala. My husband was the *tufa'ava* at your ceremony. He runs the trading store."

Blue couldn't remember what a *tufa'ava* was, but he

smiled and pretended he knew, "Oh, nice. That's nice. I'm Blue. Ronin Blue."

Mrs. Suisala anxiously looked back into her classroom. The clatter of the children grew louder.

"Mind the centipedes," Mrs. Suisala quickly said.

"The what?"

But Mrs. Suisala didn't stick around to answer him and rushed into her classroom. He could hear her yelling instructions in Samoan to her children before saying, "Mister *Lanu Moana*," which made the children laugh. The words actually meant, "blue ocean" because they believed he came from the ocean.

Blue made his way to the last classroom. He watched the hounds wrestle with each other over a papaya that fell from its tree. They abruptly stopped when someone opened a set of blinds from a small cooking *fale*. The dogs then quickly trotted to the *fale*, as if it was now open for business. A few leftovers came hurtling from inside and the dogs barked a "thank you" before scuffling for the scraps. Contented from the meager meal, they merrily moved on towards the village and their next snack-providing haunt.

The small room at the end of the school building was more of a storage unit than a classroom. The room had the distinct musty smell of mold and cockroach feces. Cobwebs hung from the corners of the ceiling. There were a few wooden desks, but half of them had some issue like a broken leg or a missing desktop. Boxes of various shapes and sizes and old paperback lesson books were piled along the back of the room. A crooked crucifix hung on the wall along with a couple of posters. One poster showed all seventeen letters of the Samoan alphabet with pictures of things that represented each letter, while another poster had the word, *Ta'aloga* in large bold letters across the top and depicted cartoon people engaging in the different sports of Samoa. An out-of-date calendar also hung on the wall, perhaps displayed the last time the room was in use.

Although the room was a bit of a dump, Blue was glad to be out of the rain. The foul air, however, made him gag, and he tried turning on the ceiling fan first by clicking the switch on the wall. It didn't work. He then hopped on a desk and tried to turn on the fan manually. It didn't work. He went back to the switch on the wall and clicked it several times. It still didn't work.

*Damn me.*

The warm, putrid air was stifling. He then moved aside desks as if he were wading through a bog to the windows and tried to open the louvers. The windows were dirty, and he wiped the dirt off the panes to reveal a verdant view of the grassy field with the jungle encroaching to the left. The *fale tele* could be seen in the distance. Blue struggled to open the louvers, as some of them were broken. But when he finally did, the view became fresher. A breeze instantly wafted through, carrying the scent of wet grass.

It was at this moment that Blue saw the seven young women in white *puletasis* standing at the edge of the bush. He leaned forward and tried to get a better look at them through the driving rain. The women didn't move and simply stood still in a row facing the village.

*Even a fool has enough sense to get out of the rain.*

Then, one of the women turned her head towards Blue. It freaked him out. He squinted his eyes hoping for a clearer view. The woman stared at him, and he felt that she looked familiar.

*Who is that?*

The woman then turned her entire body towards him. She was the only one out of the group to do so. He got a better look at the familiar woman, and instantly his body fluttered with terror, the hairs on his arms and neck standing rigidly straight.

*What the eff? It can't be. Scarlett? She's been dead for over two years!*

Scarlett Wang was Blue's only friend since he was ten years old. She lived near Blue in an unincorporated part of North San Diego County between the city of Oceanside and the Marine base of Camp Pendleton. The neighborhood was composed of sporadic, custom-built houses only a mile from the ocean, and a narrow path led to a small private cove with a beach that Blue's mother and aunt named Sabatini's Beach, because it reminded them of a setting in a Raphael Sabatini's adventure, swashbuckling books. The cove also boasted having two small, shallow caves with narrow openings that were carved out of the cliff by ocean waves. A pristine and mostly untouched tide pool teeming with seen and unseen life gurgled in front of the caves.

When Scarlett moved to the neighborhood, Blue's mother arranged a playdate at Sabatini's Beach. Blue remembered that the two played in the sand and built a sandcastle. They didn't say one word to each other that day. They just worked together to construct the castle and waited for the tide to come in and sweep it away.

"Why didn't you say anything to me that first day we

met?" Scarlet asked Blue years later when they were in their early teens.

"I didn't think you spoke English."

"Because I'm Chinese?"

"Yeah."

"I wasn't fresh-off-the-boat, you know. I was born in Los Angeles."

"I didn't know."

"You could've asked."

"I didn't think you spoke English, Scar.

"You're weird."

"Wait. Why didn't you speak to me that day?" Blue had to ask.

"I didn't think you spoke English," She said with a half-smile.

"I'm not foreign looking!"

"Yeah, but you were kinda dim witted."

"You're weird."

After their initial rendezvous at the beach a couple of weeks later, Blue was invited to Scarlett's house. When he arrived, she was practicing the cello performing the Bach Cello Suite No.1 in G Major. The suite was a rite of passage for cellist just like learning the song, "Stairway to Heaven," was for a guitarist, or playing the theme to the movie, *The Sting*, was for a pianist.

Blue was a very good pianist at the age of ten, but Scarlett was definitely a prodigy. He immediately recognized how talented she was, but the deep, moody instrument didn't seem to fit her spirited and naïve personality. Over the years, Scarlett respected Blue's playing ability, and believed he had a gift too. However, she was often confused as to why he didn't take his gift more seriously.

"What school do you go to?" Blue finally asked.

"I'm home schooled."

"You go to school here?"

"Yes."

"By yourself?"

"Yes."

"Is it lonely?"

"Not really. I have my brother and sister running around and lots of teachers. We have fun," Scarlett said, looking up to the sky. Blue would eventually learn that she always looked to the sky when she didn't mean what she said.

"It doesn't sound like fun."

"Are you home schooled?"

"No."

"Then how do you know it's not fun?"

"I have a piano teacher that comes to my house. It's never fun."

Blue played the "SpongeBob SquarePants" theme on the piano.

"What's that?" Scarlett asked. Blue was surprised at this. Every kid watched SpongeBob.

"It's Mozart." Blue grinned mischievously as Scarlett gave him a curious look.

Indeed, Scarlett's parents, who were both university professors, were very tough and were known as "tiger parents," a label that meant they governed and protected every aspect of their child and would get confrontational if anyone should get in the way. They rarely let their Scarlett and her young siblings out of their sight and dedicated their life to making sure that their children obeyed the right rules and expectations. They also brought in the right tutors and teachers to ensure unmitigated success in the future. Those with the strongest credentials were the ones that were hired. Scarlett's private cello teacher, for example, was a member of the San Diego Symphony.

At Blue's first visit, Scarlett's parents asked him to take off his shoes at the door before they escorted him to their piano. Unbeknown to him at the time, this was where he would sit whenever he visited during the subsequent years. Besides for several cousins, Blue was the only one Scarlett interacted with of her own age. This was partly because he was the neighbor boy whose guardians were often away, and despite not having much supervision, Scarlett's parents respected Blue's mother and aunt and believed that they had interesting professions that required hard work and skill. The Wangs also felt that Blue had a genuine talent playing the piano, and they felt that another gifted musician would benefit their daughter by, sadly, manipulating Scarlett and making her believe that she needed to practice more if she were to be better than her neighborhood pianist friend.

When Blue reached the age of twelve, he was asked to keep his hands on the piano keys at all times during his visits, which he thought was very strange. Scarlett's grandmother was the one who was given the task to enforce this rule and she was good at it. Besides answering the front door when Blue arrived, he never saw the grandmother again until he took his hands off the piano. Often, Blue would teasingly test how fast the grandmother would enter the room after lifting his hands. She would charge into the room like a mad woman screaming in Chinese and waving a broom, or a feather duster, or a ladle—whatever instrument she was using at the time. Both Blue and Scarlett would get a kick out of this until Scarlett yelled at her grandmother in Chinese, telling her everything's fine and that she should leave. Sometimes, Blue would even be so bold as to actually stand and walk around the room, much to grandmother's annoyance.

***

Blue hadn't thought about Scarlett for a few years, and seeing her, or a woman that resembled her, dangling on the edge of the jungle like an ornament, brought back a flood of memories. She was his only friend, and he was ashamed that he didn't think of her more often.

The driving rain made it difficult for Blue to watch the woman more closely. He straightened the glass louvers to get a better look. Straining through the rain, he saw the woman raise her arm and then point her finger at him. Blue thought it was a strange gesture, but then realized that other women were doing the same thing.

*What are they doing? Are they pointing at me?*

He tried to open the louvers more. However, the strain was too much, and one piece fell out of the window and onto the ground. Luckily, it didn't shatter. He bent down to pick it up. When he tried to replace it, he looked back at the women and saw that they were gone.

Blue shook his head and rubbed his eyes.

*Creepy women. Maybe it's a Samoan thing.*

He decided that he would forget about the women and

try to make the room a little more habitable. He piled lesson books more neatly and repositioned boxes. When he moved one box, a menacing black, two-inch centipede came scurrying out, scaring him half to death.

*What the eff was that?!*

He tried to smash it with a book but missed. The centipede made its way to the safety of a crack at the baseboard of the room. Blue waited. He armed himself with a book to see if it would reappear, ready to smash it.

*That came from the bowels of hell.*

The centipede never reappeared.

He then grabbed a chair from the corner of the room and positioned it behind the desk. With nothing else to do for the moment, he sat in the chair and put his feet on one of the desks. He looked out the windows to see if the weird women had returned, but there was nobody.

He occasionally looked back at the baseboards for the demon bug.

Then, he waited.

*What am I waiting for? Oh yeah, students.*

But no students came, and it wasn't long before he dozed off.

6

---

*B*lue quickly realized that a nap in the Pacific Islands could be a heavenly experience. The heat and humidity combined with the melodic sound of the waves crashing against the reef, or the rhythmic pattern of the rain hitting a tin roof made it easy for the senses of the human body to relax and drift away into a peaceful slumber. In the old days, most of the villagers would sleep the afternoon away only to wake when the shadows took over.

For Blue, it was morning and not the afternoon, and he was out cold. Perhaps, two full days of sleep wasn't enough for him. Maybe he was still experiencing jetlag. Nevertheless, his snoring suggested he was deep in a dream —women's cleavage bursting out of their white dresses, dogs humping in the tall grass, and Aumua eating a banana. Interweaving these sexually charged fantasies was an image of his naked self playing piano in the middle of the schoolyard. Children gathered around the piano and began chanting, "Mr. *Lanu Moana*."

"Mr. *Lanu Moana*."

"Mr. *Lanu Moana*."

"Mr. *Lanu Moana*."

As the chant became louder, it wasn't long before Blue awoke to the giggles of school children. They then repeated the chant in the real world.

Startled, he fell off his chair. The children roared with laughter that abruptly stopped when Fiame, the school's principal, approached the room yelling in Samoan and telling them to leave Mr. Ronin alone. The kids scattered to the four corners of the schoolyard.

The sun had broken through the sky and looked as though it had a stranglehold on the clouds. It wasn't going to let go until had squeezed the life out clouds like a snake coiled around a rat.

Blue quickly stood up and wiped the drool from the corner of his mouth. He was a bit groggy, but easily composed himself as Fiame entered the classroom.

"We didn't get a chance to clean the room," she said in very succinct English. "Your arrival was quite sudden."

"Oh. It's... it's fine."

"I asked a couple of teachers to clean the room, and they didn't do it," she added. "That's the problem with this village—nobody wants to do a little more to help."

Blue nodded his head. He really didn't want to get anyone in trouble.

Fiame never had an issue discussing the problems of the village with anyone who would listen, including a stranger. Her husband unexpectedly died in a boating accident, and it was a devastating loss to her and their children. He was the one she confided in about village politics. To compensate for his loss, she began to talk to any guest that came to visit, or Father Krimple. Nevertheless, nothing was ever good enough for her, and she was rarely impressed. She believed that without her, the village would succumb to a shantytown. She had been the impetus that kept everyone living the *Fa'a Samoa* and ensured that everyone played a significant role in the vitality of Vaimasina.

To her, Chief Joseph was a dreamer, while she was a doer. It was a relationship she understood and thrived in. Unfortunately, it had gone on a little too long. She had developed a love/hate relationship with the villagers. Fiame adored Vaimasina, but knew that if she should leave, there would be no one to take her place. Thus, she had grown weary and restless. She tired of being the school's principal, a post she had held for the past twelve years, and desired to move to Apia where she could take a position in one of the ministries, particularly the Ministry of Education. She truly believed that she could be influential not just for one Samoan village, but a champion for all of Samoa.

"Did someone have to ask you twice to come to Samoa?" Fiame asked, as if knowing the answer already.

"Uh... no..."

"No. Right," Fiame interrupted. "You woke up one morning and told yourself that you wanted to come to Samoa and make a difference. The people here are so indecisive."

"Well, I've been known to procrastinate," Blue said with an air of protecting people he didn't know.

"Indecision and procrastination are two different things, Mr. Ronin."

Blue felt that the principal was on the verge of getting

riled up. He'd always been good at avoiding confrontation, and it seemed that this was as good as any time to put the skill to use.

"I'm sorry. I've only been in Samoa for a few days, and I've been asleep for half of it."

Fiame snickered, which Blue believed was a laugh. He wasn't sure, but he started to feel himself sweat. The rain had stopped temporarily to, perhaps, adjust its battle plans against the sun. The humidity was on the rise, and Blue wondered when the last time was he had taken a shower.

*Do I stink?*

"How long have you been a reading teacher?" Fiame asked.

"Well, I...uh... I was an English major in college. I just graduated."

"So you read a lot?"

"Yeah."

"And those who have read much can teach reading?"

"I don't see why not."

"The Pacific Islands are oral societies, Mr. Ronin. We like to speak our stories, rather than read our stories. Does that concern you?"

Blue felt that she was fishing for another confrontation.

*Damn she's good.*

"Some things should be written down before spoken," Blue blurted out. He was unsure of what he had just said.

*Oh God, What am I talking about?*

Fiame raised her eyebrows. There seemed to be a million avenues she could explore with what the volunteer just said.

Blue remained on the offensive and rambled on before

she could get a chance to take the conversation to a deeper place.

"For example, I'm writing a novel right now with lots of dialogue. I have to write it first to see if it can be spoken," Blue added.

*What am I talking about?*

Fortunately, it was good enough. Fiame zeroed in on the word, "novel." The word was a big, meaty piece of bait dangling at the end of a fishing rod.

"What novel are you writing?" he asked. The look in her eyes told Blue she had several questions already lined up.

"It's an adventure of forbidden love on the high seas."

"Ah. Very good. I think I saw that movie when it was in Apia a few years back."

*Damn me.*

"Well, uh... it hasn't been told."

A bell rang in the schoolyard. The end of recess or lunch had come. Fiame moved towards the door.

"Splendid. You can come to my house for dinner tonight. *Sa* begins at six. *Feiloai mulimuli ane.*"

And with that, Fiame left. Blue could hear her shouting at school children in Samoan.

Blue wiped the sweat off his face with the end of his shirt and sat back down on the chair.

Still, no students came to the room.

He thought about going to the office and asking Fiame about the children he was supposed to teach, but he didn't want to endure more questions from the inquisitive, interrogating principal. He was dreading dinner as it was. It was better to remain where he was. Besides, they knew he was there, and he believed that students would come along soon enough.

Before he positioned himself comfortably in the chair, Togi quickly approached the door.

"Bro, we need your help in the church," Togi said enthusiastically. "Fast!"

Blue hopped out of the chair.

"What's up?" Blue asked.

"Father Krimple is stuck. Come. Fast!"

Blue wondered if it was a good idea to leave the classroom. He thought a student might show. He hesitated.

"Fast, bro!" Togi insisted.

Blue hurried out of the classroom, and didn't close the door behind as he left. He had a hard time keeping up with Togi, who seemed to be galloping at a horse's pace.

They passed by a two-room community center where a group of women were practicing a *siva*. Two women were in the kitchen attached to the center preparing dishes for after the practice. Blue noticed that the women floated effortlessly, as their hands softly swung in delicate positions. Aumua was part of the group, and when she saw Blue, she gave a wave to him. She then swiftly returned to the next motion of the dance in unison with the group.

Blue stopped to watch Aumua.

"They practice for Teuila Festival," Togi said. He then quickly yanked Blue away. "We don't have time to stop to watch women, bro. Father Krimple is in trouble."

When the two entered the church, it smelled of dampness and the old wooden pews seemed to creak like an old ship. The stone floor, however, felt cool on Blue's bare feet.

"Bro, there!" Togi shouted.

Blue looked towards the front doors and saw two men trying to move a small, upright piano up one of the spiral staircases to the balcony. The two men were about three-fourths up the stairs when one of the men, Father Krimple, became stuck between the end of the piano and the railing. The other man was trying to hold the piano from pushing the priest through the railing.

"Good Lord," Blue mumbled.

He and Togi rushed up the stairs and lent a hand by grabbing the piano, moving it away from Father Krimple and allowing him to take a deep breath.

"My prayer has been answered," said Father Krimple.

"Depends on which way you're going—up or down," Blue said.

"Well, which way you do you think?" asked Father Krimple.

"Up," Blue answered.

"Ah, an optimist," the priest said with a pleased smile. "You must be the volunteer that everyone's talking about, especially Togi," he added.

"Ronin Blue."

"Father Krimple. Pleasure to meet you. And the strapping youth on the other side of the piano is Lance Lafau."

"*Talofa*," Blue said, acknowledging the Samoan.

But it was in vain as Lance looked everywhere except at Blue. A little embarrassed, Blue turned his attention to the priest.

"American?" Father Krimple asked.

"Yeah."

"Go on. Don't get too many Americans around here," the priest added.

"You sound like one," Blue inquired. "I mean, your accent."

"Canadian. And we're even more rare in these parts."

Father Benjamin Krimple was a tall, well-built man with wavy yellow hair, and he looked more like a Californian surfer than a man from the cold Canadian Rockies town of Calgary where he was born and lived until he was in his midtwenties. Despite being in his late thirties, he had a boyish face that made him look younger—a trait that will be with him well into his golden years.

Father Krimple had been Vaimasina's beloved Catholic priest for the past fifteen years. He enjoyed smiling because he knew that one couldn't help noticing how his shiny, white teeth glistened in the sunlight and shone in the moonlight. He applauded when he heard good news, and he never wasted an opportunity to acknowledge a person in his congregation when they achieved something, did a good deed, or made a positive contribution to the church or village. Being athletic, he thoroughly loved playing sports and games with the villagers, particularly the children. When he was a teenager, he received a long, garish gash under his right eye. It was a gruesome tale of a crash with an opponent and a skating shoe blade that he shared from time to time with those he felt weren't too squeamish. But during these days he believed it was necessary to make the story into some kind of parable.

The priest simply spewed confidence and leadership despite not wearing the usual vestments of a Catholic priest. In fact, he was never seen wearing the typical black pants and shirt with the white clerical collar. Instead, he wore a black *lavalava* and a flower-printed shirt like the Hawaiian shirts or the *Bula* shirts found in Fiji. He went barefoot most of time because he felt it was just too hot to even wear sandals.

"Oh my, I seemed to have sliced my hand open," the priest said, observing a gash on his hand. The blood trickled down his wrist and forearm.

Togi, who was always a Johnny-on-the-spot kind of a person, rushed over to Father Krimple. He pulled out some cloth from his satchel made of pandanus leaves.

"Go on, son," Father Krimple said.

Togi tied it around the priest's hand. When he tightened the cloth, Father Krimple gave a wince but thanked him.

With Togi rushing to the priest's aid, it left Blue and Lance balancing the piano. Blue looked across the piano at his partner, and instantly didn't like the cut of his jib. The feeling was mutual, however, and would be for the entire time the two would know each other.

Lance Lafau was a smarmy, shifty-eye man in his early twenties who had a thin mustache like a 1940s actor. He was short and stocky and liked to shave the hair off his head. He did this because he thought it made him look tougher, but mostly because he couldn't stand that his hair was receding at such a young age. Lance never liked the village life. He preferred living in Apia where he could make money doing nefarious jobs such as pickpocketing tourists in the market. Lance was Fiame's youngest child, and she often made him feel guilty for being away from the village for long periods of time and only returning when he was out of money. Although nobody in the village knew what Lance was doing in Apia, they hoped that he was trying to better himself, or the village, and they accepted all his excuses for his absences.

Behind the priest and Togi's back, Lance purposely let go of his end of the piano much to Blue's surprise. Blue felt all his muscles tightening to steady the piano.

"Whoa, dude!" Blue yelped.

The piano easily pushed Blue against the railing, just as it did with Father Krimple. Blue had a panicked look upon his face as he heard one of the vertical spokes of the railing crack. He instantly looked below him as another spoke snapped.

*The fall may not kill me, but it's gonna hurt.*

Blue began sweating. Another spoke snapped like a piece of chalk. Blue could hardly keep the piano and himself from bursting through the railing and crashing below on the stone floor. He ducked downwards and dug his shoulder against the side of the piano.

Father Krimple and Togi looked behind them when they heard Blue's yip, and quickly rushed to help stabilize the piano. Even Lance lunged forward with a fake astonished look and grabbed the piano.

"Got it?" Father Krimple called out. "Everyone got it?"

The Samoans shook their heads, confirming that they had a grip of the piano.

"Last thing we need is you to be crushed to death on your first day of work," the priest said to Blue.

"I haven't been around long enough for people to write songs about me," Blue answered with a bit of relief.

"Go on, boys. Let's get it on the balcony," Father Krimple ordered. "Go on! Go on!"

Together the group shoved and heaved the piano up and around the final stairs and onto the balcony.

"Let's put the damn thing against the wall," the priest commanded. The Samoans thought the word, "damn" was funny coming from a priest. On the flat, wooden surface they moved it easily across the balcony and placed it against the wall.

Blue stretched out his sore arms and looked over the balcony. He was impressed with the view to the altar despite the heat that oppressed this higher area. The stained glass windows were putting on a late performance due to the morning storm.

"Thank you, everyone," the priest said. "Feel blessed that the Lord made sure nothing would happen to us in his house."

Lance and Togi made their way across the balcony towards the stairs. Blue gave Lance the stink-eye, which the Samoan troublemaker returned with a squint of his eyes. Behind the priest's back, Blue sarcastically stuck out his tongue at his nemesis like a petulant schoolyard child. Lance responded with a flick of his fingers before heading down the stairs.

"Do you know anything about pianos?" Father Krimple asked.

"No," Blue answered ashamedly.

Blue's fingers twitched when he looked at the keys. He told himself that he stopped playing the piano because he felt that it consumed too much of his youth. He was lying to himself.

"That's a shame," the priest said. "The damn thing's been here for years. Way before I started working here."

"Wait. Did we just move a broken piano up a spiral staircase for nothing?"

"Not for nothing. I want to move the choir up here for Masses, which will allow more space for parishioners down there."

Blue moved over to the piano. He looked at the keys. Many memories shot through his mind of pieces he had played through the years, from "Twinkle, Twinkle Little Star" to the sprightly folk dance piece, "Hungarian Rhapsody No.2," by Franz Liszt. The fingers of his left hand stretched and slowly lowered to the keys. Blue closed his eyes, picturing himself at the piano in his home performing over and over until his aunt dropped the keyboard guard on his hands and told him to play something else.

He can hear the pieces rise to a cacophony of mashed piano tunes.

"Go on," Father Krimple goaded, sensing the volunteer had a connection with the wooden music box. "It's just a little out of tune."

Blue's fingers lowered more and were only a half inch from the keys. He paused his hand just before he touched the key and grimaced.

He couldn't do it.

Blue wouldn't do it.

He promised himself not to do it.

He pulled his hand away.

Father Krimple could see the pain in Blue's face. The piano obviously struck a chord in Blue's mind.

"I don't play," Blue said.

"Maybe some other time," the priest said

empathetically. "It's getting hot up here, and you must get back to your students."

"Right."

Father Krimple patted Blue on his back.

"Thanks for your help today. Sorry to put you in such danger."

Blue nodded his head, moved towards the stairs, and stopped at the top step. He turned back to the priest.

"Music is the language of God," Blue blurted out awkwardly. "Uh- Beethoven."

Although a bit confused, Father Krimple smiled and agreed with the strange volunteer.

"Go on. Go on," the priest encouraged Blue.

When Blue returned to the classroom, there was no one there. He sat down in the chair and propped his feet up, his white feet sunbathed by a strip of sunlight that poured through the window. It only took about two minutes before he fell asleep again.

In the distance, thunder grumbled, complained, and vowed to take revenge against the sun on some of other day in the very near future.

When Blue eventually found Fiame's house, he wasn't sure if he should knock on the front screen or simply enter. He saw that Fiame's family was sitting in a circle in the front room reciting prayers in Samoan. He hoped that if he stood there long enough, someone would notice him and invite him inside. This, indeed, was what happened, as a woman eagerly opened the screen door to let him in. Once inside, he quickly noticed that it was a quaint, modest one-story western-style home with a kitchen next to the front room and a short hallway that led to the bedrooms. Louver windows were opened without screens, and the light of the room seemed to beckon every flying insect of the night. The room was lightly furnished and on the walls were mostly artwork that Fiame's children created in school and a large framed picture of Jesus Christ above a sofa.

Everyone stopped saying the prayer and looked at Blue who was still soaking wet. Fiame wasn't sure if she should be upset with his tardiness or accept him formally into her home. As Blue sat on a mat in the circle, she opted for the latter and introduced the volunteer in a lengthy speech about what she learned from him earlier in the day, told in both Samoan and English. At the end of the speech, everyone clapped and welcomed Blue. They then continued with prayers until the church bells rang, signifying the end of *Sa*. This immediately produced a more relaxed and informal atmosphere where many of Fiame's *aiga* approached Blue as if he was a celebrity and began describing who they were and who they were married to, and which children belonged to them. Blue tried to follow each and every person he talked to but became easily distracted when he heard a chorus of "Mr. *Lanu Moana*," echoing throughout the room from playing children.

The assorted aroma of food that wafted through the room teased Blue's growling stomach. He was quite famished from barely eating anything all day, and he anticipated participating in a feast that promptly began shortly after the end of *Sa*. As a guest of honor, Blue was one of the first persons served and was given a plate piled high with food that included: taro, octopus, *fa'apapa* (a sweat coconut bread), rice, and a fish (with head and tail). He often crunched on bones while eating the fish, which made him queasy. However, he would eventually push the fish aside in favor of the delectable Samoan dish, *oka i'a* (raw fish marinated in lemon juice). He was given a plastic fork but noticed that everyone else was using their fingers as utensils.

After about an hour of people refilling Blue's plate with generous portions of food, he was feeling replete. He enjoyed the company of Fiame's *aiga*, and he mostly talked about where he was from. This truly intrigued the hosts as the furthest away that any of them had ever been was to Apia.

Eventually, Fiame got a chance to see how her guest was doing, and she approached Blue, handing him another plate of food. Blue thought about declining, but he didn't want to be rude.

"What was your impression of your first day, Mr. Blue?" Fiame asked.

"It was… different," Blue answered. He didn't want to bring up the fact that not one student came to him. Fiame was perplexed by the word, "different."

"Different? How so?"

"Just different from what I'm used to."

"Different is good?"

"Well, yeah. I mean, if I didn't come here, I would've never have experienced today."

"Ah," Fiame said, still a little perplexed. She didn't let it go. "But what made today so different?"

It was at this point that Blue noticed Fiame's nephew, Lance Lafau, sitting in the corner with a mound of food on a plate and talking with his mouthful to a cousin sitting next to him.

"I… well, for one thing, I saved Father Kimple from getting crushed by a piano," Blue said matter-of-factly.

"Oh! What was he doing with the piano?"

"Moving it to the church loft."

"I swear that man. He always wants to do everything himself. He never wants to delegate. A couple of months ago, he almost pierced his foot while spearfishing in the lagoon. And last year while fixing the roof of the church, he almost fell off."

"The man likes to tease death, no?"

"Pardon?"

Fiame looked at Blue inquisitively wondering what he meant. Blue could have slapped himself for fueling Fiame's flame with his *faux pas*. Before he could explain his meaning, Fiame was called to the kitchen.

"Excuse me, Mr. Ronin. I'm needed in the kitchen."

"Of course."

"Don't go away. I enjoy talking to you."

Fiame left for the kitchen, spouting commands in Samoan. Relieved, Blue felt that this was the right time to change his environment. He placed his plate of second helpings on a tall stereo speaker and went outside.

As he stepped onto the ground of crushed coral and sand, Blue's senses heightened in the night air. The aroma of neighbors cooking in their *umus* wafted by him, and he questioned if he was actually full from the feast that was served to him. He thought about going back to his plate on the speaker, but he didn't want to risk another conversation with Fiame.

With the half-moon in the sky, the night was fairly bright and placid. Blue looked up in the sky and marveled at the ocean of stars. He wondered what the celestial heaven would look like on a moonless night. Blue felt somewhat comforted how to the night's sky reminded him of the one he was used to at his home. He would sit at Sabatini's Beach with his mother and aunt at night and try to identify the popular constellations that were protected from the big city lights.

Blue was able to make out the stars that comprised the Southern Cross, which was one of the few distinguished constellations in the Southern Hemisphere. Traditional Pacific seafarers had used the cross to help them navigate across the vast ocean for centuries. A shooting star streaked across the sky, and Blue's eyes widened with amazement. He watched it fizzle and dissolve like a firework. He was kind of disappointed that nobody else saw it, or even cared to look skyward.

*Do I wish? What do I wish for?*

Blue thought of a million wishes—from wishing he could take a shower to writing a best-selling novel. Staring up at the stars, he went through all his wishing options. In the end, he didn't wish for anything, as his neck became sore from looking up. Distracted, he noticed a group of young men smoking under a papaya tree, one of whom was Lance Lafau. Blue wanted to confront Lance for the shenanigan he tried to pull in the church but felt that this wasn't really the time or place to pick a fight. Instead, Blue thought it was best that he head back to his *fale* and get out of his damp clothes, which he just remembered he had been wearing for a few days now.

As Blue began to make his way back to his home, Lance Lafau quickly approached him and brazenly gave the volunteer a shove in the back.

"I hope you keep down what you ate tonight," Lance sarcastically said.

Blue turned around and knew quite well that Lance was referring to his incident at the ceremony a few days ago.

"If I don't, I'll be sure to find your mat," Blue retaliated.

"Just watch your back, *palagi*. We don't need you here."

"Hey! Clark Gable called, and he wants his mustache back," Blue said with a short laugh. Lance didn't get it.

"You *palagi* always come here thinking you know everything. I'm sick of you."

"Well, I got news for you, bro, I don't know shit."

Lance was a little flustered at what Blue just said and didn't know what the white man exactly meant. "You just watch your back."

"How about you watch my back for me as I leave?"

With that, Blue turned and started walking away. He had never really been in a heated argument before. He had his petty disagreements with his girlfriend or fiancé, (he still didn't know exactly what she was to him) Harper, but he wasn't opinionated enough, or met enough people, to actually get into any verbal squabbles. There was a moment when the two were face-to-face that Blue thought about slugging Lance. However, he had a golden rule ever since he was a young piano player and that was to "protect the fingers." As he was walking, he thought about the situation with Lance over and over.

*Shit. I don't play piano anymore.*

Blue stopped and braced himself from a blow to his back he thought was surely coming. It didn't happen. He turned around to see if Lance was where he left him, but the angry Samoan was gone. Blue looked up to the sky, hoping to see another shooting star. He knew exactly what he would wish for this time: that Lance Lafau would disappear for good. But a curtain of clouds closed on the stars, darkening the night. Blue continued his walk back to his *fale*. From that day forward, Blue made a conscious effort to make sure he stayed clear of Lance Lafau whenever and wherever possible.

It wasn't long before Blue passed the *fale* of Chief Joseph Tuputala, who was sitting on his mat. Blue noticed that the *fale* was more of a modern structure equipped with electricity and a bright light that hung from the center of the ceiling. A couple of older men, perhaps other chiefs, and who were close to Joseph's age, were sitting on mats next to him. Blue wondered if the mammoth man moved at all during the day. The chief was exactly where Blue left him that rainy morning. A mound of discarded fruit peels and chicken bones were piled on a banana leaf next to all three men. Although Blue couldn't understand what they were talking about, Joseph was entertaining them and all three men seemed to be having a good time, gesticulating and laughing. Blue assumed they were talking about the old times.

Aumua entered the *fale* with a *tanoa* of ʻava and set it down in the middle of the men. She then began closing the venetian blinds around the *fale*. Not wanting to be caught spying on the men, Blue ducked behind a pandanus bush when Aumua reached the blind directly in his path. She stopped for a second and peered out, as if she felt someone was watching her. As she reached to pull down more blinds, her voluptuous silhouette enamored Blue. He watched her longingly, feeling a little guilty because of her age, or just maybe, because he had a girlfriend or fiancé back home.

When Aumua began pulling down the last set of blinds, Fiame and Lance approached the *fale*. Aumua held the blinds and let the two inside. Blue noticed that the laughter had faded, and he wondered why the two had come to the Tuputala *fale*. He figured that Fiame was there on village business, but he had no idea about the reason why the village bully would tag along with his mother.

Blue tried to peer into the *fale* through some of the broken blinds. He thought that, perhaps, Lance was sweet on Aumua. What other reason must there be for his presence? Blue wasn't sure if he should feel a little jealous. After all, it's a small village and everyone knows everyone, or is related to everyone. But Blue didn't like the idea that Aumua was interested in Lance as a suitor.

Blue crept closer to the *fale*, hoping to get a better look inside. He was hoping that one of the broken slats would promise something more revealing. Peering in the *fale*, Blue felt like a fly on the wall, but unfortunately, couldn't understand anything they were saying. As he repositioned himself and looked through a wider opening in the blinds, he was able to see Aumua sitting with Lance on the ground. Blue leaned in closer for a better look and was startled when Togi's hand touched his shoulder. Aumua and Lance looked in the direction of the commotion, but they couldn't tell what was happening outside the *fale*.

"Your home is this way," Togi said. "I show you."

Before Aumua and Lance opened a set of blinds to look out, Blue and Togi were already further along the dirt road swallowed by the darkness of the night.

Upon arriving at his *fale*, Blue immediately wanted to change clothes.

"You need help?" Togi asked.

Blue looked confusingly at him. He was a little peeved at

his friend. But mostly, he was simply tired from the long day.

*Uh- I've been dressing myself since I was nineteen.*

"No. Thank you. I'm capable of changing myself."

Blue wondered if Togi ever slept.

"Shall I leave you?" Togi asked with a hopeful tone that Blue had one more thing for him to do.

"Sure. Thanks."

Togi bowed his head with disappointment and leapt out of the *fale*. He hesitated before walking away.

"Hey, Togi!" Blue called.

Togi eagerly stopped and turned around.

"Is there a shower that I could use?"

"*Ioe*! Behind *fale*." He was excited about having something new to do for Blue. "I clean it for you." He cleared the overgrown vines and grass and reconnected the hose. The makeshift facility provided only cold showers that Blue grew to never mind, particularly on those unbearable balmy days.

After Togi ran away that evening, Blue felt he wasn't alone. Although he couldn't see the mosquitos, they hummed like *vuvuzelas* in his ears. Geckos scurried along the poles looking for a spot to lie in wait for an unsuspecting insect. Every so often, they would cackle to let each other know which territory they were covering.

Blue tucked himself inside his mosquito net with hopes of escaping these little vampires and sat down on his mat. He opened his laptop to work on his novel, and a dim light was cast throughout the *fale* by the computer screen. He noticed the nightstand and wondered why a lamp was on top of it when there was no electricity in the *fale*.

Blue turned his attention to his novel. He read the latest page that he had worked on, thought about it, and then typed three words: "The next day..." He looked at what he typed and fell asleep.

Blue spent the next several days doing exactly the same thing, and quickly developed a routine. He would go to school, go on walks with Aumua, spend the evening at Fiame's house for *Sa* and dinner, and come home to a dark *fale*. Since the children never showed up for their reading lesson, he would open his laptop and try to work on his novel before falling asleep. More importantly, he used the opportunity and the room's electricity to charge his computer.

On one occasion Aumua wasn't able to take Blue on a walk for his Samoan language lesson, so he decided to go to the trading store and see if he could get himself some kind of lighting for his *fale*. It was a small convenience store with a couple of old movie posters, and a "Vailima Beer" sign hanging on the wall. Although the shelves were half full, a standing, glass refrigerator was teaming with beverages that included water bottles, canned cokes, and bottled beers.

Like most of the buildings in the village, the store had no air-conditioning—only a couple of ceiling fans, one of which was broken. Its stock was mainly snacks like chips, cookies, and candy, rice, housewares and hygiene products, cloths and clothing, and canned goods. Once a month, specialized items would come to the store and sell out immediately. No one knew exactly when these items would arrive, but word of mouth helped move the items off the shelves.

When Blue entered the store, the first thing he did was to cool himself by sticking his head in the refrigerator. He closed his eyes as a blast of cold air froze his eyelashes. Behind the counter, Savea Suisala, the owner of the store, got very excited that the village celebrity was there to patronize his store.

"*Talofa*," Savea exclaimed. He continued to say something in Samoan but remembered that the volunteer's level of understanding was not that advanced.

Blue pulled his head and a couple of bottles of water out of the refrigerator. His face was numb with coolness. He closed his eyes to relish the last few seconds of splendid iciness.

*Damn me, that feels good.*

When he opened his eyes, he was startled upon seeing Taaiti, the village *taulāsea*, standing next to him. The old woman was staring at him and smiling. Then, without warning, she began to sniff the air around his head and body and mumbled something in Samoan. Blue backed away from her, as she looked at him and nodded her head with a satisfied acknowledgment.

"You clean," the traditional healer said in English with a snort. "Good. Good boy."

As soon as she left the door, her long black and silver hair blew in the air. She left the store with a bounce and a laugh, holding a jar of chicken feet.

Blue placed his water bottles on the counter and looked back at the old healer.

*What the eff was that?*

"She only comes here for one thing—chicken feet," said Savea Suisala. "And she never pays me for them."

"What does she use them for?"

"I don't know. We're not supposed to ask."

Blue shook his head and turned his attention to his transaction.

"Hey! You know my wife at St. Cecilia," said Savea in English.

Blue looked at him. He had met a few women at the school, but had no idea who he was talking about.

"I'm Savea Suisala."

Blue still had no idea which woman he met was Savea's wife.

"I was the *tufa'ava* at your ceremony," Savea said proudly. "My wife is Vaveao."

"Ah. Okay."

"What can I help you with?"

"I need a light bulb."

"Right. A light bulb."

"Do you have one?" asked Blue.

"Yes," answered Savea. But then he thought about it. "No."

"Okay."

"I have flashlight."

"Great. I'll take one of those."

"But. Sorry. Not batteries." Savea quickly looked under the counter. "I'm out of flashlights. Sorry, mate."

"Do you have any kind of lanterns?" Blue asked getting a little frustrated.

"Yes."

Blue's eyes perked up.

"Next month," the storekeeper added.

"How about a blanket?"

"Next week," Savea stated with enthusiasm. "All colors."

Blue looked around the store. The half empty shelves discouraged him.

"Savea, what do you have?" Blue asked with a little sarcasm in his tone.

"Tin corned beef. Very tasty."

Blue wiped the sweat off his forehead and looked at the refrigerator. He wished he could just leave his head with the cool drinks for the rest of the night. He sighed.

"All right. I'll take a couple of cans of corned beef," he said, a little defeated.

Savea merrily rang the order.

"Fifteen *talas*."

Blue paid him and the storekeeper bagged the items. He thought about asking for a can opener, but he decided not to.

"*Faafetai*," Blue said.

"Don't forget, I have all your needs." Savea said, meaning every world. "You don't have to go anywhere else."

Before exiting the store, Blue stopped and turned around to Savea.

"Is there anywhere else to go?" asked Blue with a hint of hope in his tone.

"No."

That night, Blue didn't feel up to going to Fiame's house for *Sa* and dinner. Even though Fiame hosted a lot of her *aiga*, Blue knew she would find him missing. He knew he would have to be prepared to answer a few questions about his absence from school the next day. Nonetheless, on this evening he was excited to stay in his *fale* and work on his novel. Togi had given him a camping lantern that provided a much-needed, but dull luminesce, and casted eerie shadows throughout his *fale*.

In his mosquito net, Blue worked on his novel wearing only boxer shorts. From time to time he noshed on corned beef from the tin and slurped papaya. He was surprised how good the corned beef was and was glad that Togi had given him a can opener.

Another storm was brewing, and Blue could hear thunder rumbling in the distance. The air was stagnated and oppressive. The humidity rose and wrapped around him like a blanket. He wished he had a fan to circulate the air and wondered if Togi could find him one. Blue knew he would have much better luck asking Togi for things than going to Savea in the trading store.

As Blue's fingers feverishly flittered over the keyboard, sweat dripped from the tip of his nose onto the computer. Lightning flickered and lit the dark crevices of the slats of the blinds around the *fale*, and a crack of thunder, this time much closer, quickly followed. Blue looked up from his computer and waited for the next flash of lightning. Growing up in San Diego County, he didn't get to experience weather like this very often. This time, however, the thump of thunder seemed to beat the lightning to the punch.

Blue left his mosquito net and opened a row of his blinds. He was hoping that a gush of wind would blow off the blanket of humidity. But as soon as the blinds came up, the three hounds that had recently taken a liking to him came running into the *fale* as if they were spooked. Blue watched them huddle together on the other side of the room.

*What the hell was that all about?*

The rain began to pound on the roof of the *fale*.

Blue looked back across the grassy field and couldn't believe his eyes when he saw the women in white standing, once again, in the rain. This time, they weren't standing still, and in fact, were walking towards his *fale*.

*Who are they?*

One of the dogs howled, which caused Blue to turn to look at the hounds.

When Blue looked back at the women, lightning showed that they were now only twenty yards away from him. Thunder cracked.

When lighting sparked twice, Blue was able to recognize Scarlett Wang once again. He rubbed his eyes. Sweat cascaded down his chest and tickled his belly button.

*Damn me.*

Blue squinted for a better look and was thunderstruck. Without a doubt it was definitely Scarlett.

He shut the blinds and took a step back.

*It can't be.*

Blue always felt guilty about her death during Christmas break of their second year in college. He hadn't seen her since before college. Oddly, she never came home during her first year. When she came home, the first thing they did was to go to their beach at their little cove. Blue, however, instantly felt she wasn't acting like her usual self. He noticed that she was quieter and more reticent than usual. More pale than usual. Perhaps she was even a little more grown up than usual. When Scarlett decided to go into the ocean, Blue felt that it was kind of odd, as she never really liked going into the water. Besides, the water was freezing at that time of the year, and the winter waves were quick and strong. She went in slowly, as if waiting for each part of her body to get accustomed to the temperature of the water. The force of the waves would push her back, and when they receded, she would gain back the ground she lost, and perhaps a little more.

Scarlett then turned to Blue and stared at him. The waves rose behind her and seemed to grab her.

"The water's gotta be freezing! You're crazy!" Blue yelled, but he wasn't sure if she could even hear him from the sound of the waves crashing against her and the shore.

Scarlett then turned and faced the wide ocean. No matter what time of year, the sea had a way of enticing people to come to it.

Blue got bored watching her stand waist high in the water and turned his attention to setting up a board game he had brought.

When he looked back at her, she was gone.

He remembered smirking and thinking she'll be splashing out of the water soon.

She didn't.

Blue waited and inquisitively watched as each set of waves rolled roughly on to the beach, revealing nothing but occasional clumps of kelp.

A chill shot down his spine. He stood up. He thought for sure the next wave would carry her back to shore.

It didn't.

Blue yelled Scarlett's name, but the sound of the waves drowned him out. He lunged forward to the water's edge. He yelled for her again. He asked himself if he should jump in the water. He took one step and then another, his feet touching the cold water. He asked himself if he should go in after her.

He didn't.

A couple of weeks later, he attended Scarlett's funeral. It was a large family affair with many speeches. Although everyone was in solemn disbelief, Blue noticed that the strains on Scarlett's parents' faces seemed more enraged. He wondered if they would add to the eulogies.

They didn't.

---

*It can't be. It just can't be!*

Blue stared at the closed blinds of the *fale* as lightning seeped through gaps. He felt compelled to look again at the women. He had to make sure he wasn't seeing things. He had to make sure it wasn't Scarlett.

He crept to the blinds and slowly split a couple of slats open only to see Scarlett's whitish-green face with bloodshot eyes staring at him. Scared to death, he let go of the blinds and stumbled backward and onto the ground. Looking back at the blinds, a lighting flash revealed her entire body.

The hounds began to howl. Thunder clapped.

"Scarlett?"

A strong gust of wind blew the blinds inward. Blue braced himself and believed that the ghastly apparition would enter the *fale*. However, after calling out her name and acknowledging her, he was relieved that a spark of lightning revealed that the figure of Scarlett was gone.

For the rest of the night, Blue sat awake under his mosquito net with the lantern and all three dogs.

8

_______

The chilling encounter with his ghostly friend at his *fale* left Blue in a troublesome and upsetting state. Troublesome in the sense that he questioned the reason why, now, after four years of being dead, would Scarlett come to haunt him. Blue never believed in the paranormal, although he wished like hell for a few years to see his mother one more time after her untimely death. Living in an isolated village surrounded by shadows and superstitions, however, did tease his senses, and it would only get worse. He was glad to have the island hounds for company, as they seemed to be as frightened from phantoms as much as their host.

Blue spent the next few days in his *fale*. He kept the blinds that faced the grassy field closed but raised the blinds on the other side to break and move the stagnate air. Fortunately, he only missed one day at St. Cecilia because it was closed to the weekend—not that his presence was needed at the time. He probably would have missed another school day from an upset stomach that forced him to hurry to the outhouse behind his *fale* every so often. Blue blamed his diarrhea first on Savea Suisala for selling him the cans, and then on the actual corned beef cans, which he noticed were well passed their expiration date. Every time he rushed to the outhouse, the hounds got excited and would follow, sniffing him and nipping at the back of his legs. Blue couldn't believe he spent a whole day sitting in a sweltering, stinky, and fly-infested place. Blue tried to hurry himself in the outhouse—a man can only stay in that place for so long before gagging on the fetid air. The dogs on the other hand, waited patiently for him to come out, invigorated by the stench that followed.

*The Little House on the Prairie just called, and it wants its outhouse back.*

Togi knew that something was wrong with Blue when he realized that the volunteer didn't show for work. For the next few days, Togi would often visit Blue, bringing coconuts, water bottles, fish that he caught, and cold beer, which he would drink himself. Blue didn't mind, though, as he was somewhat of a teetotaler because alcohol gave him severe headaches. In fact, Togi would compulsorily use his small machete to eat the entire fish by the end of his stay. Nevertheless, Blue enjoyed Togi's company, and it never ceased to amuse him when their conversation inevitably led to Keanu Reeves.

"I think we would be awesome bros, man," Togi said with a gleam in his eye.

"Who?"

"Me and Keanu." Togi made the name "Keanu" sound perfect with his accent.

"I'm sure he would think you're a good bro."

"We have the same adventures."

"Dude, don't confuse his movie life with his normal life."

"You think he could fish?"

"Not like you."

"Ha! Nobody fishes like Togi," Togi said, stretching his head above the clouds.

"You're the man."

Togi offered some fish that still had its head. Blue looked at it and gagged.

"No thanks," Blue said.

"I can't believe you don't know Keanu," Togi added. "I know all the important people in Vaimasina."

"Dude, there's like three hundred and fifty million...who do you know that is so important here?"

Togi rambled off a bunch of names. Blue found it interesting that the list of names that Togi provided were mainly from his *aiga*. They were grandparents and great-grandparents who defied colonialism and missionaries, half brothers and sisters living abroad, cousins who were good at rugby, uncles who owned a fishing boat, aunts who were excellent dancers, and, of course, his father, Chief Joseph Tuputala. Blue understood that adhering to *Fa'a Samoa* was closely associated with honoring one's family. To Togi, his family members were the real celebrities, and he proudly went in to detail about them, as the sharing of his ancestry was an important way to show his own identity.

For an hour Blue tried to keep up with Togi's family ancestry, and often dozed off. Blue did perk up when he heard the name, Aumua, and when Togi shared the legends of Joseph Tuputala.

"Come on, Togi, no man can drown a twelve-foot shark," Blue interjected, mostly to help him stay awake.

"My father is not a man, bro."

"Are you sure?"

"*Ioe!*"

"He looks like an old man."

"He was born a legend."

"And sea serpents, sirens, and sorcerers don't exist."

"Not around here anymore."

"I think you're confusing your father with Sinbad."

"Who?"

"Just another legend."

"Someday I will follow in my father's path," Togi exclaimed while picking up his small machete.

"Does a man make the legend, or does the legend make the man?"

"I don't understand, bro."

"Neither do I. Forget I said anything."

As the church bells rang for *Sa*, the hounds came bounding in the *fale*, yipping at each other. One of the dogs stopped to chew on his tail, while the other two dogs tackled each other and rolled into the small nightstand. The lamp fell and shattered on the ground.

"Aaaiee! Bro, why you let them in here?" Togi asked with a hint of disgust in his tone.

"They're all right. They're good company."

"They'll give you fleas."

"Too late," Blue said scratching the fleabites on his leg.

"You need woman," Togi said with a hearty laugh. "Right?"

Blue was speechless and wondered if Togi meant what he said.

"I send you Taaiti," Togi added.

"No! No thanks."

"She'll cure your illness and your loneliness," Togi said with a laugh.

"Dude, I'm fine. Really."

Togi picked up a coconut and chopped the top off with his machete, leaving a hole as large as a quarter. He handed the coconut to his friend and told him to drink. Togi then picked up another coconut and hacked off the top of it. He downed the coconut water with one gulp, ate some of the inside coconut meat, and wiped his mouth with his arm.

"*Feiloai mulimuli ane*, bro," Togi said.

"Yeah, *feiloai taeao*. See you tomorrow."

After Togi left, Blue settled in his mosquito net drinking his coconut water. The water inside the nut seemed endless, and he wondered how Togi drank it in one swig. It would take him another fifteen minutes to drink the coconut dry.

He thought about Togi's offer to send him a woman, but he knew that was out of the question due to his condition. Blue was never a romantic person. He wondered if being romantic was something one learns or was it innate? His girlfriend, or fiancé, Harper, was very romantic with him. She took him out to candlelight dinners, wrote him poems, and enjoyed wearing sexy swimsuits when they went to the beach. He wasn't very good, or creative, at reciprocating that level of romance. He could've have played her an amorous Mendelssohn or Debussy piece on the piano. But the sad truth was that after dating her for almost three years, Harper never even knew he even played the piano. On this night, however, in his oppressive, yet sultry *fale*, the thought of sharing his mosquito net with Aumua seemed inappropriately romantic to him.

Blue grabbed his computer to work on his novel but couldn't help think about the genealogy of the Tulutapa family that Togi so elegantly expressed, with perhaps, a bit of exaggeration. He started to think about his own ancestry and quickly came to the conclusion that he didn't really know anything about his ancestry aside from his grandfather on his mother and aunt's side. Although Blue never met the man, he could recall how his mother and her sister would often talk about him. There were also times during his youth when he observed his mother and aunt eerily talking to their father and wanting approval from him even though he had been dead for almost two decades.

The glow from his computer screen was the only source of light in his *fale*, as the batteries of the camping lantern that Togi brought him wore out. His screen saver of different classical composers created shadows that skimmed back and forth along the rafters like little dark spirits looking for the best spot to jump to the floor. A gecko's cackling call was quickly muffled by the pack of sonorous dogs in deep sleep.

Blue sat back in his mosquito net and wondered if he could piece together his ancestors as easily as Togi did. He thought that it shouldn't be too difficult. He only knew a handful of relatives. Indeed, his grandfather, Malcolm Blue, was the only person that he could start with. Inspired by Togi, Blue believed that his grandfather's story should be passed down and even elaborated through the generations.

Malcolm Blue was born at the end of World War I and grew up in the Notting Hill neighborhood of London. His parents owned and operated the Blue's Antiques and Curiosities Shop on the famous Portobello Road. Blue loved the word, "curiosities," and often wondered if his great-grandparents sold items such as a monkey's paw, a gold lamp that harbored a genie, or a magic wand. When Malcolm wasn't in school or at home, he was helping in the store. He performed a variety of tasks such as putting price tags on items, polishing silver, sweeping the floors, cleaning the glass displays, relocating items within the store, and, at Christmastime, he would help decorate the storefront windows with the hope of enticing more customers.

It wasn't always about work, as an antique store was like a playground for children with a vivid imagination, especially in those years in between the two great wars, which Malcolm and his three younger siblings definitely possessed. They would eagerly play old board games, ride children's bikes and wagons, set up tin soldiers and knights that protected princesses and castles, donned dresses, suits, and costume jewelry, and pretended to have tea using vintage sets much to the chagrin of their parents. Malcolm's favorite pastime in the store, however, was spending countless hours producing live theater with the use of dolls and marionettes. He and his siblings would often holdshows for the neighborhood children, or for children who simply came into the store to shop with their parents.

Malcolm Blue loved the theater and wanted to be a thespian. At the age of eleven, he joined a local theater, auditioned for everything that had a boy in the cast, and enjoyed any part he could get, even the smallest ones with few lines. His parents' store also served as a used bookstore, and whenever a book donation came through the doors, he would sift through the box and pick out the plays. Although he enjoyed all the playwrights, he got particularly excited when he found plays by Shakespeare, Webster, Shaw, Wilde, Ibsen, Chekhov, and O'Neill. Malcolm would stealthily take the plays home to read, and when he was done, sneak the books back into the store.

When Malcolm was in his late teens and early twenties, he would make the short trip to the West End for roles in the numerous theaters in the area. He particularly enjoyed playing Shakespearean characters and loved speaking in the sixteenth century English. At home, he would annoy his siblings by responding to them in Elizabethan phrases. Little did he know at the time that throughout his lifetime, he would run the gambit of Shakespeare's characters from the young Romeo to the old King Lear, and every hero or villain in between.

As Malcolm was acquiring more roles and making a career for himself, everything came to a halt when Europe ignited in war. The theaters closed, and he wanted to do his part to fight for England. He enlisted in the Royal Army, and after training, was sent to North Africa. Malcolm fought mostly Italian armies at first, and he hoped that his contribution was somehow helping the people of England, even though he couldn't see what was happening at home. He knew the Germans Luftwaffe was brutally pounding London, and he prayed, even though he wasn't religious, that the Royal Air Force was doing all that they could do to minimize the destruction. He often wondered if his family and his beloved theaters were surviving air raids. He wrote to his family, and after asking how everyone was getting on, he would then ask how the theaters were holding up.

After several close, scary, and lucky calls fighting Italian divisions and pushing them back, it wasn't until General Edwin Rommel, The Desert Fox, arrived to support the Italians, that Malcolm feared his luck would run out. In October of 1942, during intense fighting of the second battle of El-Alamein, Egypt, Malcolm was wounded by German artillery. The right side of his body took most of the impact, and he couldn't hear out of his right ear, or see out of his right eye. He felt as if only half of him was alive. It took hours for medics to remove shrapnel out of the right side of his body. When he finally returned home a couple of months later to convalesce, he eventually recovered from his wounds but showed terrible scars throughout the right side of his body including the area around his chin and neck. He would recite many Shakespearean lines about death.

Malcolm didn't let his scars deter him from returning to the theater. Once he fully recovered, he was back performing and would optimistically tell colleagues that his scars could land him the roles of evil characters.

About a year after the end of World War II, Malcolm became part of a touring troupe that went to America to perform Shakespearean plays in major cities of the East Coast. This event would be life-changing for him. When the tour ended in New York City, Malcolm became enchanted with the place and decided to stay and tried to find work on Broadway. For such a gifted actor, work was easy to come by. Possessing a beautiful singing voice, he was even cast in several musicals.

It was having a role in the musical, *Finian's Rainbow*, in

1947, where Malcolm would meet the love his life, Sarah O'Sullivan, an Irish American from Boston who was cast in the same musical. She was beautiful, with red hair and green eyes, and Malcolm would call her his, "lassie of the moors." He loved the way her nose twinkled when she smiled like a fairy godmother. Malcolm and Sarah fell in love during rehearsals and would spend every second together during their run of the show. They married in a lavish ceremony surrounded by family, friends, colleagues, and the cast of *Finian's Rainbow*—including the leprechauns. Long after the two had left *Finian's Rainbow,* they would continue to sing the songs of the play to each other. They would sing the songs through good days and bad days, or times of good news or when one was trying to apologize to other. With the exception of being a soldier, his relationship with Sarah would be the only other time that Malcolm dedicated a part of his life to something other than the theater.

Unfortunately, Broadway wasn't enough for Sarah. She craved the stardom of the movies, and Hollywood called for her. She convinced Malcolm to move to Los Angeles, which caught Malcolm by surprise because he truly believed that she was happy in New York. But he wanted to see the West Coast, and before they even hopped on the train, he had already acquired a role in a play at the grand Pantages Theater in Hollywood. During the four-day train ride, Sarah talked about nothing else but the pictures, hinting that the stage was currently beneath her.

It didn't go well for Sarah in those early months of 1948, and she found it difficult to land any major roles. The more frustrated she got, the more obsessed she became. Obsession and art typically lead to misunderstanding and misbeliefs and was often on a collision course with jealousy. She became invariably envious of Malcolm, who turned down starring roles in movies because of his busy stage schedule that included roles in various theaters along the West Coast, from San Francisco to San Diego.

Sarah withdrew more and more from Malcolm's life. She would hole up for hours in the bedroom of their rented house, pouring over celebrity magazines and acting out lines from the recent hit movie. Obsessive artists seek other obsessive artists, and at night when Malcolm went to work, she would keep company with other actors trying to break in to "the business." She would engage in heavy drug use or alcohol with this group. She loved it when the group complained about auditions or sneered and derided those they knew who got jobs. On some nights, Malcolm would arrive home before her and stay up worrying until she arrived. He saw how her behavior was changing. Sarah would only be intimate with Malcolm when she was high on drugs or alcohol. He truly felt sorry for her and offered to return to New York, but she refused, stating that she was just one audition away from making it big. Obsession distorted reality.

Malcolm tried to sing songs from *Finian's Rainbow* to her, but she didn't reciprocate. When he sang a few lines, she would simply close the bedroom door.

Then life became even more complicated when Sarah found out she was pregnant. The joyous news was received with mixed emotions. On one hand, she could occupy her mind and time with being a mother, while on the other hand she could postpone making it in Hollywood. Malcolm believed that the baby kept Sarah from dying. She got off the drugs and stopped drinking. She devoted her time to the coming child, which she felt was an admirable excuse not to pursue her acting dreams in Hollywood. By the end of 1948, Sarah gave birth to a baby girl, which they named Ophelia after the tragic Shakespearean character. Two years later, Sarah and Malcolm were blessed with a second daughter who would eventually become Ronin's mother. They named her after, arguably, the most tragic female Shakespearean character of all—Juliet.

About five years after the birth of his second child, Malcolm saw an opportunity to move his family to San Diego County. He always loved performing at the Old Globe Theater in beautiful Balboa Park, surrounded by buildings and museums of Spanish architecture that were nestled under large eucalyptus trees. More importantly, he worried about Sarah's mental health, and there were times when he saw Sarah's obsessions creep up in the recesses of her mind like a ghost in a dark corner. He believed that the move away from Hollywood would benefit his wife most of all.

The next few years seemed to be the happiest in Malcolm's life. They rented a house on a hill looking towards San Diego Bay. The girls spent their free time learning instruments, writing poetry, and painting pictures. They never wasted an opportunity to share their new art, music, or writing pieces with their father, and constantly asked him for his opinions. The girls also enjoyed going to the zoo, which was quickly becoming one of the world's most famous zoos, and frolicking at the beach. In the evenings, they would sit on their porch and watch ships come and go in the bay and become silhouettes against the setting sun.

Sadly, during this time Malcolm was unaware that the demons of obsession were taking over Sarah's mind once again. The joy of motherhood had worn away, and she thought about nothing else but Hollywood. Every so often she would get a letter from one of her old acting friends telling her about the upcoming film that he or she was cast in, or she would see one of their names printed on a movie poster. She returned to her drug habit by securing them from lowlifes in Balboa Park or downtown San Diego.

In the mid-1960s, Malcolm bought a piece of land in an unincorporated part of North San Diego County between the city of Oceanside and the Marine base of Camp Pendleton. He knew that Sarah always wanted to live in her own home. He told himself that building a home they can call their own, would do wonders for the family, and would ease the strain that Sarah had been exhibiting.

Malcolm had built a two-story Tudor-style home with triangular frames and a couple of chimneys, much like one would find in Shakespeare's time. It was a fairytale type of house with modern conveniences. Malcolm was proud that his new home was unique and in an area that was protected by greedy developers who wanted to capitalize on developing neighborhoods with cookie-cutter houses squished together (to make one oozing cookie). Malcolm also anticipated that the girls would enjoy a nearby path that weaved through the California chaparral to the secluded beach that they eventually called Sabatini's Beach.

A couple of weeks after Malcolm's family moved into their new home, Sarah disappeared.

Securing a few friends to watch the children, Malcolm left to try to find his wife. He was gone for two months. His search was futile, as Sarah didn't have any family to get any leads. She was simply nowhere to be found.

When Malcolm returned home, he took the girls to Sabatini's Beach and told them the truth: that their mother was gone and was not coming back. The sky and sea were both gray that day and made it hard to decipher the horizon. The three of them sat on the sand and had a cry, which was muffled by the waves smashing ashore. Malcolm told them to sit quietly, and they should try to remember their favorite moments each had with their mother. As they did so, a flock of pelicans swooped down in single file rows, and they smoothly sailed a few feet above the ocean. Watching the prehistoric-looking birds effortlessly ease their way through the wind, Juliet solemnly stated that, perhaps, their mother was now one of the pelicans flying peacefully to paradise. It was a day none of them would ever forget.

⸻

Blue shifted in his mosquito net. A wind whistled through the slats of the blinds creating an eerie, high-pitched sound like one blowing on the edge of a piece of grass. An oppressive feeling hung in the air like floating candles in a haunted house. He had a spooky suspicion that the women in white dresses surrounded his *fale*. Blue looked at the hounds that were dead asleep. He thought that if the dogs weren't worried about the creepy sound and women, she shouldn't be either. At the moment, Blue strongly believed that if the women in white, and especially Scarlett, were to make an attempt to make another ghostly appearance inside, the dogs would know first and warn him.

Reminiscing about his grandfather made him a little homesick. It wasn't because he never got to know his grandparents that made him pensive, or even their depressing story. For all he knew, his grandmother could conceivably still be alive somewhere, and his grandfather, although broken-hearted, continued to have a successful career in the theater after his wife left him until he passed away fifteen years later from an unexpected cardiac arrest.

No, it was the fact that he still lived in the Tudor-style house that his grandfather had built, and he missed the odd-looking house near the ocean. He missed the cool marine layer that moved inland during the night and hung around until it dissipated from the morning sun. He missed the interior of his home with its floor to ceiling bookshelves, sculptors, and paintings from all over the world that made him feel as if he was in a museum. There was even a large Blue family coat of arms hanging on the wall above the piano that he can still picture in his mind the countless times he stared at it during his lessons. He missed his own room and the way his comfortable bed conformed to his body. He missed his Aunt Ophelia, who never knew his age and always treated him ten years older than he was. But most of all, he missed his mother.

At the moment he especially missed the way she spontaneously sang Broadway tunes to him, and he, like the favorite mama's boy that he was, would sing along with her. The memory put a smile on his face.

On this dark and sweltering night sitting alone underneath the mosquito net with malevolent ghosts swirling around the outside of his *fale*, he felt oddly comforted by the thought that the spirit of his mother and his grandfather were watching over him somewhere in the darkness.

Blue finally lay down on his mat and wrapped their presence around him like a blanket and didn't let go until he fell asleep.

9

It was late morning, and Blue was sitting in his classroom trying to work on his novel. The heat of the day had made him tired and sweat dripped onto his keyboard from the tips of his hair like a leaky faucet. Although there were a few children (ages eight to ten) in the classroom, they weren't there to study reading. Instead, they were climbing on boxes and looking for things to get into while they were on recess. When they first arrived, Blue made an attempt to teach them some reading, but they were disinterested. So, he returned to his novel. In fact, after several weeks at St. Cecilia, he wasn't even sure which students he was supposed to teach. The children, however, were very much interested in his computer and would ask "Mister *Lanu Moana*" all kinds of questions in Samoan. They especially enjoyed plucking the keyboard, which irritated Blue because they kept adding gibberish to his novel. Nevertheless, Blue was very proud that he could answer some of the questions and scold them in their native language.

Every so often, Blue would gaze through the windows to see if the ladies in white would make an appearance at the edge of the bush. He hadn't seen them for several days and started to believe that, perhaps, it was the heat or exhaustion, or heat exhaustion that had caused him to hallucinate the haunting female apparitions. Still, he didn't want to get caught off guard by the women, and he wanted to catch them in the act. He told himself that the next time it happened, he would go to them and confront them, especially the one that looked like Scarlett.

On this day, however, the only thing that Blue witnessed through the window was an odd moment where a woman angrily chased Togi. She was about the same age as Togi, and in one arm she carried a one-year-old baby, and in the other a traditional broom made of coconut palm leaves. The woman wildly swung the broom at Togi, and when her attempt did connect with the big man, he looked as if he hardly felt it.

Although Blue was amused at the unusual quarrel, the children in the room became even more titillated as if watching juvenile monkeys play with each other in a cage at a zoo. All the kids ran to the window and laughed or hollered every time the broom connecting with Togi. When the children laughed, Togi looked towards the classroom and pathetically smiled as if on stage.

Blue leaned back in his chair. The thought of going out there and helping his friend did briefly cross his mind, but he knew better than to get in the middle of a lover's spat— at least that's what he believed what was unfolding in front of him. He tried to listen closely as the woman berated Togi. He was able to understand some words, and he guessed that Togi was a terrible father. The revelation floored Blue. After a couple of months in Samoa, he never thought that his friend was married and had a child. In fact, he would soon learn that Togi had two sons.

Blue's hounds loved a fracas and came out of nowhere to join the fray. They barked and danced around the couple. The woman figured they were on the side of Togi and started swinging her broom at the allies. Blue felt that the woman would have a taken on the whole village if they sided with Togi.

It wasn't long before Togi slipped and fell to the ground. A roar of laughter came from the classroom. The hounds could never resist the urge of a dog pile and jumped on Togi, only to be brushed away from a wild swish of the broom.

As the dogs lost interest and scampered away, the woman reached down and helped Togi up. She then grabbed him by his shirt's collar and tugged him towards the village while occasionally slapping him with the broom. The children hooted and hollered, as a shamed Togi still managed to smile while being dragged away.

Blue was impressed how the woman was able to make a coordinated effort of dragging a boulder of a man, poking him with a broom, and all the while holding a baby. Blue raised his eyebrow and made a mental note to never cross Togi's woman.

A schoolboy blew in a conch shell, signaling the end of recess. Blue hoped that some of the kids would stay and work on their English, but they all scampered out of the classroom shouting their farewells and telling Mister *Lanu Moana* that they will see him soon.

Blue sighed and sat down in his chair. The heat rose. He looked at the broken ceiling fans and wished that they were working, spinning cool air and blowing ice cubes upon him.

About a half hour later, Blue saw Aumua heading towards the community room. He hadn't seen her for a couple of days. She had been too busy preparing for the Teuila Festival that was only a month away. Looking for an excuse to see Aumua and to leave the hotbox he was sitting in, Blue hurried over to the community room.

Upon entering the room, Blue noticed several *siapos*, or tapa cloths, strewn across the floor in various stages of processing. Women of all ages were teaching young female students the traditional and oldest cultural art form in which the cloth's main uses included clothing, burial shrouds, bed covers, and ceremonial garments. The largest and most completed *siapo* was a ten-foot by ten-foot cloth with an extraordinary Samoan design.

Blue studied the design of the large *siapo* and didn't notice Aumua approaching at a rapid pace.

"Mr. Ronin," Aumua said as if she had something very important to say. "Mr. Ronin."

"Aumua," Blue said. He loved pronouncing her name.

"Mr. Ronin. The zipper of your pants is down."

Blue looked down at the crotch of his pants and saw the gaping hole.

*Damn me.*

Blue turned his back on Aumua towards the open door. As he struggled to pull his zipper up, Fiame walked into the room.

"You need some assistance, Mr. Blue?" Fiame asked.

"No. I swear it's these pants."

"Yes. Quite."

Blue didn't know which way to turn. His cheeks turned red as a stop sign with embarrassment. At last he was able to get the zipper up. He turned to Aumua who wasn't there, and he noticed that she had moved on to help students with a *siapo*.

"How do like the *siapos*?" Fiame asked.

"They're pretty... amazing," Blue answered staring at Aumua.

"It's part of an initiative to learn our traditional customs that I implemented within the curriculum of the school about three years ago...with Father Krimple's approval, of course."

"I imagine that more schools throughout Samoa should do the same."

"Yes. We are at a point where we can't trust parents to pass down such knowledge."

"An investment in knowledge pays the best interest," Blue quoted. He then snapped his fingers. "Benjamin Franklin."

Fiame smiled and nodded. Over the past couple of months, she had become used to Blue's odd outbursts, believing that the volunteer was simply thinking on a creative level.

"We teach every step in the production of *siapos*," Fiame continued. "From the stripping, separating, scraping and beating bark from the mulberry tree. We even use traditional tools such as clamshells to scrape away remaining bits of bark."

"Unbelievable," Blue sincerely said.

"The dye you see is extracted from the bark of a... how do you say?... Blood Tree. We call it *o'a*. The *o'a* starts as a pale tan, but as it ages it becomes a dark brown."

"Where does the black color come from?"

"The *lama* comes from the kernel of the candlenut, and when it is mixed with the *o'a*- "

"*Voilá*- Black."

"Right."

Fiame always enjoyed teaching a foreigner about the customs of her Samoa. But it had been awhile since a *palagi* came to her village, so she took full advantage of Blue who was kind enough to listen. She continued with the different dyes they use on the tapa cloths, and told Blue how the red dye came from pods filled with seeds of a blooming lipstick tree. When the seeds are mixed with *o'a* and *lama* it produces the red color known as *loa*. Fiame added that the *ago*, or yellow dye, was extracted from the roots of a turmeric plant.

Blue tried to keep up with Fiame, but he was too distracted watching Aumua helping the schoolgirls with a *siapo*. Aumua, as if sensing someone was staring at her, looked at Blue, and he blushed and turned his head.

"You all right, Mr. Blue?" asked Fiame. "Your face keeps glowing red. Are you getting too much sun?"

"No. I'm fine."

Blue saw Father Krimple walking by the community room carrying a box. Blue decided to take advantage of the priest's presence.

"Excuse me, Fiame. I have to talk to Father Krimple."

"You come back then?"

"I won't be long."

"When you return, you can give scraping bark a try."

"I wouldn't miss it. I... I've been in a lot of scrapes before," Blue said and shot out of the room towards Father Krimple.

As Blue exited the room, Fiame gave him another strange look, not sure if she understood what he had just said. She shook her head saying to herself that he's just thinking on a different level.

Blue caught up with Father Krimple, which wasn't easy. Father Krimple never moved slowly. He always had a hundred and one things to do in a day, and he made sure to get them all done by dinnertime. He didn't believe in "Island Time," or "Samoa Time." They just held him back. If he got sick, he just added one more thing to do—get better.

"Father Krimple," Blue called, hoping the priest would stop.

Father Krimple didn't stop, but he did turn around.

"Ah, Ronin. Taking a break?"

"I saw the strangest thing earlier."

"Go on—lot of strange things in Samoa, my friend."

"A girl was beating up on Togi while holding a baby."

"Ah, yes. That's Togi's wife, Iris. She keeps him in line."

"She was half the size of...wait, his wife? They're married?"

"Not in the eyes of God," Father Krimple said with a hint of defeat. "They never married, at least not in front of me. But Iris is a regular churchgoer and makes sure to drag Togi with her to Mass," he added with optimism. "That's good enough for now."

Blue wondered more about the couple but surmised that

it would be as sore spot with the priest. It was best to leave the subject alone for the time being.

"You look like you could use some help, Father."

"Go on. What gives you that impression?" the priest asked. He rarely needs help with anything. But he does enjoy it when others from the community get involved. He probably could've moved the piano up the stairs to the balcony by himself much quicker than what transpired. However, Togi and Lance just happened to be walking by, and so he asked for their help.

"That's a big box you have there."

"Light bulbs. The church used to be lit up with only candles like a medieval castle. But we recently had more electricity rigged inside. The bulbs and lamps have finally arrived to give us more light."

"And God said, let there be light and there was light," Blue quoted, and then pitiably mumbled, "God."

"You know you're Bible, Ronin."

"Oh no."

"Go on!"

"I...I'm not really religious."

"Ah! We're all religious in one way or another. I've a friend whose religion is football. To him, Zidane is God. Then there are Saint Messi, and Saint Ronaldo..." The priest then saw something he didn't like, and stopped at the side door of the church. "Hey, hold this for a sec."

Father Krimple handed Blue the box. The box was a lot heavier than Blue expected, and he nearly dropped it.

"You sure you got light bulbs in here?"

The priest didn't answer. He was too concerned with a six-year-old student with a Teenage Ninja Mutant Turtle backpack who had wandered towards the church. Blue was able to comprehend a little of the Samoan that the priest was saying to the student. He was telling the boy to return to his classroom. But the boy explained that his teacher let the students go for the day.

The peculiarity of the situation then hit Blue. The boy was very light-skinned compared to other Samoan children, and he had wavy blond hair much like the priest. Blue looked at Father Krimple and then at the boy. The similarities in appearance the priest and the boy had begged questioning. Although Blue didn't know much about religion, he knew Catholic priests did not get married and lived a pious, celibate life.

Blue was able to discern that the priest gave the boy a final ultimatum to return to his classroom and help his teacher before going home.

Father Krimple watched the boy run back to his classroom before returning his attention to Blue.

"Right," the priest said clapping his hands. "Let's bring the church into modern times, eh?"

Blue looked at the priest. It wasn't his place or business to ask about the boy. But he knew if he were patient enough, he would be able to get the story through village gossip.

"Who's the boy?" Blue asked, thinking he'd give the priest a shot to come clean.

"That's Isaac. He has a habit of leaving his class early, but we usually coerce him to return."

Father Krimple opened the door of the church and stood aside to let Blue enter first.

Blue hesitated before entering the church. He stared at the priest who looked at him. It was an awkward pause, but he felt that Father Krimple wasn't going to confide in him.

"Let there be light," Blue said.

"Go on!"

Blue struggled through the doorway and jammed the box of lights against the doorframe and bounced backwards. The priest caught him.

"You got a body in here?" Blue asked.

Father Krimple smirked and guided the volunteer through the door.

Blue took the box straight to the altar of the church. The only source of light within the walls came through the stained glass windows, and the story of Saint Cecilia was now playing.

"You can put..." said Father Krimple, but realized he was too late to direct Blue who had already placed the box on top of the sacrosanct altar table. "I guess you really aren't religious."

Blue took a few steps forward away from the altar and was categorically mesmerized by the windows' story told in light and color. He thought about what kind of soundtrack would work best behind the story. Bach, perhaps, or a John Williams score, or a U2 song. Regardless, Blue's fingers itched. He thought it would only be right if he provided appropriate music from the piano.

It was the cello, however, that provided the backdrop in Blue's mind and ears. Staring at the windows, Blue cynically smiled. The music from the cello was perfect, and he instantly knew that there could only be one person who was playing. Blue glanced at the balcony and saw it was Scarlett who was creating a moody, mystical backdrop. It was intoxicating, with the music filling the church and reverberating off the walls of stone like a lonely echo.

Father Krimple noticed that Blue was lost to the mind-altering display of the windows. He thought about calling out to Blue to break him from the spellbinding affect the sun had, like a movie projector, on the windows. However, the priest let the volunteer have his moment of enlightenment, as everyone does when they get their first chance at watching the story unfold on a bright, cloudless day.

Blue thought about how much his mother would've enjoyed this unusual artistic moment. He could envision her engaged with the story that became more riveting as the music enhanced every scene. Juliet would've tried to convince her son that, although the story would be the same, the tone would change depending on the disposition and intensity of the sun.

It was the double doors to the front of the church opening and allowing light to pour into the church that broke Blue's concentration from St. Cecilia's story. The cello music abruptly stopped, and he looked to the balcony to see that Scarlett had disappeared. He then looked to the double doors and could decipher what looked to be a silhouette of a female posing like a model.

"Pardon me. But I've come to free a sexy American from this dungeon," said the silhouette.

Blue looked at the female in the doorway and smiled. A gust of wind swished through the church, and Blue wondered if the girl was responsible for creating such a breath of fresh air.

"Oh, fun," Father Krimple said to himself softly.

"Who's the girl?" Blue asked.

"It's the one and only Misi Sao. And, she's not a girl."

Amazed, Blue watched the six-foot Misi strut down the center aisle of the church as if it was a runway at the Met Gala. Misi looked sleek in a purple *puletasi*.Misi's hairstyle was bobbed and curled inward just under the chin. A thin, yet fashionable pink shawl with purple flowers was wrapped around her neck. Even the handmade satchel that Misi was carrying matched the outfit perfectly.

*How is that not a girl?*

"Misi is neither female nor male, but another gender known as a *fa'afafine*," Father Krimple added.

Blue was intrigued. He would later learn that a *fa'afafine* literally translated to "in the manner of women," and as Misi got closer, Blue could see the interesting contrast to transgenderism back home. Yet, he wondered if it was much more accepted here in Samoa than in Western society.

*Whoa. Straight out of the fa'afafine magazine.*

"Father K, are you keeping this boy all to yourself?" Misi said playfully.

"*Talofa*, Misi," the priest answered affectionately. "You haven't been home in a while."

"We haven't had a volunteer in a while."

Misi was about the same age as Blue, or perhaps a year or two older. It was difficult to truly guess Misi's age. The *fa'afafine* always acted and appeared ageless. Nevertheless, Misi was a niece of Fiame whose sister bore four sons first, and when the fifth child began to display a definite effeminate behavior, everyone recognized Misi to be *fa'afafine*.

In pre-Christian Samoa, every individual, either man, woman, or *fa'afafine* had a separate role in society and contributed significantly to families, churches, and cultural obligations. The missionaries naturally tried to put a stop to the third gender with the exception of the *taupou*. The *taupou* was a ceremonial hostess typically selected by the high chiefs. They were usually the daughter or a *fa'afafine* of a chief. They were often given the responsibility of representing the village and entertaining visitors particularly in the form of a dance. Missionaries didn't mind these hostesses because they idealized the *taupou's* virginal and virtuous qualities.

Misi Sao was an excellent *taupou* and performed the role with grace and vigor for Vaimasina. Misi was a respected celebrity within the village, and the *fa'afafine* could sing, dance, act, orate, and perform all the traditional responsibilities that women in the village are typically tasked with. The skills that Misi developed from a very young age would eventually win many *fa'afafine* pageants in Apia and other international competitions. Misi enjoyed the pageants because it brought a chance to perform while making an exaggeration and parody of the Christian-Colonial ideal through sexual humor and body language. Father Krimple appreciated the ability that Misi opened the door for discussion on forbidden and offensive topics through humor, particularly to educate villagers about sex, which was a taboo subject for men and women to discuss in public.

"*Talofa lava*," Blue said in the manner of starting a conversation.

"Ohh, he speaks Samoan," Misi said. "How cute."

"His Samoan's getting better," the priest added. "Misi, this is Ronin Blue. Ronin—Misi.

"Charmed," Misi said holding out a hand for Blue to take.

"Oh... uh...," Blue mumbled and awkwardly took her hand.

Misi quickly pulled the hand away. "This is Samoa. You don't have to be so formal, and you don't know where this hand's been, darling."

"Ronin's an author and is busy writing his book," Father Krimple said.

"How'd you know?" Blue asked with an inquisitive expression on his face.

Misi and Father Krimple looked incredulously at each other, knowing how naïve the volunteer was acting.

"Darling, it's a small village," Misi interjected. "Believe me, when I tell you that everyone knows what color underwear you wear."

"Eww."

"Black boxers," the priest added and shrugged his shoulders.

"Mm-hmm," moaned Misi and enhanced the situation by looking at Blue's bottom.

"Eww! That's unbelievably gross," Blue shrieked, and wondered if the blinds on his *fale* were broken. Misi laughed.

"So what are you writing?" the *fa'afafine* asked.

"A tale about forbidden love on the high seas."

"Mmm, how quaint," Misi stated.

"Oh, it's like that, uh... what's that... uh, story?" Father Krimple shouted with enthusiasm trying to remember the name of the popular movie that he couldn't momentarily think of.

"Yes, right, what is it...?" Misi said. The answer was on the tip of the *fa'afafine's* tongue.

*Don't say it.*

"Titanic!" Misi exclaimed.

*Damn me.*

"No, it's an epic tale that spans decades and two world wars. It's not about a lust-fest for three days on a boat," said Blue, defending himself.

Misi began to sing the song, "My Heart Will Go On," from the movie *Titanic*. Father Krimple couldn't help himself but to join the *fa'afafine*. The two sounded pretty good in harmony.

Although Blue thought the pair had nice voices, he shook his head with disgust. He hated the movie, *Titanic*, and he especially loathed the song that was synonymous with the film.

When Misi and Father Krimple finished, they both laughed. Blue wasn't exactly impressed, but he did notice how the two, despite being undeniably disparate individuals, got along so well.

"You should come to Apia, Father K," said Misi. "And do a show with me."

The two laughed even harder. Even Blue gave a short chuckle, before the priest turned his attention to the volunteer.

"Misi mostly lives in Apia these days," the priest stated.

"And Auckland, Sydney, and Singapore," Misi added.

"The dancer gets around."

"Father K, I'm appalled. You make me sound like a slut."

"Go on. I didn't mean..."

"I know, darling," Misi said and then turned to Blue.

"Father K and I were actually a good team before I left. We were the only sane ones in this village."

Blue liked the way Misi talked. Besides having a perfect accent, Blue thought the *fa'afafine* exhibited a sense of confidence and modernity without forgetting the place that created and molded the *fa'afafine's* cultural spirit and practices. Although Misi was a contemporary performer, the *fa'afafine* always included traditional customs and stereotypes in the act. Nobody enjoyed being Samoan more than Misi.

Misi reached into her satchel and pulled out a collared shirt with a Samoan design much like a Hawaiian shirt. Misi threw it to Father Krimple.

"A new shirt for you to add to the two I know you've already outworn."

"*Faafetai,*" Father Krimple said with a genuine smile.

"Now, American cowboy—turn around for me. Come. Come. Give me a twirl. I just love the twirls."

Blue hesitantly and reluctantly whirled around in a circle.

"Mm-hmm. Darling, you must be sweating your balls off in those pants," Misi stated. "Excuse me, Father K."

Misi pulled out a black *lavalava* and threw it to Blue.

"It takes a little getting used to. But darling, it's going to keep that undercarriage of yours cooler. Think of it as a kilt," Misi said and then leaned closer to Blue. "And, let everyone imagine what you got on under the *lavalava*. Mm-hmm."

"*Faafetai,*" Blue said.

"Love that accent."

The three were then instantly distracted as a group of male students of different ages including the blond boy,

Isaac, came springing into the church as if it was a shortcut they use every day. One boy was carrying a rugby ball and was tossing it to another.

"This is not a rugby field," Father Krimple said in Samoan. The boys stopped dead in their tracks. The whites of their eyes widened, and the hair stood on the back of their necks as if God himself stood in front of them. The boys quickly slowed their pace and silenced their voices. Father Krimple pulled Isaac aside so that no one else could hear what he had to say to the boy. The other boys made their way to the big double doors of the church and exited.

"I swear Father K's also the other kind of father," Misi said to Blue almost as a whisper. "Mm-hmm. You know what I mean?"

"I didn't want to say anything."

"This all happened when I wasn't around. The bugger."

"I don't know. It's gotta be a coincidence, right?" Blue asked with a tone of disbelief.

"The devil loves working in these small villages most of all," Misi said with a laugh.

Father Krimple patted Isaac on the arm, and the boy hurried down the center aisle of the church and left. The priest then turned to the others.

"I was just telling the American cowboy that he should come and see me perform."

"You won't forget it," Father Krimple said to Blue, raising his eyebrows.

"No one forgets me, darling. I'll be at Aggie Grey's and the Tanoa Resort the next few months," Misi said to Blue. "I expect to see you one night. Surprise me, though. I love surprises."

"They're making *siapo* in the center, Misi. Nobody did it better than you. Why don't you give them a hand?" the priest asked, knowing that Misi's knowledge in the skill would be beneficial to the students.

"It would be my pleasure."

"Nothing too risqué now."

"No worries, Father K. I'll be exemplary," Misi exclaimed with a chuckle.

"You want to join her, Ronin?" Father Krimple asked.

"What about the light bulbs?"

"I'll have to reschedule to replace them later. I have a meeting soon."

"I can do them for you," Blue offered.

"Thank you. There's a ladder in the storage room just behind the altar."

"Ta ta," Misi said and blew Blue a kiss.

Blue watched the two exit through the same door that he and Father Krimple entered. Misi, as if always on stage, naturally exited with a swagger.

Blue didn't hop to replacing the light bulbs right away. Instead, he sat down in a pew and turned his attention to the stained glass windows. The story of Saint Cecilia became dull and monotonous thanks to the thick clouds that covered the village. Blue wished the clouds would move on and let the light bring back the magic of the story. Blue waited and waited. He could hear the students and adults greeting Misi with enthusiasm.

Still waiting, he heard a rooster crow in the near distance, and he heard children playing rugby on the grassy field.

Blue waited a little longer. The light wasn't coming

back. In fact, it was getting darker. Probably rain would fall soon. It was then that the volunteer heard movement on the balcony. He turned and saw a shadowy figure. Although he couldn't see who it was upstairs, he knew it was Scarlett. Blue quickly turned his attention to the windows, as if telling Scarlett that he didn't care if it was there. He thought about what Misi said about the devil loving to work in small villages. He wondered how true it was. There were so many shadows for the devil to do his work in.

Blue leaned back in the pew and looked at the large crucifixion of Jesus on the back wall of the altar. He wondered how safe he was sitting alone in a shadow, even in God's house.

Melancholy, yet melodious music from a cello began to play, filling the church once again. Blue closed his eyes and listened.

10

It was one of those picture-perfect late afternoon days in the tropics when puffball white clouds glided placidly throughout the sky like parade floats. Blue and Aumua were wandering aimlessly among the beaten paths around the Vaimasina pool discussing how every plant, bird, insect, and animal was derived from one legend or another. Blue was pleased how his Samoan speech was coming along, as half of their conversation was spoken in the native language—typically until Blue didn't know a word or phrase and had to ask in English.

Blue was somewhat captivated with the way Aumua looked. Her jean shorts showed off her smooth, yet somewhat chunky legs, and she wore a T-shirt with the music band, Coldplay, blazoned across the front in bold letters. It was the T-shirt that truly intrigued the volunteer. Whenever he heard music in the village, it was either a traditional song, or a pop song that was reimagined with a reggae beat. He wondered if she was truly a Coldplay fan and if the band had ever performed in Samoa or the Pacific Islands.

Before Blue could ask about the shirt, Aumua had swiftly rushed away and playfully danced on the stones along the bank of the stream in her bare feet. Blue watched her dance with awe. Her graceful movements caught each rock perfectly without slipping in the water as if she had been dancing in that spot since she was born. When Blue caught up to her, she skipped away again to a noni tree and picked up ripe fruit from the ground. She then crashed in the shade of a frangipane tree and began to eat the noni. Blue finally reached her and sat next to her. Aumua offered Blue a noni. He accepted and took a bite. Children could be heard laughing and chattering in the pool just a short distance from where they were.

"Togi says you have girlfriend," Aumua stated in Samoan.

*Damn it, Togi.*

Blue hadn't thought about his girlfriend, or fiancé, or whatever she was in a while now.

"It's... uh, complicated," Blue answered, hoping that she wouldn't want to continue on the subject.

"Do you miss your girlfriend?" Aumua boldly asked.

"No?" Blue answered with a question, trying to be cute.

Aumua giggled when Blue answered her question with a question. Although her hair was up in a bun, a few black strands frivolously and flirtatiously fell across her forehead and covered her left eye. Blue wanted to kiss her.

"What's her name?"

"Who?"

"Mr. Ronin, your girlfriend!"

Blue hated it when the villagers, especially Aumua, called him, "Mr. Ronin."

"Harper," answered Blue, swatting a mosquito on his arm.

"Harper," she repeated.

Blue loved the way she pronounced the name with an accent, but he could tell it was a strange name for the island girl to comprehend. She repeated the name under her breath.

"Is she pretty?"

Blue sighed and dropped his head. The romantic moment he created in his imagination had faded, and he was forced to think about his girlfriend, or fiancé, back in the States.

*Damn it, Togi.*

Blue glanced at Aumua, who waited patiently for him to answer. She noshed on some noni, and tossed what she didn't want to eat into a bush.

The truth was that Harper was more than just pretty. She was a stereotypical gorgeous California girl with long sandy-blond hair and a beauty mark on her left cheek. Her hair simply amazed, and the natural light and dark streaks shined in the sunlight. She flaunted her figure in tight skirts and jeans, and never missed an opportunity to wear crop tops even on those chilly California days. Harper was the epitome of a surfer girl from upscale Solana Beach and spent most of her time at the beach. It was always unclear to Blue if she actually surfed. She never had time to hit the water, as she was too busy socializing with everyone she knew—and she knew everyone. Blue never really cared, however, if she ever hit the waves. Her body looked incredibly curvaceous in a wetsuit in the sea or on dry land. Harper was born with the gift of gab, gossip, chitchat and chatter. She made friends easily, boyfriends easier, and jealous girlfriends easiest. The Beach Boys used to write songs about a girl like her.

Blue and Harper met at San Diego State during their junior year. She sat next to him in an English Literature class, and she was always amused how she got a better grade on an essay than him, even on the ones she wrote the night before.

Harper was never shy and easily struck up conversations with everyone sitting around her. She was usually the focal point of the classroom. Even the teacher pulled her in during the lecture to start dialogues and discussions about the topic of the day, especially when the other students just sat there staring into space. Blue was always peeved at how this girl, who had everything, was also quite intelligent. Indeed, there was no doubt that she had school smarts too. School came easy for her. Her father was a lawyer, and her mother was a pediatrician. Harper was destined to be a college student. She was a political science major with an eye towards law school.

By coincidence one morning, the two found parking next to each other in the school's parking structure. Blue would never forget the day. As he was about to get out of his small green Toyota Echo that his mother left him, Harper, driving a dark green BMW sped into the parking spot next to him and almost took off his door. She even had the audacity to honk at him as she aggressively maneuvered her car into the slot.

Blue got out of his car in the hopes of getting a good look

and making a snarky remark at the Mr. Toad who so brusquely bullied their way to a parking spot.

Harper got out of her car and Blue's flaming head immediately cooled. She was wearing high heels, a pink skirt, and a gray-and-pink polka dot long-sleeved sweater.

*All she needs is a rat-like dog in her purse and she could pass for the "Legally Blonde" girl.*

"Sorry. I hope I didn't scare you. Parking spots are so hard to come by these days. I just got excited when this one was open," Harper explained.

"Yeah. The… uh, parking gods are looking favorably upon us today."

Harper sniggered with a snort. She never laughed, but only sniggered with a snort.

*Damn me. Even her snort is cute.*

The two started to walk towards the campus together.

"Were in the English Lit class together, aren't we?" Harper asked.

"Yeah."

"The professor's pretty awesome, isn't she?"

Blue didn't really like the professor. He found her a bit pretentious and her grading style difficult.

"Sure," Blue lied.

"You get a lot of "C's," don't you? I like the letter, "C," and I like writing them. I only get "A's," but I think they're uglier than the letter "C." My best friend, Myna, thinks the letter "G" is the best letter, but she only says that because her last name is Gross."

"What's so gross about her last name?"

Harper giggled.

"No, dorkus. That is her last name—Gross."

"Eww."

"Right. She needs to marry and change her name."

"Sometimes that could backfire though. She could marry a guy with the last name Bird."

Harper thought about what Blue had just said for a few seconds. She ran the names in her head a few times. Blue could feel the synapses of her brain flaring and fading like shooting stars. Despite her good looks, charm, and money, Blue loved her poise most of all.

Harper sniggered and snorted a couple of times.

"Myna Bird. I get it. That's so funny. I'll have to tell her that. Oh! There she is!" Harper exclaimed. "Come on."

"Wait—really?"

*Oh, shit.*

"Yeah, come on. Let's tell her. Come on."

Harper picked up her pace. Blue followed her for a few feet and then stopped.

"You know, I have to see a professor about a grade," Blue lied.

"You do?"

"Yeah, but, but I'll see you in class."

"Okay, Charlie Brown," Harper giggled. "See you in class."

"Uh... excuse me?" Blue asked a little confused.

"That's what the letter "C" reminds me of—Charlie Brown. He always got "C's" on his tests."

"Right."

As Harper hurried away to her group of friends, Blue realized that he never got her name. But more importantly, he hoped that she wasn't calling him Charlie Brown to her friends.

And that's how their relationship began. Harper was the second girl that ever talked to him after Scarlett. This was a Mr. Toad meets Charlie Brown chance encounter. It was odd. It was fast. To Blue it was totally romantic, and he couldn't wait for class.

---

Blue got hit by a flying piece of noni that forced him to break from his rapid reminisce. He looked at Aumua who smiled mischievously at him.

"Well, can she?" Aumua asked in Samoan.

"Is she pretty?"

"No."

"Can she climb a coconut tree?"

Aumua picked herself up and quickly went to a coconut tree. Although the tree wasn't quite fully grown, the coconuts grew about thirty feet from the ground. She grabbed the trunk of the tree and hopped on it. Her strong legs wrapped around the trunk like a snake coiling a death grip around its prey.

"This is how a Samoan girl climbs," Aumua said, and began to shimmy up the trunk of the tree.

Blue watched with concerned astonishment. He thought about calling out to her to get her to stop, but he knew it would be futile. To him, climbing a tree without branches was a foolhardy thing to do, but to Aumua it was easy and something she had been doing since she first started to walk. He also knew that Aumua was one of the few village girls who were athletic enough to climb a coconut tree.

Blue understood that the island girl wanted to make a

point that she could do something that his American girlfriend most likely couldn't do. At first, her attitude seemed rather childish to Blue until he thought how competitive the villagers were with each other and how they intuitively strived to be remembered for something they had done or achieved.

When Aumua reached the top of the tree, she grabbed a coconut, pulled it free, and threw it down. The coconut hit the ground with a thud and flipped over at Blue's feet.

Blue then looked up and saw Aumua slither down the trunk of the tree as easily as she went up. Towards the bottom of the tree she jumped, and Blue caught her in his arms.

"Easy," Aumua said in English with a smile. A little stream of sweat trickled down the side of her temple.

Blue held on to her waist, and she let him. He wanted to kiss her. She wanted him to kiss her. Confusingly, Blue thought of ole' wishy-washy Charlie Brown, and a snorting Harper, and... Togi.

Blue puckered his lips like a fish and closed his eyes. He leaned towards her and missed.

Aumua wriggled herself free of Blue's hands. The moment was lost. She picked up the coconut, and demurely walked away.

*Damn it, Togi!*

The island girl recognized that she had something Harper didn't have. It wasn't beauty, or money, or a first world sophistication. Aumua had what all islanders never take for granted—the present. The present was mundane to a Westerner—just another day another dollar. However, to an islander, the present was essential to living and so much depended upon it. Aumua knew that Blue was part of her present. He was here with her and not with Harper.

As Aumua led the way back to the village, Blue followed, hanging his head ashamedly low. He was a little embarrassed from failing to kiss her. The birds seemed to cackle even louder from the branches of the tree, and the temperature felt like it rose a few hundred degrees. Blue started sweating profusely and swatted away a couple of mosquitos that hummed around his head.

He thought the best plan was to strike up a conversation to make it seem like nothing had happened like the botched kiss was no big deal.

"Aumua," Blue said hoping she would stop walking. "Are you and Lance Lafau a couple?" he asked, and why not? He thought if she could ask about his girlfriend, or fiancé, or whatever she was, then he could ask about her love life.

Aumua didn't stop. She kept walking.

"Aumua, did you hear me?"

"Please, in Samoan"

Blue asked the question again in Samoan. He butchered it, but she understood.

Aumua stopped, turned to Blue, and coyly giggled.

"He's sweet."

"Lance? Sweet? Are you kidding me?" Blue asked incredulously. "Uh, the devil just called, and he wants his son back."

"The devil?" Aumua asked with a concerned look.

"Sorry, it was a joke," Blue said and felt like a boorish tourist. He should have known better than to say that Lance Lafau was the spawn of the devil to a superstitious, pious young lady.

"He likes me, *ioe*, but he's not around much."

Blue watched her turn her back on him.

It was true. Lance Lafau was hardly around. In fact, Blue was thinking how nice it had been at Fiame's house during *Sa* the past couple of weeks because Lance was in Apia probably committing all kinds of crimes. Nevertheless, Blue felt like a jerk for his outburst. Although he was a bit relieved with the revelation that Aumua and Lance were not an item, he wished he could stick his head in Savea Suisala's drink refrigerator.

*Damn it, Togi.*

Togi was the first person that came to his mind to blame for his *faux pas*.

It was at this moment that Blue looked across the stream and saw the women in white staring at him. They were only about twenty feet away, and Scarlett stood in front.

The women startled Blue, and he stumbled backwards into Aumua.

"What?" Aumua asked.

"Do you see them?"

Aumua looked around, but didn't see anything.

"See who?"

"Those women in white dresses."

Although Aumua didn't see anyone, she had a hunch what Blue was experiencing.

"White dresses?" Aumua asked.

"Yeah, I've seen them a few times."

"*Sau loa! Tatuo o!*" Aumua demanded. "We should go!"

Aumua turned and started to walk briskly away. Blue kept up with her.

"Do you know those women?" Blue asked. "Aumua? Aumua!"

Blue finally stopped the island girl. She turned around and Blue could see the fear in her dark eyes.

"Aumua, do you know them?" Blue asked again.

"Yes. You see the *Teine Sa.*"

"The what?"

"*Teine Sa.* Spirit women."

Blue looked back at the women in white to see that they had disappeared. But he believed Aumua. After all, one of them, Scarlett, was dead.

"We must go. If not, they make us suffer. Make us sick," Aumua added.

"Wait. I don't see them anymore."

"They are jealous, spiteful spirits. They will seduce you and hurt you."

Blue thought that the last thing he needed was to be seduced by a ghost. He looked back at the spot where he saw the *Teine Sa*, but he still didn't see them. A wind eerily picked up and blew, which dried the sweat from his skin. The birds fell silent, as if hiding from impending doom. When Blue turned back to Aumua, she was gone.

Blue caught up with her on the grassy field.

"Mr. Ronin, you should go to church and pray the *Teine Sa* will leave you alone."

"Look, Aumua. I think I was just seeing things. It was the way the sunlight hit the boulders that made it look like people," Blue explained. "I'm sorry I scared you, but it's okay. There was no one there."

Blue didn't want to make a big deal out of this. He knew that the villagers were very superstitious and would easily get the heebie-jeebies. Eventually, everyone in the village would hear about the event with the *Teine Sa*, and he would have to deal with their judicious stares and a surfeit amount of questions. Most importantly, he really enjoyed his walks and talks with Aumua, and he didn't want to compromise his relationship with her.

"I'm really sorry," Blue reiterated. "It was just sunlight playing tricks on me. I swear."

"Don't swear."

"Right. Sorry."

Aumua stared at the volunteer. She didn't really believe Blue, and she knew that the *Teine Sa* had been haunting villages across Samoa for centuries. However, she knew the best way to deal with them was through prayer.

Aumua hugged Blue. It was a quick hug, which felt as if she was trying to say, "Good luck. You're screwed." Despite the fact that the hug lacked passion, it still felt nice to Blue who hadn't been hugged for a long time.

"*Feiloai teaoa*," Aumua said. "See you tomorrow."

"*Feiloai teaoa*," Blue repeated.

Blue watched Aumua walk away towards the church. He sat down in the grass. A group of teenage girls, still in their school uniforms, were laughing as they attempted to dance a *siva* combined with at Western-style dance. Further down the field, a group of boys were playing rugby near the *fale tele*.

Blue was, well, blue about his outing with Aumua. He sighed, as he saw her enter the church. It was a rough afternoon, and he hoped he didn't ruin his relationship with the girl. The lessons with Aumua were what he looked forward to the most each day.

Then as if they knew that their best friend was feeling down in the dumps, the three hounds came running out of nowhere with their tongues hanging out of their mouths and jumped on Blue. Blue rolled in the grass with them.

"Hey, you mutts!" Blue said with excitement. "The rats just called, and they want their fleas back!"

Blue hopped to his feet and stood still. The dogs became motionless waiting intensely for Blue's next move. Then, Blue dashed this way and that way, and the dogs rousingly nipped and barked at Blue's every movement.

Blue played with the hounds until the sun dropped below the hills and the bells of the church rang for *Sa*. As Blue ran towards Fiame's, the dogs followed, jumping up and down at his side like dolphins playfully following a boat. Blue cherished the thought that no matter how bad of a day he could have, the dogs were always excited to see him. Blue was one of the pack, fleas and all, and hungry.

They all wondered what tonight's fare would be at Fiame's house.

11

It was early one Sunday morning that Blue finally fell into a deep sleep after a restless night of tossing and turning on his mat. Sleeping on the ground the past several months had given him a bothersome backache. Sometimes his back hurt so much that he tried sleeping by leaning against a pole away from the protection of his mosquito net. Unfortunately, this didn't help much, as he would either slide off the pole, or, most likely, the mosquitos would have a blood-sucking orgy on his body. The persistent sound of the mosquitos buzzing in E major past his ear inevitably ticked him off and drove him back to the safety of the mosquito net. When he lay back down on his mat, he would speak for his back and let out a groan. Blue's movements and moans only managed to force the hounds to crack an eye open before they shifted or turned for a better snoozing position.

It was within this much-needed, deep slumber that Blue saw a vision of himself standing behind Aumua who was sitting in a chair in the middle of a *fale*. Her long, black hair draped over the back of the chair, and a garland of flowers was wrapped around her head. A cello was nestled between her legs, and she began playing the haunting Camille Saint-Saens piece, "The Swan" from "Carnival of the Animals." A group of St. Cecilia's school children sat or leaned on their knees in front of Aumua and keenly watched her play the instrument they had never seen before.

Blue amorously approached Aumua with the desire to show how much he loved her. He leaned his face close to her head and sniffed the flowers of the garland, then sniffed her hair. With a delicate touch of his hand, he gently moved her long hair aside from her neck and began to kiss and suck the back of her neck. Although Aumua continued to play the piece, Blue could sense that she was enjoying the sensual kisses from his lips. He imagined that her eyes were closed. With each kiss, she moved her head from side to side, her body increasingly building in ecstasy.

Aumua quickly stood. As the cello crashed to the ground, the music kept playing. As Blue pulled her body close to his, he continued to rapturously kiss her neck. Her hand then lustfully reached for her lover, grabbed the back of his head, and began to rub his hair. She moaned when Blue's hand lifted her dress and began stroking her thigh.

All the children ran out of the *fale* except for one little girl. Blue opened his eyes to see the little girl in her St. Cecilia's uniform watching them sexually ignite each other. He didn't know who the girl was, but he didn't care. He didn't want to lose this feeling and this moment with Aumua.

Aumua slowly turned her body to kiss Blue on the lips.

Blue closed his eyes and readied himself for a moment he had been waiting on for a long time. She kissed him, but it didn't feel right. It felt wet. It felt cold. It felt lifeless, with a scent of mold. When he opened his eyes, Aumua's face was a pallid green. Her eyes were bloodshot, and the skin around her mouth looked as if it had been chewed away. An open sore on her cheek oozed pus and blood.

Startled and disgusted, Blue escaped the embrace and began to slowly move backwards. For a brief second, he thought it was Scarlett. He quickly glanced at the little girl, who simply sat down, picked up the cello bow, and began waving it like a conductor to the rhythm of the piece.

Aumua raised her hands to Blue, beckoning him to return to her arms. But he continued to slowly retreat. Angrily, she flew upon him and was face-to-face with Blue within a second. He fell, hitting his head on the ground.

Blue awoke and sat straight up on his mat.

*Damn me.*

Music came from his open computer, and he groggily realized that the tune was "The Swan."

Blue reached for his computer to close it and stop the music. As he did so, a pain shot up his back that forced him to return to his upright sitting position.

*Damn me.*

He was famished too.

The other day after *Sa,* Fiame curiously wanted Blue to leave after she had just piled a plate of food for him. The only explanation she gave him was that some of her family members felt uncomfortable being in the same place as him for that evening. A bit dumbfounded, Blue asked her what the reason for this was, although he didn't really want to engage her in an open and profound conversation.

"Fear... by association."

"Fear of me?"

"Not you. But..." She was trying to find a nice way to put it. "But by what you may bring."

"My dogs? I can tell them to..."

"It's just one of those nights when people's superstitions are," Fiame searched for the right word. "Well, heightened."

"Ah."

The word, "superstitions," hit Blue. The event with the *Teine Sa* in the jungle must be the cause of this unprecedented premature dismissal. He felt a little foolish and naïve that he didn't see this coming. After all, rumors spread like wildfire in a village. Blue found it hard to believe that Aumua would tell anyone. She wasn't the kind of girl to gossip, and least of all, tell others about somebody else's misfortune.

"I'm sorry," Fiame sincerely said. "Take the plate with you."

Blue defiantly piled more food on his plate, and as he made his way out of the house, he noticed that everyone was staring at him.

It was with some difficulty that Blue traveled down the dark road trying to balance his large plate of food. Only the faint lights of people's *fales* or homes guided him along the way. Soon, his hounds found him and joyously sniffed the air around the plate of food.

"Yeah, yeah. Don't worry. I got some extra taro for you guys."

The dogs anxiously followed Blue back to his *fale*, anticipating a great meal when they got there.

It would be their last feast for a while, as the *fale* mates would subsist on fruit and tinned meat that Togi dropped off.

"The Swan" started over through his computer, and Blue wondered how the song began playing in the first place and why it was on repeat. He never really liked the piece, but he remembered that it did consume most of his freshman year in high school when Scarlett asked him to accompany her on the piece for a youth cello competition in Pasadena, California. She lived and breathed competitions, as most prodigies do. Scarlett had participated in every music contest from San Diego to San Francisco. Throughout her high school years, she would compete nationally and even internationally on rare occasions. She won them all.

Blue hadn't heard the piece since he and Scarlett performed it together in Pasadena. He smirked at the thought of that performance, which was the first of many times that he accompanied her. Naturally, she won with ease. However, it was the lead-up and rehearsals in Scarlett's living room that Blue remembered quite fondly. It was probably the first time he noticed how spoiled, stressed, and frail Scarlett was. The piece and the competition meant everything to her.

"You're too slow," Scarlett said in a scolding tone.

"Dude, it's "The Swan." I can't play it any slower."

"Play it right."

"We've played it a hundred times."

"And we'll play it a hundred more times until you get it right."

"Uggh. Aren't your fingers sore?

"No."

It was true, Blue thought. She could play the piece a hundred more times. He swung around from the piano to face her.

"You're as callous as the tips of your fingers," Blue stated.

Scarlett thought about that for a second and smiled. She threw her small block of resin at him.

"You're such a dork."

Blue liked it when she joked with him. Scarlett was such a tautly wound girl, that when she did loosen herself, she could be quite fun.

"Let's take a break and play cards or something."

"No."

"Hands on piano!" Scarlett's grandmother ordered. Blue often thought that there were holes in the walls of the house to watch his every movement.

Blue sighed and turned his body to face the piano and indignantly placed his hands on the keys.

"What does she think I'm gonna do to you? Strangle you with your bow?"

"That would hurt," Scarlett said, staring at her bow.

"I've been coming here for years, and she still doesn't trust me."

"She's just being overprotective."

"I gotta go soon anyway," Blue said. "There's a dance tonight at school."

"A dance?"

"Yeah, some kind of event for freshman."

Blue played a few notes on the piano before he realized

that there was an awkward pause in the conversation. He turned his body towards her.

"Do you dance?" Scarlett asked.

"I don't know if what I do would be called dancing. It's more like a, uh, boogie."

"Boogie."

"Yeah." Blue turned back to the piano and started playing the song, "Staying Alive," from *Saturday Night Fever*. "It's all good fun. My friends and I like to boogie just for laughs. The girls don't really dig it though."

Blue stopped playing and turned back to Scarlett.

"What are the names of your friends?" she asked.

Blue quickly wondered why she would care about the names of his friends. He could hear the desperation in her tone. He could see the loneliness in her eyes.

He knew that, except for going to Sabatini's Beach on occasion, or going to a competition, she rarely left the house. Everything, everyone, every thought, and every expectation was brought to Scarlett, and Blue felt sorry for her. Despite all her talent, she had so little to look forward to.

"But, I, uh, will probably just stay home tonight," Blue added.

"You will?" Scarlett asked. Blue noticed a tiny hint of elated relief at the possibility that he, like her, will not go to a dance tonight.

"Yeah, my mother is, uh, getting sicker, and wants me to be with her," Blue lied. His mother always wanted her son to be active and experience things. She never missed a school dance during her youth, and she would be appalled at the thought of her son missing an event on account of her. "My aunt was supposed to go to Timbuktu but decided to stay home too. Doctor said my mother won't make it to Christmas."

"That's so scary. I don't know what I would do without my mother."

Blue looked at her. It was true. Scarlett wouldn't know what to do without her mother. Her mother did all the thinking, planning, and dreaming for her.

"Yeah. It's, uh... yeah."

Blue gathered his music off the piano and stuffed it in his backpack.

"Hands on piano!" the grandmother screamed.

"I'm leaving!" Blue responded. "Damn me."

Blue picked up his backpack and started to leave.

"You'll come tomorrow for practice, right?" Scarlett asked.

Blue stopped and turned to the prodigy, and he saw that she was loosening and tightening her bow. He knew that she had a couple more hours of practice in her.

"Yeah... sure," Blue answered.

Blue stared at Scarlett who began to perform "The Swan" with more verve and passion. A rare smile formed on her usually frowning face. A grandfather clock somewhere in the house began to strike six o'clock, but it didn't seem to faze the young cellist.

The toll of the grandfather clock was replaced by the ringing of the St. Cecilia's church bells, signaling the start of the six a.m. Mass. Blue fought through the pain to reach outside his mosquito net to slam his computer closed. He hoped to never hear "The Swan" again.

Blue rolled out from under the net and slowly stood and tried to stretch out his back by raising his hands high in the air. The stretch felt good, and he thought about being bold enough to try and touch his toes. It was worth a try, but he had to stop halfway down.

*Whoa. Too much too fast.*

It was then that he heard a thunderous knock on the post of his *fale*. The knock caught Blue by surprise, and he wondered who it could be since everyone should be on their way to church.

"Mr. Ronin..." a deep voice bellowed from outside and was followed by two massive hands trying to separate the blinds of the *fale*. "You there? I have something to show you," the voice added in Samoan. "Mr. Ronin..."

Blue didn't recognize the voice but was nevertheless peeved at the stranger's presumption of producing a show-and-tell at the crack of dawn. Plus, Blue felt that there was a lack of privacy once again, and then remembered that there was no privacy in this small village. It was considered rude to do something privately.

The hounds, on the other hand, awoke with tails wagging at the thought that a visitor had come to see them. One of them gave a short bark as if saying good morning.

Blue quickly wrapped a *lavalava* around his waist and shuffled towards the area of the *fale* where the voice was coming from. He irritably pulled the cords and opened the blinds. Blue was somewhat shocked to see the huge frame of Chief Joseph that easily eclipsed the early morning rise of the sun. It had been awhile since Blue had seen Joseph, and when he did, the chief was usually sitting in his *fale*. He didn't know that the big man could even walk.

The hounds briefly greeted the *matai* with a bark and a sniff before eagerly bouncing from the *fale,* excited about the breaking of a new day and the awaiting adventures.

"*Talofa*," Joseph said. "Come walk with me."

"You're not going to church?"

"I don't need a church to talk to God."

Blue thought that if there were any mortal man on earth that can actually talk to God, it would probably be Chief Joseph.

"Yeah, I like Father Krimple, but those pews are uncomfortable."

"Mmm," Joseph grunted. He had helped numerous times over the decades renovating the church and can remember a time when parishioners only sat on mats during Mass. Joseph spent hours and days carving new benches to replace old ones a couple of times, and he didn't like to hear the volunteer complain about the pews. Joseph felt that Blue was still a visitor and had no entitlement to criticize the work of the village and especially the effort of his own. But the chief didn't call out Blue on his statement. He felt that if the volunteer had to watch everything he said in the village, he would never say anything. At this point in Blue's visit, it was better for him to speak honestly than to speak appropriately. But one thing was certain for Joseph: someday the chief would stroll over to the church, which he hasn't done in years, and sit in a pew and judge the comfort of the seats for himself.

"Come. We go to the plantation," Joseph commanded.

"Right. I'll be ready in a sec."

Blue dug through his suitcase and pulled out a T-shirt that he had cut the sleeves off to make it cooler. A cockroach followed the shirt, which startled him, as it darted in a straight line for the edge of the *fale* and freedom.

*Damn those things!*

Joseph observed Blue's *fale* without even moving his head. His dark, scrutinizing eyes covered the entire house with a single glance. With a lack of furniture, everything had to be placed on the cement floor. Clothes seeped out of an open suitcase like a giant clam rejecting a meal and were also strewn on the ground throughout the place. Full and used water bottles and whole or partially eaten papayas were piled in such a way that it seemed to be the only décor in the *fale*. Two red plaid towels and a couple of pairs of underwear were draped over a string that was tied between two posts. A stalk of bananas hung from the rafters and was an enticing attraction for the flies and gnats.

"Ok. I'm ready," Blue said as he slipped the makeshift T-shirt over his head and shoulders.

"Mmm," Joseph grunted, not really impressed with Blue's appearance. "You need a haircut."

"Yeah, it's getting shabby," Blue answered, running his hand through his hair.

"I'll send Aumua later."

"Oh, uh, you don't..." Blue started to object. But, before he could finish his sentence, the chief was walking away.

Blue hadn't seen Aumua for a few days after their awkward encounter with the *Teine Sa* near the pool. Although he still felt a little embarrassed about the event, it was more about how Aumua seemed to distance herself from him since the incident that bothered him the most. He tried to convince himself that the visions he was having of the whitewashed women must've been occurring because of something he had been eating. Additionally, and more rationally, he believed that Aumua had been too busy preparing for the Teuila Festival, and that kept them from being together.

Blue searched his *fale* for his sandals. He didn't want to leave in his bare feet—his feet were simply too prissy to handle the rough terrain of the island. He looked under piles of clothes and stacks of papayas before finally finding them under his sleeping mat.

*Damn me. No wonder my back's killing me.*

Blue quickly slipped his feet in the sandals and rushed out of his *fale*. He eventually caught up with the *matai* on the grassy field. The chief was heading towards the bush, and Blue couldn't believe how fast the big man was moving even with an ornate, wood-carved walking stick.

It was the itches on his legs that forced Blue to stop and scratch them. After a few yards, Joseph realized that his companion wasn't with him, stopped, and looked back.

"Sorry. Flea bites," Blue revealed. "Mixed with mosquito and fly bites. Throw in a cockroach bite and a centipede sting. They all really like gnawing on us white boys."

"Mmm," the chief mumbled, and continued his walk.

Blue caught up with him once again near the entrance of the church. Aumua, dressed in a yellow *puletasi* with a Samoan decorative design was greeting churchgoers as they were entering the building. Although her hair was rolled into a bun on the top of her head, a breeze blew a few loose strands of hair across her face. She noticed Blue walking by with her father and gave a long, cold stare at the volunteer. Blue stared back at the girl until he fell behind the chief.

*Damn. That's the coldest I've felt in months.*

Before the jungle would swallow the two, Blue looked back at Aumua but was disappointed to see that she had already entered the church. His hounds, however, then came frolicking to the front of the church, and he was amused at the way they tried to play with the stragglers who were late for Mass.

The two progressed upon a well-beaten path with overgrown tropical foliage. Blue didn't recognize the trail, and wondered if, perhaps, it was a sacred route.

"So, where we going?" Blue asked.

Joseph didn't answer and kept walking. Blue looked at the chief, who felt quite comfortable in this lush and leafy environment. Butterflies fluttered and led the way, birds sang, and the tree branches separated for the venerable chief and his companion. Blue wondered how many times the chief had traveled along this path over the past eighty years or so.

The trail meandered to a steep hill. A couple of African tulip trees, which were not indigenous to the island, flanked the path on either side. Despite being an invasive species, they were in full bloom with beautiful red-orange flowers.

Joseph trampled up the hill as easily as a weekend hiker. Blue was impressed how the old man didn't slow down, and actually gained momentum the closer he got to the top.

When Joseph reached the top of the hill, he stopped, looked below, and smiled. Blue caught up with the chief and stood next to him.

"The Tuputala legacy," Joseph said with a laugh.

In the valley below was a cocoa plantation with about thirty cocoa trees covering almost an acre of land. On either side of the plot stood two tall breadfruit trees that provided shade for the cocoa trees throughout the day. An open-wall hut with a thatch roof made from coconut palm leaves was positioned in the middle of the plot and contained a couple of crudely made, rustic wood tables. Blue thought how the verdant valley created such a picturesque scene that any impressionist painter would have loved the opportunity to recreate on canvas.

"What are those trees?" Blue asked.

"*Koko Samoa*," the *matai* answered and started down the hill. "Come."

As the two walked along the rows of the cocoa trees, Blue reached out and touched some of the pods.

"My grandfather bought a few trees from the Germans in the late 1800s," Joseph said in English, making sure that Blue would understand him. "My father added dozens of trees, and then I planted more. There are about forty beans to a pod, and each tree produces about thirty pods."

Blue was attracted to the reddish pod like a hummingbird to a flower. As he reached for the pod, the chief used his cane to slap Blue's hand away.

"The cocoa plantation is the village's main livelihood. It has been our most successful form of income for the past several decades. Without it, the village would die."

Blue found the word "die" a bit dramatic, but he didn't question it.

The *matai* moved on and sat on the ground in the shade of the breadfruit tree. Blue followed and sat next to him, swooshing with his hand at the pestering flies that circled his head.

"We used to ferment, dry, and grind the beans into a paste in that hut before we moved the process to the village where there's more space," the chief proudly said. "Everyone loves the Vaimasina cocoa. We sell it in the markets of Apia. Some people travel here from as far away as Australia or Japan or China, just for our cocoa."

"I've had the *Koko Samoa* at Fiame's house," Blue said. "It's so rich it made my toes curl."

"Mmm."

The chief always liked to hear the kind compliments of his family's cocoa. He loved the plantation as much as he loved his children, and he would do anything to continue its growth and success.

"Who will oversee the plantation after you?" Blue asked delicately, without mentioning the chief's inevitable death.

"My sons live abroad these days."

"Togi?"

"Togi is a nitwit," Joseph said in an honest tone, but immediately felt that he was being too hard on his son. "Togi is better on the sea than on the land."

"The dude loves to fish."

"Aumua is more suited to run the plantation when I'm gone. The problem with Aumua is that she is woman."

Blue raised his eyebrows with concern. He knew Samoa was a patriarchal country, but the chief's statement and belief seemed completely unjust and archaic.

"With all due respect, sir, I believe Aumua would do a great job," Blue stated in defense of his tutor, or rather, the girl he had a crush on. "She's smart and determined as hell. I mean, come on." He then pointed at himself and spoke in broken Samoan, "She taught this idiot how to speak Samoan."

"Mmm," the chief grunted with a half-smile.

"Her love and devotion to the village is unsurpassed. She would be the first one that I'd ask to oversee all of these plants."

"Trees."

"Right."

"But the girl will marry and have babies," Joseph added.

Blue was obviously peeved at the remark, and defiantly stood up. He wondered if the chief was purposely goading him. But for what purpose he didn't know or even cared about at the moment.

"So what if the girl was married and had ten babies!" Blue said hotly. "I have no doubt that she would ensure that this plantation would continue to produce for the village for years to come until one of her children was ready to take over."

"Sit. Sit," the chief demanded.

Blue hesitated before he sat back down. He rarely lost his cool.

Joseph stared at the cocoa trees, as Blue, who was still fuming a bit, swung his arms violently at the flies that antagonized him.

"Fiame wants us to partner with a cocoa company from Australia," the *matai* said with a bit of apprehension in his tone. "They say they could modernize the plantation. They would add moisture meters, pruning equipment, and fermentation boxes. They say they would double our productivity and double our money."

"They'll exploit the village," Blue said grumpily.

"Mmm."

"I don't know. I'm no businessman," Blue admitted. "But history has shown that whenever a white man's company moves into a developing country to do business, nothing good really comes from it."

"Fiame is convinced that Vaimasina will benefit greatly from the partnership. She and her son come to my *fale* often and try to persuade me to let them in. Perhaps, she's right. There's nothing more than I would like to see before I die than the village to prosper."

Blue now understood the nightly visits of Fiame and Lance at the Tuputala's home. It was all about village politics, which he never wanted to get mixed up in. He knew the politics were a complicated web, and it was practically impossible to comprehend when blended with *Fa'a Samoa*. Besides, Blue had only lived in the village for less than a year. He was a foreigner, a volunteer, and he thought that he had no business getting involved with village politics. He wasn't interested in them and certainly didn't feel like he had the intelligence to be included in any village decisions.

Blue also thought about Lance's involvement. To Blue, Lance was a trouble-making punk. He knew that Fiame's son had no interest in the village. In fact, he was hardly ever here. Then it hit Blue. It was like the machinations of a medieval European aristocrat looking to marry his children to better the family, perhaps, Lance was only sweet on Aumua for a higher position in the village. The combining of the two *aigas* would be a powerful step in controlling the main source of the income of the village. Blue grinned and thought he was overthinking all this. He had read too many fantasy books.

*What is this? Game of Thrones?*

"Sometimes you gotta do what your heart tells you to do even though you lose money," Blue said, thinking that his statement was a lame attempt to placate the chief's uncertain and confused thoughts on the matter of the cocoa plantation.

"Mmm."

"I mean, uh, Vaimasina has been around for a couple of centuries. I don't think it's going anywhere any time soon, you know."

The *matai* didn't say a word. He only stared at his plantation. He had been part of the village for nearly a century. He had seen the changes over time. Missionaries, colonialism, globalization, and modern technology have all had their chance to influence the *Fa'a Samoa* of Vaimasina for better or for worse. Yet, he knew the volunteer's odd statement was true. Despite the changes, the village grew, his *aiga* grew, his children grew, and his plantation grew. It was reassuring to know that it would all continue to grow without him.

Blue slapped a mosquito on his arm.

"You see the *Teine Sa*," Joseph said in Samoan.

"What? No," Blue said, his cheeks turning red with embarrassment.

"Mr. Ronin, do not let them seduce you," the chief demanded in English. "They will hurt you."

"I don't believe in ghosts."

"Mmm."

"Who told you this?" Blue asked.

"Togi."

*Damn it, Togi.*

Blue knew that Togi was only partially at fault for spilling the news of the events that took place in the bush. Blue thought that since Aumua was the only other person there, she must've told Togi. Yet, he was comforted by the thought that it was Togi who blabbed it to the village and not his sister. Blue also preferred to think that Aumua "confided" with her brother. The word, "told," seemed too bold, and Togi's mouth was a gaping gap of gossip.

"It was just a bunch of kids playing in the pool," Blue explained, hoping that he could convince the chief of not being crazy.

"The *Teine Sa* will hurt you," Joseph firmly reiterated. "They will try to rip your eyes out as they make love to you. They will harm Aumua."

Blue looked at the *matai* who was staring forward at his trees. He noticed the chief mentioned Aumua's name. Blue wondered that if Aumua weren't with him that day, would the chief have said anything to him.

Blue wanted to ask about Joseph's encounters with the ghostly white females. He had heard the stories about how the chief had made love to a siren and lived. However, Blue began to overthink it. Sirens were different from the *Teine Sa*, weren't they? He became confused, and he thought that he was mixing legends.

*Hey! The Grimm Brothers just called; they want their fairytale back.*

Blue snorted a quick laugh. He decided to change the subject.

"So I gotta know. How'd you drown a shark with your

bare hands?" Blue asked. He thought the topic would be way more interesting than the subject of plantations.

The chief looked forward and thought about the question. Nobody had ever asked him that before because everybody had already heard the story, and they had accepted the story, which became a legend.

"I was teenager—thirteen or so, when a long-haired preacher from England came to the village holding a Bible in one hand and a cane in the other," the matai said in Samoan. Blue knew he had to listen really carefully if he was going to understand the gist of the story. "In those days, lots of priests and missionaries came from many denominations- mostly *palagi*. They all wanted their own flock and a little piece of land in the village to control. This English preacher was *tautala lelei*, good talker. Samoans— we like good talkers. We believe in good talkers. He promised people God will give us things and keep us safe from the Japanese. He would control people with his eyes. He... what's it called when you control with eyes in English?"

"Hypnotized," Blue answered, wondering what this has to do with sharks.

"Mmm."

"I think that's what you mean."

"The English preacher didn't control me with his eyes. I was already big and strong."

"I have no doubt."

"He became a bad man and drank a lot. He drank people's home brew and then scolded them for making it because it was sin. Eventually, his good talk was no more, and he used his cane to talk. He beat people when he got mad. He enjoyed beating people. He beat me for all kinds of reasons. It didn't hurt; I was big and strong. When my father was working in Apia, the English preacher wanted to baptize me. I refused and he beat me. My mother tried to intervene and protect me, and he beat her too. That was when I had to make sure he and his cane talked no more."

"Shit. It's like a Jack London story."

"To answer your question on how I killed a shark with my bare hands, it was easy," the chief confirmed. "I lured the predator away from the place where he lurked the most. Then, I dragged him to shallow water, and with my hands, held him still under the water until his *mana* flowed up my arms and into my soul. It didn't take long because I was big and strong."

Blue looked at the chief with dumbfounded disgust.

"Did you eat the shark?" Blue asked.

"No. I'm not Fijian," the chief said with a wry smile. "I pulled the shark to the deep sea and let the other predators feed off his flesh."

Blue looked away confused. He couldn't tell if the *matai's* story was true. However, it would be months later when he finally put the allegory together.

Blue found it fascinating how violent even the most peaceful and gentle Pacific Islands' villagers could easily become. They were well-known for being fierce warriors, headhunters, and cannibals.

A wayward cloud darkened the sky over the little valley. A heavy breeze followed and forced the cocoa trees into a rain dance. When the cloud ultimately opened up and showered the earth, every living thing widely opened its leaves to receive the water.

The two men remained unfazed by the downpour, protected from the rain under the broad leaves of the giant breadfruit tree. They sat watching the cloud slake the thirst of the trees, bushes, and grass.

Blue and Joseph would remain there for some time until after the shower dissipated, until the chief finally thought it was time to leave.

12

<hr>

Blue was sitting in his classroom at St. Cecilia's School with his laptop open on his lap. He was having a difficult time concentrating on his novel, as the school was abuzz with activities in preparation for the weeklong Teuila Festival in Apia that was to begin in only a few days. The choir was practicing in the church and was accompanied by a pianist. Blue cringed at the sound of the out-of-tune piano, and he winced every time the player stumbled with the notes and chords. When Blue looked outside his door, he could see villagers that included Father Krimple playing volleyball. School children ran amok to and from other happenings on the church grounds. Anything was better than being cooped up in the classroom. Beyond the volleyball court the *siva* group was fine-tuning their dance routine in the community center. Indeed, it was an exciting time for the village.

In Blue's classroom, a group of nine, ten and eleven-year old girls were using the desks to make headdresses of flowers for the *siva* dancers and choir. Vaveao Suisala, the teacher, was supervising them. They were stringing the bright red, skinny *teuila*, the Samoan national flower, among white gardenias to create a colorful crown. As they focused on their creativity, some of the girls would sing along to the song that the choir was singing in the church. One girl would stop what she was doing and happily practice a portion of the *siva* dance, only to be corrected by another girl.

Blue liked that the students were using his classroom to make the headdresses. For one thing, they kept him awake in the heat of the afternoon. But he genuinely liked the company. He was also momentarily relieved that they weren't staying away from him because of the rumor that he saw the *Teine Sa*. Other villagers, sadly, have kept their distance from him since that day in the jungle, particularly Aumua, which has caused him great concern and sleepless nights.

Blue watched the girls in the classroom closely and was impressed with how well they constructed the flowery festive festoons. They worked quickly and diligently and gave Blue the impression that they made these garlands all their lives, when, in fact, they were taught by Vaveao not more than two hours earlier.

"Who is ready to practice their reading in English?" Blue asked in Samoan. He was half being sarcastic and half taking advantage of actually having students in his classroom. "It's a good afternoon for reading."

The girls giggled. Blue must have mispronounced a word.

One of the girls then stood, went to Blue, and placed a

recently made garland on his head. It was like her way of putting a sock in his mouth to get him to shut up about reading.

"Oh, *faafetai*," Blue said.

The girls giggled.

"Would you like to learn how to make an *ula*, Mr. Ronin?" Vaveao asked in English.

"Thanks, but it looks complicated. And I'm all thumbs."

The girls giggled again.

"You learn quickly," Vaveao said.

"Really. Thanks. But I'm actually gonna leave."

"You want me to make you a lei that keeps ghosts away?" Vaveao asked. The girls stopped what they were doing to hear Blue's answer.

*Damn me.*

Blue sighed. Was she telling a joke? Blue looked at the teacher who looked back at him with a sincere look. She honestly wanted to help him.

"What's it made of? Garlic?" asked Blue sardonically.

The girls giggled.

"No," said Vaveao with a laugh. "Taatiti taught me. I make one for my husband, Savea. Ghosts follow him all the time. He sells them in the store."

"He sells ghosts?" Blue asked.

The girls giggled.

"No, the leis, silly."

*I wish he sold actual stuff one needs in store.*

"Thanks, Vaveao. I, uh, don't believe in ghosts."

"But you see the *Teine Sa*. You need lei."

Blue looked at the girls, who were staring at him. Their frivolous facial expressions turned to an unforgiving frown.

Blue was a little embarrassed. The moment confirmed to him that the entire village knew about his encounter with the devilish white women.

Blue was left speechless. However, he felt saved and pretended to be distracted when Togi walked past his classroom carrying a large carved *tanoa*.

"Togi!" Blue yelled. He turned his attention back to Vaveao and the girls. "I have to talk to him. Please close the door when you leave."

Blue hurried out of the room and into the schoolyard, trying to catch up with Togi. His path took him towards the volleyball game.

"Togi!"

Togi stopped and turned. He greeted Blue with his usual, casual smile.

Before Blue could take another step, Misi Sao approached him in a traditional outfit with a high headdress of colorful feathers and flowers and was followed by a small entourage of teenaged females with the same headdresses that looked like a row of peacocks.

"I hear you had a fling with some sexy spirits," Misi said teasingly. Misi had always enjoyed the superstitions of the villagers and had spent many hours helping Father Krimple calm the fears of those who felt that they had somehow become the wrath of a vengeful ghost. Misi believed, however, that when a Westerner got involved with the supernatural, it was often something extraordinary. Nevertheless, the rumor was simply too titillating to not say something.

"My eyes were playing tricks in the heat of the jungle,"

Blue answered annoyingly. He started to feel as if he was running out of excuses.

"It's so cute."

"Yeah, real cute, Misi."

"They must be beautiful," Misi added.

"You don't strike me as one who believes in that spooky stuff."

"In this village, darling, a ghostly girlfriend is like a grey hair—once it's plucked, you never know when and where it will return."

Blue stared at Misi.

*Are you kidding me?*

He wasn't sure if the *fa'afafine* was being profound, or mockingly provoking him.

Misi added, "I don't envy you, darling. The dead talk back worse than the living." She laughed and continued on the way, followed by the entourage of peacocks.

Blue watched them file away in a straight line. Then, Misi abruptly stopped and turned back to Blue. The line collapsed on itself.

"You should see Taaiti," recommended Misi.

The line regrouped and continued walking.

"Bro, let's go fishing," Togi said with enthusiasm. Fishing and talking about fishing always excited him. Blue only stared at Misi. "Bro?"

"Togs, you got a big mouth," Blue said angrily, with a crack of frustration in his tone.

"I know," agreed Togi and bowed his head with shame even though he didn't know why his friend was angered with him.

"You're always creating rumors about me. Now everyone

stares at me and looks at me like I'm some psycho *palagi*. Fiame didn't even let me eat at her house last night. You know how hard it is to settle and fit in here? I feel like I gotta start over now."

Togi felt bad. He got reprimanded a lot during the course of the day. His father, his sister, Iris, and everyone else he encountered never wasted a moment to lecture him. But this time, the scolding came from his best friend, and it hurt even more. He kicked the ground like a petulant child.

"Do... do you want to go fishing? Togi asked, as if it was a way to make it all up to Blue.

"Are you...? Do you under...?" Blue stopped himself and sighed. "Yeah, I'll go fishing," he said defeatedly.

Togi's smile grew from one ear to the other ear.

"Bro. We'll catch a boatload!"

"Why are you carrying such a ridiculously large *tanoa*?" Blue asked.

"It's our *'ava* bowl when we're in Apia for the festival."

"You guys gonna swim in the *'ava*?"

Togi laughed and almost dropped the bowl.

Father Krimple was still playing volleyball when he saw Blue talking with Togi. He made a slamming hit for a point that brought cheers from everyone playing and watching. He then made his way to the two young men.

"Ronin. Ronin. I need to talk to you."

"I'll see you at the beach, Togs."

"Boatload, bro. I can't wait," Togi said and hurried away.

"Let's go to my office," the priest said.

Father Krimple's office was a small room that was attached to the community center and a short distance away from the volleyball court. A louvered window opened up to the school's yard and curtains made of *siapo* provided most of the color in the room. The walls contained a framed picture of Jesus and several photos of various sizes of Father Krimple with the Archbishop of Samoa, along with portraits of the priest attending different meetings or synods around the island, Samoa, or the Pacific Islands. A desk was pushed against the far wall and was littered with paperwork, a laptop, framed photographs, and a small Canadian and Samoan flag that drooped over a specially carved wooden bowl. Hanging on a nail near the door was a hat made from faded pandanus leaves.

Blue felt like he was entering the principal's office and readied himself to be reprimanded. He had a hunch that Father Krimple wanted to talk to him about the *Teine Sa*, and thus decided to go on the offensive, pleading his innocence.

"I know what you want," Blue started to say, but instantly stopped when he saw a rectangle box above the window. "Is that air-conditioning?"

"Yeah."

"You have air-conditioning?

"Yeah," the priest repeated with a perplexed look.

Blue quickly grabbed the air conditioner remote off the desk and began to overzealously push the down arrow key. The temperature display on the unit went from twenty degrees Celsius to sixteen degrees Celsius.

"Oh my God," Blue said with relief, as he moved directly under the blow of the unit. He thought that this had to be the only room in the village with air-conditioning. He closed his eyes and stretched out his arms, letting the cool air blow on his armpits. Blue clicked the remote to fifteen degrees Celsius. "Oh my God."

"Please give me the remote," Father Krimple irksomely said. He took the remote out of Blue's hand and began raising the temperature to its previous setting. "You know how hard it is to get someone here to fix it if it breaks?"

"I would never, ever, ever leave this room."

"Listen," the priest said. "I brought you in here to ask you about the rumors of you talking with ghosts."

Blue was really sick and tired of the whole thing and was quickly becoming indifferent about the entire affair.

"And what if I did?"

"Did what?" Father Krimple asked, wanting to hear the volunteer admit what he had done.

"Talk to ghosts," Blue said, then added, "My favorite ghost is Scarlett. She loves Broadway tunes and we sing the song, *All I Ask of You*, from *Phantom of the Opera* together."

"You don't have to be so facetious, my friend."

"You haven't lived until you've heard us sing the entire Phantom musical."

"Go on. Look—you know how superstitious the villagers can be. If you're not too careful, they'll shut you out. They won't invite you to dinner. They won't ask for your help. Students won't come to your reading class."

Blue raised his eyebrows on the priest's last sentence.

"You've developed a good reputation thus far," Father Krimple continued. "Everyone likes you, and I'd hate to see someone like you get shunned."

"Sweat got in my eyes, Father K, and it made me see things in the jungle."

"Perhaps, your ghosts were blurry then."

"I don't believe in ghosts."

"Go on."

"Besides, isn't your religion like founded on superstitions and holy spirits?"

Father Krimple stared at the volunteer with an expression on his face that read, *Please God, don't strike the man down because of his stupidity. He knows not what he says.*

"I mean, it must've been easy for the missionaries to convert in this part of the world," Blue continued. "Since the villagers already believed in ghosts, adding a few revered and exemplary spirits to the mix simply helped in their evangelization."

"I believe your definition of the Holy Spirit is too literal, my friend," the priest said calmly. "Think of the Holy Spirit as an active force that God places in man. It's the presence of God in the life of a believer. I like to think that the Holy Spirit reveals God's thoughts, and guides believers into all truth, including knowledge of what is to come."

"Hey, the Pope just called. He wants his lecture back."

The priest scoffed and looked at Blue. Father Krimple could have easily continued to preach about the Holy Spirit. After all, evangelizing was his calling. It was what he did best, especially to those who didn't belong to a church. When he first arrived in Vaimasina, he spent most of his days teaching and changing attitudes about the Bible. It was a slow process that took time and patience like an artist sculpturing from stone. He believed his people were the block of stone, and his words were the hammer and chisel. Today, however, Father Krimple wasn't as fervent as he used to be when faced with the challenge of converting a non-believer. There were so few left in the village who weren't affiliated with some denomination. Ronin Blue was a new block of stone, and for the first time in a long while, the priest felt invigorated to dust off his sculpting tools.

"Was that a joke?" Father Krimple asked.

"Not a good one."

"We can talk for hours trying to unravel the meanings and symbolism of the Holy Spirit."

"I get the feeling that if you ask ten different clergymen what the meaning of the Holy Spirit is, you'd get ten different answers."

"Go on. Probably so."

Father Krimple went to a duffel bag that was on a chair and pulled out a T-shirt. As he began to change out of his sweaty shirt, Blue grabbed the air-conditioning remote, pointed it at the unit, and lowered the temperature back down to fifteen degrees Celsius. His eyes closed with pure, uninterrupted relief.

"One thing's for sure, Father K, this room's heaven on earth."

"I tell you what I'll do, Ronin. I'll speak for you during my sermon this Sunday and tell the congregation that your experience with the *Teine Sa* was a misunderstanding. I'll tie it in with the scripture readings of the Mass."

"Yeah, you'd do that for me?"

"That, or you can go see Taaiti. She knows how to handle ghosts."

"I don't wanna see that crazy lady. She'll sniff me and make me drink something green."

"Go on!"

"She scares me."

"She once cured my aching plantar fasciitis with that green stuff."

"I think I like your idea better."

"Okay, but you have to do something for me."

"What?"

"You have to attend Mass this Sunday."

"Oh, uh... I don't know."

"It would be good for the villagers to see you there."

"Yeah... I don't know. It's so early."

"The one who loves God, believes in God's strength, and who is protected by God will have nothing to fear from the *Teine Sa*."

"All right," Blue said reluctantly.

"Go on, lad!" Father Krimple said enthusiastically and patted the volunteer on his back. "After Mass, those who are in the choir will be heading to Apia to sing in the choir exhibition. It usually kickstarts the Teuila Festival. You can come and play piano for us."

"I, uh... I don't play piano."

"Oh that's right," Father Krimple said. The priest still had a gut feeling that Blue was keeping something about playing the piano to himself and studied the volunteer with a penetrating stare that he hoped would uncover the truth.

"Well, Father K, I'd stay here all day, but Togi's waiting for me."

"We'll chat soon."

"Yeah... sure."

Blue left the office feeling a little uneasy. The deal he made with the priest didn't sit well with him. The lie about not playing the piano wasn't going to give him any bonus points with God either. However, he wasn't entirely too sure that he believed in God, and he could always feign illness on Sunday. He got sick so often that he knew there was a real possibility he wouldn't even have to pretend he was sick. It was just going to happen.

As Blue made his way to the beach, the village seemed quiet. Most of the villagers were at the church grounds preparing for the Teuila Festival. Every adult seemed to have a role for the festival, and every child was needed for support.

Blue didn't mind the walk through a practically empty and peaceful village. He enjoyed listening to the sound of the coconut palm trees crack and creak as they stretched themselves back and forth in the wind. In the distance, he could also make out the roll and growl of the angry surf ferociously grinding the reef. A group of pigs groveled in a pen as they fought over a small amount of scraps, which Blue concluded was most likely the highlight of their day.

Passing the trading store, Blue noticed that there was a handwritten sign in the door's window with the Samoan word, *tapuni,* (Closed). Blue wondered if the store was closed because Savea was at the church like everyone else or was it because the trader had nothing on the shelves to sell. Regardless, Blue couldn't help but peer inside through the window to see if there was anything for sale. He had a whole list of stuff he wanted for his *fale*, but every time he came to the store, he left with only tin meat that inevitably made him sick.

With the brightness of the afternoon, Blue couldn't really tell what items were on the shelf. He could, however, see the light of the drinks refrigerator, which reminded him how thirsty he was at the moment. The thought of drinking a Coke and rubbing the icy cold bottle on his chest like an actor in a sexy American commercial sounded scintillatingly refreshing to him. If he wanted to, he could simply walk in and grab a bottle. Because there was no crime in the village and everyone seemed to share everything, he knew that the door would be unlocked. In fact, the door wouldn't even have a lock.

*Why not just take a drink?*

Blue believed that there would be no problem walking in and taking a drink. He could just pay Savea for the bottle when he saw him next, or even better, he would simply leave some coins on the counter. No one would mind.

As Blue turned the knob and opened the door, it was a group of children's laughter that made him rapidly close the door. The laughter seemed to be coming from the building next door.

Blue headed towards the laughter and saw another handwritten sign on a large piece of cardboard that read in English, "Traitors Internet Café" and it was leaning against the wall next to an open door. He thought the word, "traitors," was odd. For one thing, it was missing an apostrophe.

Upon entering the room, Blue saw a group of four children around age twelve, still in their school uniforms and sharing one chair, playing a game on a desktop computer monitor. They must have escaped the activities at the church and school grounds and were elated knowing that it would probably be hours before their parents realized that they were missing and came looking for them. Noticing the figure standing in the doorway, they all quickly and worriedly glanced at the man, hoping that it wasn't one of their parents that had come to take them back to school. Relieved to see the volunteer, they all said a quick, "*Talofa, Mr. Lanu Moana,*" and then turned their attention back to the computer screen.

"Shouldn't you kids be at school helping your parents?" Blue asked in Samoan.

"We take a break," one of the boys answered in English.

"Yes, we save world from aliens, Mr. *Lanu Moana,*" another boy followed up. They all laughed.

Blue thought, *who was he to stop them from saving the world.*

The room contained three other desktop computers with screens. Blue approached one of the computers and hit the keyboard, hoping that the screen would fall out of sleep mode. Nothing happened. He hit the keyboard again. Nothing. He tried holding down Control-Alt-Delete keys at the same time. Still nothing. He was about to move to another computer, when Savea came through a door that seemed to lead from the trading store. He was excited to see Blue.

"Ah, Mr. Ronin. It's good to see you."

"Savea. When did you open this place?"

"Yesterday."

"Really?"

"No. Two days ago."

"Huh." Blue found it hard to believe that a new place would open in the village without much ado, fanfare, and pageantry.

"Last month," Savea said.

"Did you mean to call this place, Trader's Internet Café?"

"Yes, like the store."

"I think you're using the wrong..." Blue stopped. He wasn't really in the mood to go off on a tangent about the differences of the word, "traitor," and "trader." Perhaps, he would some other day.

"You can send letter to your lover."

"You mean email."

"Yes. To your lover."

"And friends, family members, acquaintances..."

"And lover."

"Sure."

"Five *tala* for fifteen minutes. No porn!" Savea pointed to a sign on the wall. Indeed, the sign was handwritten with the words, "5 *talas* 15 minutes. No Porn."

Despite being engrossed with the game, the children laughed at the word, "porn."

"Do you have Internet?"

"Yes."

"On this computer?"

"No."

*Oh my God.*

"How about that computer?" Blue asked pointing to another computer.

"Yes."

"Great."

"But not today."

*Shit.*

"Savea, can you tell which computer has Internet?"

"Yes. But no porn!"

The kids laughed.

"Savea, I promise to adhere to the sign."

"This computer here."

"Thank you."

Blue sat down at the computer and hit the keyboard, and a desktop popped on the screen with a couple of folders and icons. He hovered the mouse prompt over the Google tab and clicked on it. It took a while, but it loaded. Blue got excited about this. He hadn't checked his email since he arrived in Samoa, and he was bracing himself to view hundreds of unread messages. Sadly, when his email account finally opened, he was a bit disappointed to see that he had less than a hundred messages. Most of these were spam messages that made their way to his inbox, and a few messages from his Aunt Ophelia. The rest were from Harper.

"Wow, Mr. Ronin. You have lots of lovers," Savea said, leaning over the volunteer's shoulder.

"You mind, Savea? These are kinda personal."

"Yes. Personal. I get you, Mr. Ronin."

Savea pulled himself away from behind Blue with a creepy smile and went over to the children. He yelled at the kids, telling them how they were going to burn their eyes out for staring at the screen too long. He had no compunction, however, of squeezing in the middle of the group and taking over the playing of the game.

Blue opened one of Harper's messages and it instantly peeved him. It was long with a sappy, soppy, and syrupy tone. He tried to decipher the ramblings as if he was trying to break a code. There was something about a dog named Gidget, who belonged to a friend of hers and who knew how to surf. They would put Gidget on a surfboard and push the board out to the waves where the dog would either ride the waves with someone or by herself. It was the coolest thing that Harper ever saw, and the dog was so incredibly cute in its wetsuit. Harper couldn't help jest that Gidget learned how to surf quicker and better than Blue.

Blue took a minute to delete the rest of her messages without even opening them.

The messages from Blue's aunt were short, direct, and typically ended with a cynical pun or inspirational quip. Blue cracked a smile when he read his aunt's emails, which were just like her personality. She ended her latest message by saying, *"Your silence tells me that you have been successful."* Most parents, or guardians, would grow worrisome and fret when they didn't hear from their child for a long period of time, but not his Aunt Ophelia. She didn't think that way. To her, silence meant that her nephew was keeping busy and assimilating into a new culture. Even when her own mother left her family all those years ago, she never feared the worst. She would regularly remind her younger sister, Juliet, that their mother was simply adapting to a new environment and that someday they would all be together again.

Aunt Ophelia was much different than her sister. Juliet mollycoddled Blue, but Aunt Ophelia was always more down to earth and pragmatic towards him. She appreciated the arts. It was her upbringing too. In fact, she turned out to be a tremendous writer. In her late teens, she took a job as a correspondent for the Associated Press and traveled the world covering mostly hardcore events such as wars, political upheavals, coups, riots, takeovers, and indigenous displacements. Ophelia saw it all and loved being on assignment even when it meant covering the harsh and cruel events. She was there during the fall of Saigon, the fall of the Berlin Wall, the fall of Yugoslavia, and the fall of the

Twin Towers. She enjoyed listening and writing the facts, the stories of reality, the human saga. As she got older, she believed that fiction was just a way to escape the veracity of life. She never sugarcoated the truth, even when she gained full custody of Blue following the untimely death of her sister. She was tactfully honest with him, sometimes brutally.

On the day Blue left for the Pacific, his Aunt Ophelia gave him one bit of advice. "Remember," she said, "to have a good sense of humor." At the time, Blue didn't know what she meant and thought that it was just some kind of traveler's adage. Nevertheless, he saw on her face how proud she was for him to leave and see a part of the world. She wanted him to join the American Peace Corp upon college graduation, but he found the application process too lengthy and cumbersome. On the contrary, the Helping Hands Volunteer Program submission requirements were simple and inviting, and he had the feeling that they would pretty much accept anyone who applied.

There were two questions that his aunt asked in the messages that seemed to be on the forefront of her mind. The first question was: do you need money? Although Blue brought some of his savings from playing the piano at the resorts, he had on many occasions forgotten that he even needed any cash. He hadn't gone anywhere since he arrived, and he was using the *fale* free from any kind of rent. The village also provided him with a bounty of fruits and vegetables, which he often picked and ate when he was out and about. There were times, however, where he had to be cognizant as to what plot of land that the fruit tree or garden was growing on and who owned it. Additionally,

Blue would often return to his place with plates piled high of leftovers from dinners at the Sao house. Fiame would never allow him to leave without taking an appropriate amount of food. And much to his annoyance, he had saved a lot of money from not being to able to buy anything in Savea's Trading Store with the exception of some tinned meats and a few cold beverages.

"How are you getting on in Samoa?" was his aunt's second most asked question. Blue couldn't wait to dive into a response. He had so much to tell her, and he wanted to tell her everything. He started with the day he arrived and brought her up to speed to almost the precise moment of him sitting in the chair at the "Traitors Internet Café." He tried not to leave out any details. He believed that his aunt was a very sagacious woman who had gained a lot of knowledge from all her travels, and didn't hesitate to ask her questions regarding living in a foreign country. It was the longest email he had ever written.

By the time he had finished his letter to his aunt he didn't realize that the children had left. He clicked on the "Send" button and looked away from the computer. He had worked up a sweat from the constant typing.

Savea, who had waited patiently for Blue to finish, had a grin that went from ear to ear like a clown.

"How long have I been here?"

"One hour."

"An hour?"

"Twenty *talas*," Savea enthusiastically said. This was probably the most he had ever made in a single day at his Internet Café.

"Shit, Togi!"

Blue reached into his pocket but remembered that he was wearing a *lavalava* with no pockets. He didn't have any cash on him.

"Savea, I'll pay you back later."

Savea's grin grew limp with disappointment.

"Twenty *talas*."

"I'll pay you tomorrow. I swear. I'll give you twenty-five *talas*."

Savea's frown turned upwards in the shape of a "U."

"Twenty-five *talas* tomorrow."

"You got it. I swear."

Blue hastily exited the room. Once the volunteer was out of sight, Savea sat down at the computer and began clicking on desktop icons opening up the Internet. He wasn't too far along viewing a sex site, when Blue popped his head back in the doorway.

"Savea, no porn!"

Savea quickly logged out of the Internet and stood up.

Blue gave the storeowner a sly smile before moving along to meet Togi.

The beach wasn't very far from the trading store, but Blue continued at a brisk pace, hoping that Togi didn't leave without him. The late afternoon sun was casting long shadows from the houses and the giant mango and breadfruit trees that towered over the village like age-old sentries.

Joseph Tuputala's homestead wasn't far from the trading store, and when Blue passed it, he could see the chief sitting on a mat eating from a bowl. A floor fan was blowing directly upon him. Blue wondered who brought him the bowl, as Aumua and Lupesina were at the schoolgrounds preparing for the Teuila Festival. Perhaps there was another family member attending to his needs that Blue couldn't see. Still, everything and everyone comes to the *matai*. He didn't have to make that effort or sweat to get up to fetch what he needed. Everyone knew what he needed and when he needed it. Even though the man was simply sitting on mat doing nothing, Blue could feel that the chief was truly the heartbeat of the village, and he could have watched the big man for hours.

Passing Taaiti's *fale*, Blue saw the old lady standing on the steps watching him. She was naked from the waist upwards, and her sagging breasts surprised him. Taaiti was the only woman in the village who often went topless, particularly on those extremely hot and uncomfortable days. Nobody seemed to mind with the exception of, perhaps, Father Krimple, but even he never made a big deal of it.

Blue quickly glanced at Taaiti and noticed leaves, garlands, flowers, strings of shells, and what looked like fish bones hanging from the rafter of her *fale*.

*Damn, she gives me the heebie-jeebies.*

When Blue looked back at her, he was surprised to see her point at something behind him.

"*Teine Sa* follow," Taaiti mumbled. She then counted in Samoan, "One, two, three, four, five, six, seven..."

Blue looked back and saw no one. He then looked back at Taaiti and noticed that she was calling for him by curling her finger back and forth. He simply picked up his pace and headed to the beach.

---

$\mathcal{I}$t was one of those picturesque, idyllic days on the beach of Vaimasina that was typically captured in travel brochures enticing dreamers of a South Seas vacation. The turquois water of the lagoon stretched along the coconut tree-studded coast and was broken by large patches of cobalt blots. A white wall of foam continuously rolled over the reef, sending a watery mist into the atmosphere only to evaporate when it hits the warmth of the air. Billowing puffs of cloud reached high in the sky on the horizon and the tips looked as if they would break apart and fall into the indigo sea.

Blue took a moment to gaze upon the tranquil, tropical scene. It deserved nothing less.

*Damn me.*

He thought how much his mother would have loved the lagoon view. The two often hoofed it to Sabatini's Beach, hoping to catch the vibrant Southern California sunset before twilight's curtain descended. Although they knew it was air pollution that produced the prettiest sun setting shows, it was, nevertheless, always worth the out-of-breath rush to the water's edge of the cove. No place on earth had a more stunning sunset than on their beach. When Blue's mother passed away, he continued to hurry to the beach on those evenings when the marine layer didn't move ashore and covered the sky with a grey blanket.

Blue often invited, or insisted, Scarlett to take a break from practicing and accompany him to view the sunset. He would threaten to take her expensive cello with him if she acted indifferent to his idea. To her, watching sunsets was a waste of time and wouldn't help get her into college. Blue always knew how to persuade his friend. He would try to entice her by telling her that she might even witness the optical phenomenon called The Green Flash, which was a green spot or flash visible at the top edge of the sun during sunsets. Blue would reiterate to her that the only way to see the green flash was to be present at the beach during sunset. Scarlett enjoyed watching the sun slowly dip into the sea like a donut sinking in a cup of coffee, and she hoped that during one of her visits she would catch the green flash. She never did. However, she was inspired to eventually write a music piece for cello and piano titled, "The Spontaneous Spot." Blue genuinely thought the piece was pretty good and enjoyed playing the warm and delicate dangling notes that deceptively danced above what he interpreted as a cold, churning sea.

"Bro! Over here!"

The call broke the motif of the "The Spontaneous Spot" that was playing in Blue's mind. He hadn't thought of the piece for a couple of years.

"Bro, let's go!" Togi yelled.

Blue saw his friend at a manmade pier of coral and stone placing a bucket of live tackle bait in a small three-bench rowboat. The light blue paint was scraped off in various areas of the boat from hard use and scraps with the coral.

He wondered if his island friend would be mad at him for being late, but then he remembered: Samoan time. There was no such thing as being late.

"What's the name of your boat?" Blue asked.

"Huh?" Togi said. The question confused him.

"What do you call your boat?"

"Nothing."

"I think we should christen it *Calypso*."

Togi didn't try to repeat the word.

"To live on the land, we must learn from the sea," Blue quoted. "Uh... John Denver!"

"What?"

"You know, John Denver. *Calypso*."

"Bro."

Blue started to sing what he knew of the John Denver song, *Calypso*:

"Aye Calypso, the places you've been to

The things that you've shown us, the stories you tell

Aye Calypso, I sing to your spirit

The men who have served you so long and so well."

Blue then continued the song in his best yodel:

"Hi dee ay-ee ooo doo-dle oh

Oo do do do do do doo-dle ay yee

Doo-dle ay-ee."

Togi's four-year-old son was in the boat naked as the day he was born. He laughed at Blue's yodeling as he fidgeted with a small fishing pole that looked as if it was carved from a branch of a tree. The boy was large for his age, and it was obvious that he had inherited Togi's build and dexterity. In fact, the boy hopped around the boat with such ease and coordination that it looked as though he went fishing every day, which he probably did.

"Get in," Togi commanded Blue.

"You brought your boy?" Blue asked, even though the answer was obvious.

"Yeah. It's Kobe," Togi said, and then told his son in Samoan to shake Blue's hand. As Blue waddled in the boat, Kobe dropped a handful of fishing bait in the bucket and reached his hand out to Blue.

"Whoa. Uh…"

*Oh, what the hell…*

Blue grabbed the slimy hand and shook it. Kobe's smile was just as infectious as his father's.

"Don't tell me your boy's named after Kobe Bryant?"

"Of course he is. His younger brother's name is Keanu." Togi said proudly with a laugh.

"Your woman let you name your children?"

"Nah, bro. They got Samoan names too."

"I thought so."

"Yeah, Iris kicks me in the ass every time I call them by their non-Samoan names," Togi laughed.

Blue took a seat on a bench seat at the bow of the boat facing the beach. He kicked aside several coconuts to make room for his feet. After he got as comfortable as he could, he looked to the shore and could see several outrigger canoes resting against the sand embankment and nestled underneath the coconut palm trees. Blue could've have sworn that he saw this exact scene on a poster in the airport.

Togi pushed the boat several yards away from the pier and then lifted himself up out of the water and into the boat. He sat with at the stern with the land at his back. The boat seemed to sink a little with the added wait of the bulky islander.

"Dude, is this boat safe?" Blue asked, a little concerned.

"Yeah, I fix myself." Togi answered and grabbed an oar. The islander started paddling the boat further in the lagoon towards the reef.

"Fix?"

"Togi builds all the outriggers. I'm the best boat builder in the village."

Blue didn't doubt that Togi was an excellent and able boat builder. In fact, he thought it was rather remarkable that his island friend was keeping up with the traditional practices that seemed to be lost in modern society. Blue remembered how the *matai* of the village were keen on holding on to their traditional customs and ensuring that the knowledge was being passed down to the next generation. Nevertheless, Blue was kind of wishing that they had taken an outrigger canoe instead of the fixer-upper boat that looked as if it washed upon the shore like a piece of unwanted driftwood.

As the beach grew further and further away, Blue closed his eyes and felt the breeze on his face. The swaying of the boat along with the melodic mumbling of the waves crashing over the reef made him sleepy, and he would've easily had fallen asleep if he let himself. Instead, he thought of the classic song, "Sleepy Lagoon," by The Platters, and began humming a few bars, adding actual words of the song when he remembered them.

"What are you singing, bro?"

Blue opened his eyes. His personal tranquil time was snapped.

"Just an old..." Blue noticed the Coldplay T-shirt that Togi was wearing, which was similar to the one that his sister was wearing on the infamous day of the *Teine Sa* visit at the pool. The only difference was that Togi had cut off the sleeves to turn the shirt into a tank top. "Your sister was wearing that shirt the other day."

"Yeah, man. Savea got another shipment in today."

"Today?"

"Yeah. Bunch of stuff came in."

"Today."

"Yeah."

*Damn me.*

"The store was closed," Blue stated.

"Just for you. You talk to ghosts."

"Oh... for God's sake."

"Everyone was at the store this morning, bro. Whenever a shipment comes in, the whole village goes there. Even Father K got a shirt like this."

"Really." Blue pondered this missed opportunity that would've made his life a little easier. Sometimes that was what living in a small village with very few resources was all about—finding things to make one's life easier. "He let me use the Internet Café."

"Five *talas* for fifteen minutes?"

"Right."

"Did you pay?"

"Well, not yet."

"Nobody pays for the Internet, bro."

"Really?"

"No. You just go in and use computer."

"He expects his money tomorrow."

"Cuz you *palagi*. Savea knows you will pay."

"Why wouldn't he let me use the store then?"

"He doesn't want *Teine Sa* in his store that everyone uses."

"But... uh..."

Blue's head hurt trying to make sense of all this. He slumped on his bench seat. It suddenly got very hot despite being on the water. He waited for another breeze that he hoped would not only refresh his sweaty forehead but would also cool his scorching frustrations.

The lagoon at Vaimasina village was the widest of Upolu Island. Togi and his tree-trunk arms, however, managed to row across it with ease and speed. It wasn't very long until the voyagers made their way through a break in the reef and to the ocean just beyond. It was the only break for a couple of miles in both directions, and the one that for centuries was used by visitors to Vaimasina and the other villages in the vicinity.

After making it through the break of the reef, Togi rowed across the choppy sea to a spot that had proved fruitful in catching fish in the past. He pulled in the oars and secured them on the bottom of the boat.

"Anchor," Togi called out to Blue before turning his attention to his son and telling him to prepare the bait.

It didn't take long for Blue's stomach to become topsy-turvy in the undulating sea. And watching Kobe attach live squirmy fish by piercing them on a hook didn't help.

"Bro, anchor!"

Blue realized that his friend was yelling at him. He quickly reached down for the anchor, and the quick movement almost made him hurl. Once the queasiness dissipated a little, he grabbed the small anchor. It was heavier than it looked, but he managed to pick it up and throw it overboard.

Blue tried to look to see how far he was from land. It was deceptively far, maybe a mile or so. But it was hard to tell with the crashing waves over the reef and the rolling waves. Holding his head up and looking towards the village made him gag. His face turned as green as the verdant coastline. Finally, there was no stopping his seasickness, and he leaned overboard and vomited.

Togi and his son were too busy casting their fishing lines to notice that their companion was sick. It was the second or third time when Blue hurled into the sea that Togi noticed his friend wasn't right.

"You good, bro?"

"Splendid," Blue said sarcastically raising a thumb's-up and leaning back in the boat.

"You throw up a lot," Togi just had to add.

Blue tried to hold his head up and look at his friend. He could only get as far as the picture on Togi's shirt.

"Do you even know who Coldplay are?"

"Huh?"

"Coldplay. Your shirt."

Togi looked at his shirt and raised his arms as if asking, "what are you talking about?"

"Bro, you been drinking the seawater?" Togi asked.

Blue chuckled pathetically. He thought it was a funny remark coming from someone who didn't joke very often.

Taking a glance at the inviting lagoon beyond the reef, Blue wished they were floating serenely on its calm waters, and he remembered how much he disliked being in the ocean. Although he regularly gamboled at Sabatini's Beach especially when he was younger, he rarely went in the water. He wasn't a good swimmer, and he instinctively distrusted what lay unseen in the dark, murky water. Perhaps, he saw one too many shark movies. But even the few pool parties he attended in his youth ended up with him suffering from earaches that would last for a couple of days.

Blue leaned over the side of the boat and gagged again.

"Maybe we should head back to the lagoon," Togi said with a little disappointment in his tone.

"I'm getting... better." Blue answered, hoping that Togi would have him raise the anchor and row back to the lagoon.

It was at this time that Blue noticed that his feet were soaking wet. He looked down and saw about an inch of water in the bottom of the boat. He didn't think much of it at first, however, believing that a wave must have washed aboard while the boat dipped into the sea. Instead, he was more concerned about having Togi head back to the lagoon in a way that didn't make him sound like a wimp.

"Don't you think it's a little dangerous for your boy to be out here in such rough seas?"

Togi laughed.

"We've been in rougher water, bro."

Blue didn't doubt it.

*Today's a picnic for them.*

"Wouldn't the boy be better off in the lagoon?"

"I told you. He's a great fisherman. I taught him everything I know."

"Come on. He's, like, two years old, dude."

Just as Blue finished his sentence, Kobe squealed and pulled in a nice fish.

"Oh shit!" Blue exclaimed as he watched the caught fish flip and flop on the floor of the boat.

Togi laughed again proudly.

"I told you!"

The boy was eager to remove the fish from the hook, bait the hook with new live bait, and cast it back in the ocean, and Togi shouted instructions in Samoan to help his son quickly achieve this.

For the next forty-five minutes Blue watched (when he wasn't vomiting) with awe and admiration the bounty of fish that the two islanders were catching. Although most of the fish were on the small side, Togi did manage to catch a couple of good-sized snappers and one twelve-pound albacore using a more modern rod and reel. With each fish that was pulled into the boat, a chant and a cheer was enthusiastically exclaimed by the exuberant fishermen. Blue tried to understand the chant, which had something to do with thanking God, or a god. Despite whoever was being extolled, there was one thing that was clear: the fishing God or gods were kind to the fishermen today.

Blue wanted to participate in the sport. He thought that his companions made fishing look fun. But he knew that if he made any sudden movements, nausea would sink in and force him to the side of the boat.

The water in the bottom of the boat that now covered Blue's feet, along with a stronger wind that gave Blue an unexpected chill. Black belly clouds that rode on the back of the wind blotted out the sinking sun from time to time and threatened rain, but not a drop fell. The God, or gods of the fishermen, wouldn't allow it to rain. Not now. Not today.

The sea turned rougher too, and Togi thought it was best to head back to the lagoon. Togi told Blue to pull up the anchor. Kobe let his dissatisfaction be known by angrily throwing his fishing pole in the bottom of the boat until Togi placated his son by telling him that they will return tomorrow to catch even bigger fish. There was also still time to fish for octopus and eels in the lagoon, which immediately brightened the boy's attitude.

Togi struggled to row through the break in the reef. The heavier sea and wind conditions, and the extra weight from the water in the bottom of the boat made the journey slower. Naturally, Togi optimistically believed that it was the abundance of fish that was caught that slowed the boat, and he didn't mind the extra muscle he had to use with each stroke of the oars. From time to time to goad himself onward he would proudly mutter out loud, "A good haul!"

Blue became a little more concerned with the rising water in the bottom of the boat, but none of his companions seemed to care. He tried to shrug it off as well, believing that it probably happened every time they took the boat out.

"Togi! What's with the water in the boat?" Blue asked. He couldn't let it go.

As Togi was busy navigating the break in the surf to return to the lagoon, he was too distracted to hear the question from his boatmate. Even though Togi had done this all his life, an exhilarating rush came to him every time.

Finally, a wave helped Togi push the boat into the lagoon, and he rowed to another favorite and fruitful spot.

"Drop anchor," Togi commanded. Apparently, the area was still deep enough to merit the use of an anchor.

Blue threw the anchor into the water.

"Calmer waters, my friend." Togi said with a laugh.

Although the sway of the boat was much gentler, Blue could still feel the rocking. He looked towards the horizon and wondered how low the sun was behind the clouds. The day was growing darker, and he was ready to return to land. The day, the outing wasn't ending fast enough for him.

Kobe had already baited the poles with smaller, brighter fish and handed one to each of the men.

"Oh, uh..." Blue mumbled. He had really just come along for the ride.

"Throw it in there," Togi said. "Just see. You catch something."

It wasn't long before Togi and his son were pulling in smaller fish then repeated the feat again and again.

Blue wondered what the deal was with his bait. He waited and waited while his companions were filling the boat with a cache of fish.

Then, a bite and a tug.

Blue got excited and leaned forward.

"I got something!"

"Told you, bro!" Togi bellowed.

"Pull it in!" Kobe exclaimed in Samoan with enthusiasm. "Pull it in, bro!" He said again emphasizing the word, "bro," in English.

Blue struggled with the fish.

"It's a fighter." Blue said with a wince.

"Maybe you have a shark."

"What?"

Kobe leaped over to Blue, grabbed the pull, and tried to help Blue pull the fish up. When the line came out of the water, there was a rather small lionfish dangling on the end of it.

"Bro, you struggled with that?" Togi asked with a laugh.

"It sure is ugly."

Blue went to grab the fish.

"*Leai! Leai!*" Kobe screamed.

Kobe quickly interfered and pushed away Blue's outstretched hand, which forced the volunteer to drop the fish and the pole into the lagoon.

"What? What? No?"

"*Leai!* It hurt."

"The fish is poisonous," Togi nonchalantly added. "The stingers are painful."

Blue sat down on the bench of the boat and took a deep breath.

*Damn me. I hate fishing.*

It wasn't long before Kobe got excited and began to jump up and down in the boat.

"*Malie!*" Kobe yelled, pointing to the sea. "*Malie!*"

Blue knew the word, "*malie*," meant shark, and he quickly straightened himself to look over the side of the boat. He saw a school of black tip sharks that darted in a zigzagged pattern attracted to the fishing activity that was happening on their boat.

"Uh... I think we got company," Blue said, watching the

sharks with a little awe at how fast they could change directions.

"A nuisance, bro." Togi followed, cursing under his breath at the predators who wanted nothing more than to steal the fish that they caught.

The sharks were on the small size, mainly one to three feet long. However, a four-foot species would majestically glide by every so often to remind that there was a boss overseeing the late afternoon's work.

"They're harmless." Togi added and readied himself to fight for any fish that he pulls from the water. "Just a nuisance."

Blue watched with amusement when the sharks stole Kobe's bait every time he threw a new line into the water. The sharks were pretty savvy on stealing the bait right off the hook without being snagged themselves. He wondered how many times it would take before Kobe gave up. Meanwhile, towards the bow of the boat, Kobe's father was cursing at the swindlers who arrogantly and easily stole what wasn't rightfully theirs without even thanking the master fisherman.

*Who's gonna argue with a shark?*

It was a field day for the pompous predators. Every time Togi and his boy cast a line into the sea, the sharks would inevitably steal the bait, or better yet, the larger fish that were caught and helplessly dangling on the end of the line.

Blue had a hard time keeping his laughter to himself. It was the funniest scene he had witnessed in a long time. In fact, he had even forgotten all about his seasickness. However, much to Togi's chagrin, Blue couldn't hold in his laughter and let out a few chortles through his hand that covered his mouth.

"Buggards," Togi frustratingly said and finally gave up. He angrily brought in his pole and threw it in the bottom of the boat. Eventually, he would laugh along with his companion.

"I guess we know who owns the day," Blue said with a laugh.

As Blue turned his head to watch the sleek, silvery thieves crisscross each other, his laughter instantly faded when he saw a six-foot tiger shark slither near the boat. His dorsal fin protruded and cut through the water with ease. The shark entered the area like a bully coming for his lunch money, forcing the smaller black tip sharks to scramble away. Petrified, Blue leaned away from the water, thinking of the proverbial and stereotypical, movie quote: *We're gonna a need a bigger boat.*

Kobe, too, saw the shark and started screaming. He ran to his father's arms and climbed up the branches to the man's protective shoulders.

Togi promptly knew that the tiger shark was a different problem. They were a lot more aggressive and don't shy away from attacking unsuspecting and suspecting villagers. The shark often comes through the break of the reef looking for the easy snack, disrupting the peaceful balance of the tranquil lagoon.

As the shark circled the boat, Togi sat down on the bench towards the bow, picked up the oars, and tried to row. The boat was too heavy, and Togi realized that it had probably taken on too much water. Blue also noticed that the water was above his ankles and looked at his companion with a horrid expression.

"Are we gonna sink?"

Togi defiantly stood up in the boat with his boy on his shoulders and began shouting in Samoan at the sea and the shark with a threatening tone. Blue was able to understand some of the sentences that Togi was spouting, which was a declaration that he was the son of the man who could drown a shark, and he wasn't afraid. Togi continued that he had the blood of his father, and he, too, could drown a shark, although he hoped it wouldn't come to it because he respected and revered all sharks. As Togi gesticulated his proud warning, Kobe was almost flung into the lagoon.

"Dude, what are you doing?" Blue asked, peeved at the situation. "Give me the child."

Togi handed Kobe to Blue, and the boy clung to him like a starfish grips a sea rock.

"Next time, can you put some pants on the boy?"

"We need to bail," Togi demanded.

"Really?" Blue asked horrified. "Are we sinking?"

Togi picked up the bucket that had the live bait in it, and chucked the contents in the sea, which attracted the black tip sharks until the tiger shark muscled his way among them. Togi handed the bucket to Blue.

*Damn it, Togi.*

"Bail!" Togi ordered.

Blue put the boy down in the middle of the boat and began using the bucket to drain the water out of the boat. Togi emptied the contents of another bucket that had the larger bait and joined Blue in pumping the water.

Despite the hurried efforts to remove the water, the hole

in which the water was coming into the boat seemed to get bigger. The boat felt as if it was dropping below the waterline.

"Where's the hole?" Togi asked.

"I don't know. It might be back here."

Togi leaped towards the back. The little boat could hardly handle his heavy frame.

Blue looked across the lagoon. He could see the triangular dorsal fin of the tiger shark break the surface of the water for a few seconds before sliding gracefully underneath, its whereabouts then unknown.

Blue stood up in the boat to try to find the shark and keep track of him. Kobe also joined him by standing on top of the bench and searching the water.

"Found it!" Togi cried. "I think it's at the waterline."

Togi grabbed a small machete that he usually used to cut fishing line and gut fish. He took hold of the knife and picked up one of the coconuts. Togi quickly began carving the shell until he was satisfied with the size he believed he would need.

Without thinking of any consequences, Togi then jumped overboard into the water. The strong list of the islander's weight was strong enough to knock his son into the water on the other side of the boat.

"Shit," Blue said as he hung on to the rocking boat.

As Togi searched for the hole in the boat, Blue looked for the boy. Although Kobe was a natural born swimmer, he seemed to be struggling in the water. Blue looked to see where the shark was but decided that it didn't matter. He was going to jump in the lagoon for the boy anyway.

*Damn it, Togi!*

Blue took hold of Kobe. A black tip shark skirted by, and Blue could feel its presence, which freaked him out. It was the deepest part of the lagoon, and he really hated dangling helplessly in the sea that seemed to have no bottom. He thought that it could only get worse if the tiger shark decided that this was the moment for his supper.

Blue guided Kobe through the lagoon and the boy lifted himself out of the water and flopped into the safety of the boat. Blue hastily followed Kobe, almost falling on top of the boy.

After gaining his composure, Blue located Togi who was still in the water. The tiger shark was attracted to the commotion that was taking place around the boat, and decided it was time to investigate the possibility of fulfilling its predatory means. Blue saw the dorsal fin rise out of the water and head right for the boat, picking up speed every second.

"Uh, Togs- the shark is heading right for us."

"I almost got it, Bro."

Togi momentarily stopped trying to jam the piece of coconut into the hole, and looked to see if he could see the shark.

"You better get back in the boat!"

"Hand me my knife."

Blue looked at the shark and saw the dorsal fin submerge in the water.

"Bro, give me my knife!"

Blue searched under the water but couldn't find the knife.

"Where is it?!" Blue asked frantically. He then shouted to Kobe in Samoan to help. "Kobe, find the knife!"

"Bro, hurry!" Togi said. Using the gunwale of the boat, he lifted himself partially out of the water and saw where the shark was.

Togi knew he didn't have time to pull himself in the boat and braced himself for the inevitable collision with the shark. Togi started chanting that he was the son of the man who drowned a shark...

As the shark got within fifteen feet of Togi, it suddenly steered away when a splash in the water attracted him like a better proposition suddenly presented itself.

Blue had thrown the large fish in the water that Togi had caught, and the shark was pleased with the unexpected, easy snack. Blue continued to throw the rest of the fish in the water, hoping it would give Togi enough time to get back in the boat.

Instead of pulling himself in the boat, Togi went back into the lagoon.

"Bro, bail the water!"

Blue and Kobe began draining the water out of the boat. Blue kept one eye on the lagoon, hoping that the gift of fish was enough to satisfy the insatiable shark's hunger.

Togi fidgeted with the piece of coconut until at last he was able to plug the hole. He pulled himself back into the boat.

"Don't know how long it'll hold." Togi said. He then picked up the oars, and with his massive, tattooed arms, began paddling towards the land. He knew that if he could get the boat to shallow waters, the shark would not pose a threat to them.

Blue and Kobe continued to desperately drain the water with the buckets.

Blue looked back and saw the dorsal fin of the shark circle a couple of times, and it looked as if the predator was finishing off the free fish that was generously provided. But the shark wanted more, and he decided to turn towards the boat, perhaps inquisitively wondering what other tasty treat the hapless boat would provide.

*How much can one shark eat for God sake?*

As the shark picked up speed, Blue increased his pace of shoveling out water from the boat. He looked behind him and saw the killing machine coming straight for them. Even Kobe stood and pointed at the shark and yelled, *"Malie!"* Being low in the water, Blue felt vulnerable. He imagined the shark leaping out of the water, bearing teeth, and snatching him in midair.

"Uh, Togs- can you paddle faster?" Blue asked, feeling like a jerk. He knew Togi was doing the best he could, but the situation seemed a little dire.

Togi rowed quicker and wilder, his arms growing tired with each stroke. Despite his superhuman strength and heroism, he was no match for the shark's speed and innate athleticism.

"It's not gonna jump on the boat, is it?" Blue asked.

Blue crouched in the boat and lifted the bucket up to protect his head. He took hold of Kobe, who promptly wielded his father's machete, and pushed him down. Blue was impressed with the naked island boy, whose odds of surviving seemed better than a man with a bucket. Together, the two readied themselves for the fearless flying marauder. They weren't going down without a fight.

The shark leapt and landed on the back of the boat with a clunk like a sack of potatoes. Blue swung his bucket, hitting the shark on the snout, while Kobe sliced it with a swish of the knife.

"Get it off!" Togi screamed. "He'll swamp the boat!"

"Shit!" Blue cried.

It took a lot of persuading to let the shark know that wasn't wanted on the boat, as Blue and Kobe vigorously swung their weapons at the predator.

Blue got a glimpse of the shark's eye. It was black, cold, and full of impending death.

"Keep swinging, Kobe!" Blue screamed. "Push it in the sea!"

Finally, the shark chomped on the bucket and dragged it into the sea.

Blue was horrified. He never believed in his wildest imagination that a shark would actually jump on the back of a boat. That was the stuff only seen in movies.

*What kind of creature jumps on the back of boats?*

It wasn't long before the dorsal fin broke the surface of the water again and headed straight for the boat.

*Damn me.*

Blue and Kobe cringed at the impending threat. They were exhausted. And Blue had lost his weapon.

"Kobe, give me that coconut!" Blue commanded in Samoan.

Kobe obliged and handed him the coconut. The two faced the stern of the boat and readied themselves for another round.

The shark seemed more determined and swam faster, reaching the boat in a matter of seconds.

The predator then leapt out of the water again and landed on the back of the boat. This time, the weight of the shark halted Togi's rowing, as Blue fell backwards towards the bow. The heavy thump knocked Kobe off balance, and he was flung toward the mangled, razor-sharp teeth of the unwanted shipmate.

Miraculously, Blue caught the boy at the same time as jamming the coconut in the shark's mouth.

The shark retreated to the sea crunching, trying to spit out the coconut.

"Drain the water!" Togi shouted and continued rowing.

Blue and Kobe looked at each other. They knew the buckets were lost. Blue frantically curled his hands like a cup and started tossing small amounts of water overboard. Kobe tried to emulate his companion, but his hands were too small to be effective.

Without warning, the boat jolted and jilted and almost threw everyone into the water.

Tobi had reached the shallow water, and the coral practically halted the forward movement, ripping the coconut plug loose and gashing a larger hole in the boat. Water slowly and steadily began filling the boat.

Blue looked behind and saw the dorsal fin of the shark leisurely make its way towards the break in the reef and back to the open sea. Blue thought that the "top of the food chain" fish must've had his fill of buckets and coconuts.

"Jacque Cousteau called, and he wants his man-eating shark back." Blue said.

Nobody laughed.

The three of them were tired and took a moment to watch the shark disappear in the break of the reef. Togi then shimmied to the stern of the boat to check the hole. This time, he knew it was hopeless to fix. The three of them sat down and let out a deep breath.

"I'm never getting in a boat again," Blue commented.

"Looks like we have to swim," the islander stated with a dejected tone.

Blue looked to see how far the shore was from them. Fortunately, it was close. Oddly, he saw a woman standing on the beach holding a baby and wondered if she witnessed their heroics.

"Who's that?" Blue asked.

"Iris," Togi said and dropped his head.

"Mama!" Kobe exclaimed with excitement. He was the first to jump overboard and swim to the shore.

"Dude, I'd rather take my chances with the shark," Blue added.

"Yeah," Togi agreed.

When the three reached the beach, it wasn't long before Iris was kicking sand at her man and chastising him for endangering and almost drowning their son. Blue kept his distance from the two and pretended that he couldn't understand what was being said.

"Mr. Ronin, why my husband such a moron?" Iris asked in English.

"He saved us from a..."

Togi grabbed Blue's arm and squeezed it. There was no need to go into any details at the moment. The less she knew, the less beating and scolding he would have to endure.

Iris took Kobe by his hand and haughtily led him away. The boy looked back at his father and the volunteer and waved. Blue returned the sentiment with a wave of his hand.

Blue and Togi sat on the beach and stared across the lagoon. Dusk prepared the day for the coming of the night.

"Your son was very brave."

"Yeah."

"I mean, anyone who can fight off a shark in the buff— that's as tough as you can get."

"Yeah."

"And the shark jumped on the back of our boat. You can't make that up."

Blue could sense Togi's extreme disappointment. The islander had lost his fish, his boat, and temporarily, his woman… no doubt that he probably thought of the losses in that order.

The two sat silently for a moment as the water of the lagoon peacefully lapped the shore.

"You know, I once saw Keanu Reeves on TV catch a marlin off the coast of Baja," Blue said.

"I knew he could fish."

"Dude, it weighed, like two hundred and fifty pounds."

"Keanu can do anything, bro," Togi added with a bit of vigor in his tone.

"Took him three hours to reel it in the boat."

"Ah!" Togi smiled and laughed. "Togi could do it in two hours!"

"You're darn right. Togi could do it in two hours."

A coconut fell from a tree and hit the ground with a thud not far from where the two were sitting and rolled a couple of feet towards the water's edge.

Blue and Togi sat staring forward, thinking about what they had just endured until darkness blanketed the lagoon, calling an end to the adventure.

14

The front door of the church was propped open as villagers filed in for Sunday Mass. The church bells tolled their final rings letting everyone know that Mass was about to begin.

Blue stood about five yards from the open door staring into the church. He couldn't help noticing that the bells tolled in the key of G major. Visually, however, he was spellbound by the color and pageantry of the event, as everyone was wearing their Sunday's finest clothes. The men wore their "*tanoa*," shirts, or a collared shirt with a flowery print and/or Samoan design, and *lavalavas*. The women were dressed in their vibrant *puletasis*. Piano music streamed from the balcony inside the church, greeting the parishioners as they entered and took their seats. Blue's dazzled senses of the weekly and lively tradition clouded his assessment that the piano was still out of tune.

Most of the villagers who believed they were running late to Mass passed Blue without acknowledging him and entered the church. He wasn't sure if the snub was because of his affiliation with ghosts, or if they were genuinely concentrating on getting to the church services on time. Nevertheless, the frantic pace of the parishioners made Blue feel that he was late.

He took a couple of steps toward the door and was able to see straight down the middle aisle to the altar. To his shock and disbelief, he saw the group of women in white, the *Teine Sa*, standing around the altar table. Scarlett was front and center, beckoning Blue to enter the church. He felt like he had swallowed his heart. He hadn't seen them since the time in the jungle with Aumua.

As he took a couple of steps backwards, he choked and started to cough. He wondered if any of the parishioners sitting in the pews could see the wraiths. After all, the priest told him that this Mass was supposed to be in support of his actions in the jungle. Together with Father Krimple they were going to denounce the *Teine Sa* and prove how easy it was to be tempted by the devil—a theme ripe for a village to comprehend.

The next group of people that was in a hurry for Mass was Togi's family. Iris, carrying Keanu, was leading Togi and Kobe. All her boys were wearing the same purple collared shirt that matched her dress, which she had obviously made.

Blue took a few more steps backwards to allow the family ample space to enter the church, especially Togi and Kobe who couldn't seem to walk in a straight line. Iris shot Blue a sharp accusatory stare before entering the church. She was obviously still fuming at the thought of her boy being placed in danger in an unfit boat.

"*Talofa*, Mister *Lanu Moana*," Kobe said to Blue with a smile. Blue was glad to see the boy was wearing clothes, and he returned the smile with a nod of the head. He held out his fist and Kobe bumped it with his fist. Blue made an explosion sound, and the boy laughed. Blue had and would always have a fondness for the boy who helped him fight off the man-eating shark.

Iris wasn't going to let her son have any kind of camaraderie now and pulled Kobe by his shirt into the church.

Togi, on the other hand, stopped and looked apologetically at his friend. Blue noticed how uncomfortable the mountainous man looked in his *lavalava* and collared shirt that seemed too small for his large frame. Togi found the words that he wanted to say very difficult. Before he could say anything however, Iris quickly tugged her man away by his shirt and treating him like another son, scolding him as they went inside.

Blue followed the couple until he reached the doorway. Once they were out of the way, he looked for the *Teine Sa* at the altar and was relieved to see that they had disappeared.

Blue turned around to leave just as Father Krimple, wearing green vestments, and three altar boys in white robes approached. One of the altar boys was holding a long altar cross. Like every Sunday Mass, they were going to proceed down the center aisle.

"Ah, Ronin," Father Krimple said. He was pleased to see that his sermon topic had come. "You're going to join us?"

"After you."

Blue stepped aside.

The piano player began the opening song, and the choir began to sing the entrance hymn, "Here I Am, Lord."

"*Tatou o!*" the priest shouted to the altar boys.

The altar boys began to make their way down the center aisle of the church closely followed by the priest.

Blue watched them head down the aisle, as the parishioners were singing in full voice. He thought the singing was immaculate, and that the villagers were naturally gifted singers. Blue had heard the singing before, but usually it was from a distance. However, on this day, he was close enough to feel the genuine harmonious passion and emotion that couldn't be matched anywhere else on earth. It didn't matter how out of key the piano was, the singing just simply streamed up to heaven, becoming the soundtrack of a glorious day. Blue couldn't believe how lucky God was to be serenaded and moved by such melodious and modest music every Sunday morning.

When the priest and the altar boys reached the altar, Father Krimple turned around to face the congregation and waited for the end of the hymn before he would open Mass with the sign of the cross. As he waited, he saw the silhouette of Blue standing in the doorway against the brightness of the morning.

The song ended.

Father Krimple paused, hoping Blue would enter the church and take a seat among his fellow villagers.

Blue stared at the priest. He tried to take a step within the church, but he couldn't do it. It just didn't feel right. Despite the long history of traditions of the Church, he didn't believe in its doctrine. Losing his mother and friend didn't help matters either. It seemed unfair and arbitrary.

Although he grew tiresome with the old cliché that he was angry with God for losing the ones he cared for, the fact was, that when he died, he would have a lot of questions for the man upstairs.

The awkward moment made some of the parishioners question each other with a raise of the eyebrows, or a shrug of the shoulders.

Blue cursed the priest under his breath for putting him in this position. He also cursed the village for the way that many of them unnecessarily treated him for the past week or so. He felt that he didn't deserve any of this.

Father Krimple would have waited for as long as it would have taken for Blue to come to Mass. He was patient. He prayed that the Lord would enter Blue and show him the way forward.

Father Krimple waited.

The parishioners waited.

Blue did not.

Father Krimple watched with extreme disappointment as the silhouette of Blue closed the door.

Blue placed his head on the door, and he could hear the priest promptly begin Mass.

"In the name of the Father, the Son, and…"

Blue removed himself about thirty yards from the church and sat down on the edge of the grassy area. He felt a little dejected. He thought about catching the next flight home. He also wished that the *Teine Sa* would run amok within the church, disrupt Mass, and force folks to flee for their souls while Blue watched with an "I told you so," smug look on his face.

Before long, Blue's hounds came bounding about, taking

advantage of their best friend sitting down on their level. They jumped, nudged, and licked Blue on the legs and face. The island dogs were now almost full-grown and skinny, but by no means were they small in stature. Blue thought they had a sixth sense in knowing when he was feeling a little sad. This wasn't the first time that they had searched for their crestfallen companion to cheer him up. Blue appreciated the dogs' enthusiasm, and the dogs appreciated the opportunity for a rousing game of dog pile.

"Come on, you mangy mutts," Blue said, pushing the dogs off him. "I need to listen." The dogs understood and decided to wrestle with each other close enough that if Blue needed them, they would be prepared to literally jump on him, which of course, would make their day.

Blue attempted to focus on the Mass as it progressed to its ultimate conclusion of feasting on the blood and body of Christ. He could hear the mumbled words of the scripture readings and the melodic tunes of the choir singing the communion song and all the other pious musical pieces that passionately and dutifully moved the Mass along to its end. Most importantly, however, he tried to listen to Father Krimple's sermon. The priest mostly used English. He also could've sworn that he heard his name mentioned, particularly when the priest raised his voice. Despite not attending the Mass, he undoubtedly believed that Father Krimple would keep his word about vindicating Blue's actions in the jungle.

When the Mass ended, the door opened. Blue stood and could hear the closing hymn, "How Great Thou Art," pouring out of the blackness of the open door. It wasn't long before the altar boys emerged, followed by Father Krimple.

The boys didn't stick around and quickly went around the church and returned to the sacristy to change out of their robes. The quicker they rushed, the quicker they could begin their day of frolicking and eating.

Father Krimple on the other hand, positioned himself to greet the congregation as they exited. He was pleased when he saw Blue sheepishly standing there as if being part of a lost flock. The priest understood Blue, and he was embarrassed for trying to persuade a man to church under false pretenses. The deception hit him while he was saying his sermon. This wasn't like him. This wasn't how he operated. Nevertheless, he knew something had profoundly affected Blue to act detached and unforthcoming, and he wanted to help him as much as could. Father Krimple needed to put his trust in God and God's will to enlighten the volunteer to open up.

As the final hymn came to a close, people started filing out of the church.

Blue clumsily sputtered towards the priest.

"Heard you had a bit of a fright with a shark," Father Krimple said, breaking the awkward moment.

"Yeah. It was, uh, unbelievable. The crazy thing jumped on the back of our boat."

"Scary."

"What kind of psycho shark does that?"

"Never heard of it happening before."

"It was Togi's boy slashing away with a knife like a swashbuckler that saved us."

"Fearless boy, isn't he?"

The first group of people to greet the priest was a few members of the Lafau family led by Fiame. As they approached the two men, Blue felt a little uncomfortable. After all, he had been designated as a dubious delusory character, although Blue believed that they should check on the questionable activities their own dear Lance was engaged with in Apia. Nevertheless, Blue was thankful for the interruption, thinking that the priest at any second was going to morally lecture him about not attending Mass after an agreement was made that his presence was part of the plan for the village to accept him again.

"That was wonderful service, Father," Fiame stated. She stared at Blue and added, "I think your sermon was quite well received. It is easy to forget how difficult it could be when someone leaves home and goes to a foreign place for a long period of time."

"*Faafetai lava,*" the priest said.

"I am also reminded of Romans, fifteen seven: Accept one another, just as Christ also accepted us to the glory of God."

"Amen."

"And Jesus left his home at a young age to places unknown to talk about God. Did he not find it difficult to be accepted?" Fiame pressed the issue.

"You can say that Jesus was a volunteer endeavoring to do his best," the priest replied.

*Are they talking about me?*

"Have we taken you for granted, Mr. Ronin?" Fiame asked Blue.

"Oh uh..." Blue wondered if it was a loaded question.

"We often do when we get skilled and educated volunteers. If anything, we need to appreciate you more."

Blue felt guilty. He hadn't really done much since he

arrived except sit around all day and sweat. He hated the thought that he hadn't taught a single child to be more proficient in their reading. But was it his fault that no student came to his classroom? Was learning to read in English that important? They kind of read as they learned English.

*Are we still talking about the Teine Sa here?*

"Mr. Ronin would you accept my invitation to attend our *toonai?*" Fiame asked with the intent of reinstating the volunteer to her *aiga.*

"Um…"

"He would love to," Father Krimple interjected on behalf of his friend. The priest knew this was the way back to normalcy for Blue. Along with the Tuputalas, the Lafau family was a large and influential *aiga* of the village, and other villagers tended to follow their lead. To be seen having lunch with the Lafaus would be a favorable scenario for an instant reacceptance.

"And Father, you are invited too, of course."

"Thank you, but after the next Mass, I'll have to get the music ready for the choir to take with them to Apia."

"Of course," Fiame agreed. She was also part of the choir singing in the church choir exhibition that had become part of the Teuila Festival, and she reminded everyone how the exhibition was a big occasion that kicked off the festival week.

"Mr. Blue, however, has decided to travel with the choir this afternoon."

This was news to Blue. He looked at Father Krimple and tried to guess if the priest was sincerely inviting him to the festival, or if he was simply getting even because Blue did not attend Mass. Though, it truly didn't matter. Blue knew he would thoroughly enjoy listening to the music.

"But remember that I don't play piano or the organ," Blue added as a cheeky reminder to the priest.

"So you've said," the priest uttered with a smile.

"Well, come along Mr. Ronin. You can help with the *umu*."

As Blue walked away with Fiame and her family members, he looked back at Father Krimple. Isaac had run to the priest and tried to hide behind him. It wasn't long before Isaac's friends found him and chased him around the priest. Father Krimple playfully tried to protect Isaac before all the children ran off to the grassy field. The priest then looked back at the volunteer. Blue felt inclined to sincerely thank the priest for helping him gain the villagers' trust again. He worried about how or when or where he would display his gratitude. Father Krimple nodded and smiled at him, and Blue knew at that moment that there wasn't anything else to be said ever again.

The *toonai* at the Lafau house was much livelier and more relaxed than the usual nightly dinners after *Sa*. They often had *toonias* on Sunday after Mass, which were typically a brightly attended brunch, and Blue always enjoyed the different types of food that wasn't available during nightly suppers. Whenever he tried a new food, he prayed it wouldn't make him sick later, which inevitably, it did. However, after several months of eating Samoan fare, he learned which foods made him sick, and which ones that didn't. His hounds, on the other hand, never discriminated against the food that Blue discarded and appreciated every morsel.

A group of men were playing acoustic guitars while their young daughters danced and tried to eat ice-cream cones at the same time. Another group of people sat on mats talking animatedly about the recent Sevens rugby matches, especially the ones that team Manu Samoa were involved with and remembering great players from the past. Everyone seemed to be munching on *fa'apapa* or *panikeke*.

Blue was standing near the *umu* with a couple of men drinking a beer and watching them cook on the above-ground oven of hot volcanic stones that were heated in a fire before the food was placed on top. Blue didn't really like the taste of alcohol, but on a hot mid-morning such as this one, the chilled Vailima bottle of brew was quite refreshing to him, although he doubted that he would partake in a second bottle.

Most of the food, which consisted of octopus, chicken, taro, and vegetables covered with coconut cream, was cooked in banana leaves or put into half coconuts. Blue remembered the first time he participated in eating from an *umu* and couldn't help but think of another dumb joke: *Hey, the Stone Age is calling, and it wants its cooking methods back.* Indeed, after eating the delicious, tropical-flavored *umu*-cooked dishes, he never made fun of the unique cooking method ever again.

Blue could eat anything smothered in coconut cream, and when they gave him a coconut shell full of chicken to eat, the juices dripped down the sides of his mouth like a salivating dog. Since he hadn't eaten such good food for days, he didn't even care that the liquescent extract dribbled down his chin.

As he turned to chuck his coconut shell onto a discard

pile, Aumua walked by with her friend, Maeva, who was a niece of Fiame.

Aumua's presence took Blue by surprise.

He quickly wiped his mouth with the sleeve of his shirt, and he instinctually, yet somewhat surreptitiously, checked the zipper of his shorts to ensure it wasn't pulled down. He was relieved to know that he was wearing a *lavalava*.

Maeva giggled at the sight of Blue into Aumua's shoulder. Blue was never really interested in Maeva, but always made sure he acted kindly to her. After all, she was Aumua's best friend. The two had known each other since birth and had grown up together. They had done everything together from schooling, dancing, singing, playing sports, listening to pop music, and everything else that two village girls could do to entertain themselves at the edge of the world. Although she was the same age as Aumua, Blue thought that Maeva acted more immaturely, like a frivolous teenage girl.

"Heard you gave a shark a ride on your boat," Maeva said in Samoan with a giggle. Aumua playfully slapped her friend for what she believed was an insolent remark.

Blue wasn't amused. The shark incident was a terrifying event. One wrong slip by any of the three in the boat, and the shark had dinner even though two of them were related to the man who drowned sharks. Nevertheless, Blue was glad that people were talking about the flying, chomping shark instead of the *Teine Sa*.

"Yeah, but he was not invited, so we threw him back," Blue hopefully answered in Samoan. He wasn't sure exactly what he said.

The two girls laughed. He obviously mixed up his words.

The shake of Aumua's head with amused disappointment kind of stung the volunteer.

"Were you trying to say that the shark threw his invitation on his back?" Aumua asked.

"Uh, something like that."

Blue sighed.

*Damn me.*

As Maeva pushed her friend away from Blue, Aumua looked back at him.

"At least you understood what she asked," Aumua stated.

Blue smiled. He selfishly wished Maeva would go away because he wanted to talk to Aumua alone. He knew there would be no chance of that now, since the two were usually inseparable.

Blue desired to walk along the bush with only Aumua.

Blue desired to continue his Samoan lessons with only Aumua.

Blue desired only Aumua.

Blue stared at Aumua as she entered the house. When she got to the doorway, she turned and looked back at him.

Embarrassed that he was caught staring at her, he quickly jerked around. The coconut juice from the shell he was holding accidentally splashed on an approaching Fiame.

"Aiiee!"

"Oh my God. I'm sorry," Blue apologized.

"No worries," Fiame said. "Didn't you pull your zipper up in front of me once? Seems I need to be more careful when I approach you."

"That's when I started wearing *lavalavas.*"

Fiame grabbed a towel off a nearby clothesline and tried to wipe the juice off her blouse.

"I have to leave soon to get ready for Apia," Blue said, hoping that it would stop a conversation with the host before one even started. "Thank you for the invite. The food was delicious as usual."

"I noticed you sometimes go to the coco trees with Joseph."

Blue's plan didn't work, and he wondered if Fiame was being obtuse or stubborn.

*Or is she purposely being both?*

"Just one time."

"Did he tell you that I proposed to bring an Australian company in to make the plantation more profitable for the village?"

"Yeah, he mentioned something like that."

"And what do you think?"

"Oh I… uh, I don't know if it's my place to think." Blue said, hoping that this would put an end to the conversation.

"By the grace of God you were brought to this village, Mr. Ronin," Fiame sincerely commented. "Past years I have seen volunteers come here and work, but then they leave, and we do not hear from them again."

"You don't think I will do the same?"

"No. I believe you are here for a higher purpose. I can tell you are more rooted in our village. I have seen how you interact with everyone. You are the only volunteer to bother to learn Samoan."

Although Blue wondered where this sentiment was last week after the *Teine Sa* incident, it was true that despite the heat and the fleas, and the mosquitos and not having electricity, and the weird white women, he rather liked Vaimasina. The poetic balance between the villagers and the environment charmed him. They lived their lives dependent on the attitudes of the earth and sea, but also dependent upon each other. Overall, the village had a soul that evolved, changed, and lived for centuries, embracing every day as the touch of a newborn child, because without people it would fall dormant like the buzz of a bee at night. A soul despises the night.

Blue knew he was going to remain in Vaimasina for another year. Will he still love the village then? Will he be ready to return to Harper, his girlfriend or fiancé? When he does leave, will he ever return? Blue reminded himself of a Stevenson quote about the South Seas that he read before he ventured to the region: *The first experience can never be repeated.* As for now, everything he sees, smells, and touches is a first experience. But how long was the "first experience" supposed to last?

"What is it you want from me?"

"I want you to be there when they come to look at the plantation."

Blue couldn't help but to admit that Fiame was a very perceptive woman. Was she getting involved to genuinely help the village? Or was it for personal family gain?

Perhaps both.

"I know nothing about plantations."

"Yet you agree that it could be a major source of income."

Blue agreed with a shrug of his shoulders.

"There's something to be said about doing things the

traditional way," Blue said, hoping Fiame would like his thought.

"Of course there is."

"And you advocate to do everything *Fa'a Samoa*."

"Yes. But sometimes it is good to turn on a light switch," Fiame said.

*Touché*

"Do you not want to see this village thrive?" Fiame asked.

"Well, yeah."

"Your support to modernize the plantation will be a valuable asset to persuade Joseph's stubborn stance," Fiame said. Her eyes widened at the unlimited possibilities. "We have the best cocoa beans in Samoa and the entire Pacific. Think how our chocolate will put Vaimasina on the map."

Blue actually wondered if Vaimasina could be found on the map of Upulo Island, Samoa. He couldn't help but think of another joke, *Hey, the Samoa map of 1863 just called, and it wants Vaimasina back.* He didn't say it out loud, however. Fiame was very rarely in a flippant mood.

"Besides, what happens when Joseph passes away?" Fiame asked. "His sons have all moved away except that oaf, Togi, and he has no interest in the trees."

*Poor Togi.*

Blue finally acquiesced for the moment. Naturally, it would be Samoan time. It would be weeks or months before anyone foreign company came to look at the plantation.

"I, really, uh... will be your obedient servant," Blue said. "I want what's only best for the village."

"*Faafetai lava.*"

Fiame hugged him and headed back to the house.

"On your way out, please take some food for yourself and, I guess, your dogs too."

"The dogs will love you!" Blue exclaimed. "They will sing songs about you!"

"Yes, rather."

***

Blue hadn't been on the Vaimasina bus since the day he arrived in the village. He often saw the distinctive purple and black transport come and go to the village, but never once bothered to take it for a ride.

He took a seat and recalled the time when he and Lola were sitting on the bus. He felt a little guilty that this was the first time he thought about the program administrator since that first day in Samoa. Blue thought that she should've had her child by now and wondered if he would see her during the festival. In fact, he actually hoped that he wouldn't see her because he would have to lie to her when she asked him how things were going at the school. He briefly worried, knowing that someday he will have to answer to a progress report.

The bus was mostly filled with choir members and their families. Blue could see that Aumua and Maeva were sitting two rows in front of him. Aumua's hair dangled and curled over the back of the seat, and Blue wanted to run his hand through its thick locks.

The bus driver turned on the music and a reggae version of Willie Nelson's singing his classic song, "Always on My Mind," blasted through the bus's speakers. Blue wondered how many miles away one could hear the song.

The last family that stepped on the bus was the little blond boy, Isaac, and his mother who was wearing sunglasses. Blue often tried to guess who the boy's mother was and was a bit surprised that it was a woman named Maria who worked in the church office. Incredulously, Maria's husband, Lemanu, followed them both. Lemanu was big, bulky, and bald. Blue didn't know much about him, as he worked for a bank in Apia and was often gone during the weekdays, most likely working long hours and not bothering to take the lengthy bus ride back to the village.

Blue had often interacted with Maria at school. She seemed young, in her late twenties, but was very timid with a soft voice. She was a pretty, slim, but frail woman. Everything she did seemed dainty—the way she walked, the way she sat, the way she ate. Even her voice was dainty, which perturbed Blue because he constantly found himself asking her to repeat what she had just said. Maria rarely smiled and every time something didn't go her way, she acted downtrodden like a kicked mule.

Blue wasn't really the type of person to get involved with gossip or in the habit of making moral judgments, but the family dynamic of Maria and Lemanu was intriguing. He would love to ask other villagers who they believe was Isaac's true father. But nobody seemed to care. He never heard one person mention the oddity with the exception of Misi.

Indeed, the family didn't sit together on the bus. Isaac went running down the aisle and into the arms of an aunt. Lemanu sat with a friend in the front of the bus, while Maria took the seat next to Blue. Blue nodded to Maria and could see that she had a black eye underneath the sunglasses. She reminded him of the Samoan version of Hester Prynne.

*Where's her letter "A"?*

But that was unfair, and he knew it. It was most likely just all coincidence—just unbelievable, saucy, torrid coincidence.

Maria turned her head, not wanting Blue to notice her shiner. As she turned, however, she exposed a black and blue mark on her neck. Sensing that her seat partner could see her wound on her neck, she shifted and pulled up a scarf, wrapping it more securely around her neck.

Before the bus driver closed the door, Father Krimple jumped on the bus and said a quick prayer, which was followed by words of encouragement and village pride. When he finished, everyone clapped and cheered. The priest smiled, pumped his fist, and jumped off the bus, the door practically hitting him on his bottom as it closed.

*Apia or bust.*

The church hall in Sogi, on a peninsula that jutted out from the town of Apia, was brimming with spectators who spilled out from the doors and windows to watch the church choir exhibition. People had to wait for church services to end before the singing began, which probably felt like a lifetime for the nonreligious observers and tourists. But the wait was well worth it, as once the singing began, one conjectured that heaven closed so that its souls could listen. Hopefully, not a person would die worldwide in the next two hours because St. Peter himself would be off duty at the gates and listening to the melodious music from mere mortals.

Blue sat towards the back but near a window to catch a

breeze when one became available. With the heat and the occasional whiff of air through the windows, he had a hard time staying awake during the services. Now that the singing had begun, the ambiance turned from one of prayer to one of prideful elation. Whenever one of the choirs took the stage, their friends and family members cheered with flattering appreciation. Only a handful of choirs were selected to perform, and Blue was impressed to learn that the choir from St. Cecilia Church in Vaimasina had been chosen to sing for the last few years. It's an honor that the villagers never took for granted, practicing all year long. He had often heard them rehearse and expected the choir to showcase their voices for the next several years.

Blue looked across the audience to try to pick out those he knew either by the bus he was on or by personal cars that many of the villagers owned. When he saw someone he knew, he wondered why he or she wasn't sitting next to him, and then wondered if they wondered the same thing. He then thought that it was too hot and exhausting to wonder. It's time to relax and enjoy the music. He did wish, however, that his mother was here. She would've adored the color, enthusiasm and singing. Perhaps, she would be one listening from heaven with St. Peter.

Shortly before the St. Cecilia choir performed, Blue spotted Lance Lafau in the audience. The sight of the devious man gnarled his nerves, and he believed that Lance's only motive to be there was to kiss up to his mother. Blue hadn't seen his nemesis for several weeks, which he hardly minded, but he was upset with himself for not taking advantage of Lance's absence and spending more time with Aumua.

Lance was talking to a short, sweaty Caucasian man who wore a red bandana around his head. He was muscular and wore a dark blue tracksuit. The man looked to be older than Lance by a few years. Blue tried to guess whether he was either an Aussie, Kiwi, or a Yank. He also surmised that the white man was one of Lance's nefarious partners practicing whatever petty crime to make a fast payday in a town full of unsuspecting residents and tourists. Indeed, as they were sitting there, Blue witnessed the Bandana Man casually picking a pocket of a tourist sitting in front of them, and together with Lance, laughing at stealing a quick ten *talas.*

When the St. Cecilia choir began to sing, Blue was thunderstruck by the way they looked and sounded, especially with a tuned piano. The choir was dressed in the purple and white colors of St. Cecilia's school. The women wore the same purple *puletasi* with white hibiscus flowers while the men wore collared shirts of purple and white flowers and black *lavalavas.* Their singing was even better than in the village and their voices vibrated throughout the church. Blue also succumbed to village pride while listening to them. They were phenomenal. He could understand why they were asked to participate year after year.

Although Blue knew just about everyone in the choir, he mainly focused his attention on Aumua. She was standing front and center, flanked on both sides by her sister, Lupesina, and Maeva. Aumua sang with such enthusiasm that it was like she was singing the songs for the first time. He could tell that she was enjoying the moment—a moment that only came once a year. Aumua filled out her dress in an athletic way—all muscle. Indeed, there was a feminine charm about her that Blue found attractive. He thought she looked utterly voluptuous and enchanting, like an opera singer.

When the St. Cecilia choir finished their set, an eruption of applause and cheers filled the hall. Blue wondered if there were many relatives and acquaintances in attendance that lived in Apia. Nevertheless, they represented the village very well, and Blue thought that Father Krimple would have been delighted with their performance, albeit not surprised. However, he thought that it was rather odd that the priest didn't come to watch. Perhaps, Father Krimple had heard the songs a million times and didn't need to travel to Apia. Regardless, he missed an extraordinary evening.

After the exhibition, everyone was meeting their respective family performer outside the hall to receive even more accolades. Blue saw Aumua standing with a couple of her fellow singers. He started to go to her, but quickly stopped in his tracks when he saw Lance Lafau ooze out of a crowd like toothpaste from its tube and approach her. Blue watched the two talk with each other. He knew that Lance was sweet on Aumua and began to believe that he, the outsider, wasn't truly part of their culture and probably shouldn't disturb the natural balance of their homogenous island lives.

When Aumua suddenly looked at Blue, Lance also got his first look at the volunteer in several weeks.

Blue blushed and was glad that his red cheeks didn't flare in the nighttime. He quickly looked away and noticed that he was standing near the tourist that the red Bandana Man stole money from. Blue tapped the man on his shoulder to get his attention.

"Pardon me, but I think you dropped this inside," Blue said. He then pulled a ten-*tala* bill from his pocket and handed it to the tourist.

"Cheers, mate," the man said with an Australian accent. "Bloody hole in my pocket."

Blue looked back at Aumua and saw her and Lance walk away together. His arm was gently placed upon the small of her back as he guided her away. Blue wondered how much she would tell him about the *Teine Sa* incident. Most likely he had already heard about it.

It was a searing night, and the streets sizzled from the heat of the long day. Blue walked across the street, through a park, and sat on a seawall. A full moon effusively glared across Apia Bay, happy that its job took place only at night instead of the bright day. The pale lights of the town's buildings twinkled like fireflies.

Blue was feeling down and dejected. The sight of Aumua walking off with Lance played over in his mind, reminding him how lonely he truly was in this faraway place. The South Seas were composed of lonely islands and emphasized with the melancholy traveler. A light breeze softly kissed his cheek as if the island was trying to console him. Although it felt good, it didn't ease his personal perception of being nothing more than a foreigner—a *palagi*. Blue pathetically chuckled to himself over another Stevenson quote, "There are no foreign lands. It is the traveler only who is foreign." He contemplated what his life would be like if he had stayed at home. He sighed.

*Even at home I'm a foreigner.*

He also pondered how he would return to the village. He never saw the bus again after it dropped everyone off at the station. He thought about getting a hotel room. It certainly was an enticing consideration. After all, there were several resorts along the peninsula alone, and the rooms would definitely have air-conditioning—sweet air-conditioning. But with the festival to about to fully begin in the morning, he doubted that there would be any rooms available.

Blue wasn't alone on the seawall. Other people walked by either heading to Apia or just out for a nightly stroll. Some of the people he greeted in Samoan, and sometimes they reciprocate the acknowledgment. After a while, it became rote, and Blue stopped saying hello to anyone who walked by.

A person then walked up to him and stopped. Blue didn't bother to look up. He picked up a rock and threw it in the bay.

"Why are you here?"

It took a few seconds for Blue to recognize Aumua's voice. Turning around, he saw the lovely outline of the village girl.

"Aumua," Blue said with an embarrassed crack in his voice from the surprise visit.

"Are you not lonely?"

"Uh... no." Blue answered. He thought how strange it must've looked to Aumua that he was sitting by himself. Like most villagers, Aumua had never been alone in her life. There was always someone around her. Even though privacy was a very difficult act to achieve, Blue wasn't quite sure if anyone really wanted it. Besides, the island wouldn't allow it.

"I thought you left with uh... with the others."

Aumua knelt down to sit next to him. It was a little difficult in a tight-fitting dress.

"Most of us are staying with relatives around town. You can stay with us at my auntie's home."

Blue was relieved that he had a place to stay, although he probably could've easily fallen asleep from the gentle, cooling breeze on the seawall.

"You sang beautifully tonight."

"*Faafetai.*"

"I was thinking how much my mother would've enjoyed it."

"She likes singing?"

"Yeah. Well, she did. She, uh, she passed away a few years ago."

"Oh. *Malie lou loto.*"

"Thanks. I'm sure she was listening to you tonight."

Aumua leaned away.

"You see *Teine Sa* again?"

"What? No." Blue didn't want to start another *Teine Sa* incident. "My mother was way too cool to be a *Teine Sa.*"

Aumua shuffled closer to him.

"My mother left when I was young."

"Where'd she go?"

"Back to her village."

"Didn't she love your father?"

"Yes. But she liked her village better. She missed her family."

Aumua's mother was the last woman that Chief Joseph had for a wife. Although the couple had Togi and Aumua, Blue doubted that the woman was the love of the *matai's* life. He was a high-ranking chief who enjoyed seducing a young, impressionable woman from another village probably for the last time. The relationship was fun until it wasn't, and that's when Aumua's mother left.

"You didn't go with your mother?"

"No. My aunties raised me."

Sometimes the village dynamics blew Blue's mind. Blue had heard that it was customary in the region for grandmothers and aunts to raise children instead of the mother. Blue had witnessed this tradition being practiced on occasion since his arrival. In fact, he rather liked how everyone got involved in raising a child. The old proverb, "it takes a village to raise a child," was never more true than in Vaimasina.

"Plus, I had Maeva, Lupesina, and Iris," Aumua added.

Blue took a deep breath. He wanted to place his arm around her small, but broad shoulders.

"Aumua, I miss our lessons in the jungle," Blue commented with a sudden urge to be forthright.

"We can make lessons anywhere," Aumua replied with a smile. She nudged a little closer to him.

Blue could feel her leg against his.

The breeze subsided and the air stagnated. Blue began to sweat.

*Should I do the old stretch move?*

"The moon is mesmerizing tonight," Blue said.

"Sina lives in a tree in one of the dark spots of the moon," Aumua said.

"Sina the goddess."

"She is not a goddess. She is...*taumafa*..." Aumua tried to think how to translate the word in English. "How do you say?"

"Uh, deity?" Blue asked.

"*Loe*. Deity of love and beauty."

"I read she was a bit promiscuous."

"Pro-mis-cus?" Aumua asked, not understanding the word. Blue had no idea how to translate it into Samoan.

"Naughty."

"Oh- *loe*," Aumua said with a slight laugh. "She had many lovers."

"Well, maybe she'll be active tonight," Blue said.

There was an awkward pause for a moment as the two stared at each other. The breeze blew a couple of strands of Aumua's hair across her face, which always flirted with Blue. He reached up with his hand and brazenly moved the hair strands behind her ear.

Before he knew it, Aumua kissed him.

Blue couldn't believe his luck. Perhaps she felt connected to him in some strange, cultural way that he didn't understand. Or perhaps, Sina had simply possessed her. Whatever made her kiss him, Blue certainly didn't care. It was bold display and in public to boot. Blue was completely caught off guard. He loved it when Aumua was capricious. The kiss was extensive, electrifying, and it definitely felt a little naughty.

Blue asked himself if this was Aumua's first kiss. If so, he hoped that his slimy puckered kisser wouldn't disappoint her. If so, she was a natural at kissing. If so, he was glad that fate had brought him to this tiny village in Samoa.

He always thought that his girlfriend, or fiancé, Harper, was not a good kisser, though she had sumptuously glossy, yet stiff, lips for making out. He actually thought that kissing her was like kissing a pair of Tootsie Rolls. When they first started dating, he continuously believed that it was his fault for not making out as often as they should. But the truth was, she never enjoyed kissing her boyfriends beyond a few pecks. Perhaps Blue could be proud of the fact that his lips lasted the longest upon her lips.

Although Blue enjoyed the kiss with Aumua, he forced himself to back away. Naturally, a million thoughts ran through his mind that ranged from thinking about her age, Harper, his mother, Lance Lafau, Chief Joseph, Togi, Fiame, and even Taaiti. He wasn't sure why Taaiti would be in his mind at that moment. Perhaps she concocted a love potion for Aumua. Anyway, the old woman was in his thoughts grinning at him and showing a mouth full of missing teeth.

Aumua leaned towards him. Blue gazed into her black eyes, which shimmied and shined like obsidian. Without provocation, she grabbed the sides of his face with her large hands, pulled him to her and kissed him again. Blue questioned if this was wrong. But the kiss was strong and passionate, and he didn't back away. If it was Sina, he hoped that the deity would never leave her soul. His mind finally relaxed and settled only on one thought: Aumua.

No other words were exchanged between the two for the rest of the night. They only kissed and caressed each other until Aumua snuggled into his arms and fell asleep. Blue held onto his island girl enjoying every minute, with their silhouette entwined by the light of the moon on the seawall. For an hour or so he tried to translate every word about love from English into Samoan until he eventually fell asleep.

15

It was as if the entire island had come to a stop for the weeklong celebration, participating in and observing a splendid amount of pageants, parades, and artistic cultural practices. The Teuila Festival, which began in 1991, had developed into one of the country's most celebrated events, and had become one of the biggest festivals in the Pacific Islands region. *Teuilas* were prominent everywhere, and places and people were festooned with the vibrant red ginger flower.

For the next couple of days, Blue basked in the sights, sounds, and smells of the festival. He made a concerted effort to watch and support any Vaimasina villager who participated in a competition or event and sometimes was surprised to see someone he knew competing or demonstrating his or her skills.

For example, at the *Siva Afi* competition on the main stage at Malae Fatu Park, Blue was impressed with how Savea, the Vaimasina trading storeowner, handled himself when he danced with a knife that had burning flames at either end. First of all, Blue couldn't believe how fit the trader looked wearing only a *lavalava*. His sculpted and toned body moved aggressively to the beat of the drums. Most of all, however, Blue was awestruck with how Savea fearlessly twirled and tossed the knife with such conviction and composure. He knew that just one small slip could mean a slight to substantial burn. Blue wondered when the trader had time to practice. The only time he saw Savea was in the store or the Internet Café. Perhaps, it was after his website "explorations" when the storekeeper found time to play with fire.

Blue also enjoyed visiting the Samoa Cultural Center where demonstrations typically took place. On one occasion, he witnessed Lemanu's wood-carving Samoan patterns and aquatic animals. Again, Blue was impressed with this cultural display of talent. Although it took Lemanu many hours to complete his design, Blue checked periodically so that he wouldn't miss the finished product. On his last visit, he saw a crowd of tourists and Samoans gathered around Lemanu, asking him questions about his design. It was quite a spectacle. In fact, all the carved creations were amazing. Examining the detail in Lemanu's piece, Blue couldn't help but wonder if Father Krimple knew how well the burly artist wielded a machete.

For Blue, the highlight of the week had to be watching the *Siva* competition that took place over two nights on the main stage where other performances such as the *Siva Afi* competition and the musical acts took place. The *sivas* were graceful storytelling dances that traditionally were performed by young women. The movements were slow and fluid with small steps and delicate hand motions. Blue especially enjoyed the different traditional matching outfits and *puletasis* that the women wore. The *Siva* competition was the second most popular and well-attended event at the festival, perhaps falling just short of the Miss Samoa Pageant that typically closed the weeklong festivities.

The young women of Vaimasina were involved in two of the main dancing categories. The first dance they performed was the one from a sitting position, *sasa*, which Blue became aware of on his first day in the village. The second dance was known as the *maulu'ulu*, which artistically expressed the everyday activities of village life. Blue was particularly intrigued by how the *maulu'ulu* dance's formation was in three distinct positions. The front row dancers sat cross-legged, while the middle row knelt, and the back row of dancers stood. The performers would then transition between seated, kneeling, and standing positions with a graceful, flowing motion like gently cascading water. Indeed, the word, *maulu'ulu*, could be translated to "light rain," in Samoan. Elegant finger and hand movements accompanied the smooth footwork, and all along, the dancers kept a glowing smile upon their faces.

The villagers of Vaimasina had a history of producing talented dancers through dedication and tradition. The older women and men would pass down the knowledge to girls and boys as soon as the children were old enough to walk, leading to generations of very talented performers. Blue was amazed when he eventually learned how Fiame was a champion dancer in her youth, and now she enthusiastically taught the children. On the few instances that Blue had witnessed Fiame teaching, he could see the passion in her lessons. He also believed that her ardent instructions were a way for her to continue dancing the dances she had known and loved since she was three years old.

To get a better look at Aumua, Blue made his way closer to the stage. He loved watching her elegant movements. Aumua, like the other dancers, was very familiar with the routines. The hand and foot motions were second nature to her. There were times during the performances where Blue could've sworn that she acknowledged him with a wink. He thought about blowing her a kiss, but he wasn't that type of man. Instead, he would fervently cheer for the entire group at the end of their dance with the intent of locking eyes with Aumua. This happened after each performance, and when their eyes did meet, the world became blurry.

On the second day of the *siva* competition and while waiting for the Vaimasina group to take the stage, Blue noticed something odd happening on the fringe of where the audience was watching the dancers. Lance Lafau and the Bandana Man were talking to a teenage Samoan girl. Blue guessed that the girl was about fourteen or fifteen years old, and she appeared to be uncomfortable in the presence of the two men. It looked as if the men were trying to persuade her to do something for them. The Bandana Man even touched her hair and ran his hand down her arm. Blue got a creepy vibe watching them and wondered what kind of trivial crime the men were trying to recruit her to do. Blue asked himself how much he cared to get involved. Aumua and her group were supposed to take the stage at any moment, and he didn't want to miss his sweetheart of Vaimasina.

When Lance placed his hand on the girl's back and led her away, Blue quickly made up his mind and furtively followed them at a distance. They stopped behind a twenty-foot shipping container, and Blue knew instantly that something wasn't right.

*Nothing good ever happens behind a shipping container.*

Blue snuck to the corner of the container and intermittently stuck his head out to see what was transpiring among the group. He saw a smarmy, balding, and tall Caucasian man in his forties approach from the other side of the container. His introduction to Lance and the Bandana Man was quite saccharine and insincere. He was obviously some kind of customer. Lance then introduced the girl to the man. It quickly became apparent to Blue that the blithe man didn't care much about Lance or his partner and was quite intent on solely talking to the girl. The customer's sunburned head blazed like a neon sign as he placed his arm around the girl's shoulders.

"She's a beauty," the customer said in an Australian accent.

The girl appeared to be intimidated.

The customer handed the Bandana Man some cash, which was quickly counted.

"Two hours, right?" the customer asked.

The Bandana Man shook his head.

"One," Lance responded.

"You said that would be enough for two, mate."

"One!" Lance growled.

"What? You fuckin' greasy islanders are nothing but a bunch of dirty, fuckin' liars."

"Fuck you!" Lance retorted.

The Bandana Man agreed with his cohort with a scowl, and he tightened his fists ready for a fight. Blue saw this and wondered if Lance's muscle man could even talk.

Lance's venomous remark was the first time that Blue ever heard a Samoan swear. It didn't sound right even coming from the mouth of the Vaimasina villain.

The customer acquiesced.

"Shit," he defiantly said. "Come on, gorgeous, let's get the fuck out of here."

The customer started to lead the girl away.

Blue couldn't believe what was happening right in front of him and in the middle of the festival. He didn't really know what a prostitution ring looked like, but he knew whatever was going on behind the container at this moment wasn't right.

"Uh. Hey, wait!" Blue called, stumbling over his words. "Uh, girl!"

The customer and the girl stopped and turned to Blue.

"Yeah, girl. Uh, Amela!" It was a made-up name that suddenly popped in his head. But it sounded legitimate to him. "Yeah, your mother's, um, looking for you."

"What the fuck you doing, *palagi*?" Lance asked under his teeth.

"Yeah, sorry... uh, there's this mother looking for her daughter wearing jeans and a yellow crop shirt."

"She don't got a mother," Lance said with a spit.

Blue could feel the heat of Lance's anger.

*Just wait till you hear that I stole your girl.*

"Yeah, she's, uh, by the stage," Blue said obtusely. He quickly turned his attention to the girl. "Come on. I'll show you."

Although the girl was unsure who Blue was, he could tell that she was relieved to get away from the men. She approached Blue and kept walking past him, keeping her eyes fixed on his. Once she got a few feet beyond Blue, she picked up her pace without looking back.

"Thanks. Her mother will be thrilled to find her," Blue said to the men.

He turned and walked back towards the festival grounds. He didn't want to look back, and he kept expecting that some kind of blow would strike the back of his head. After all, he felt that he was some kind of a girl stealer, a deal breaker and a cock blocker—and in that order.

Fortunately, the blow to his head never came.

As Blue walked away, he could hear the Australian man vehemently demanding the return of his money despite Lance's placations that he had another girl for him.

Blue didn't like getting involved with other people's affairs, especially in a foreign country. But he knew what was transpiring between Lance and the girl was wrong, and he felt even more loathing for the man. There were so many Vaimasina villagers doing wonderful things at the festival and showing their pride in their village and their culture that the thought of Lance trying to take money from tourists disgusted Blue. However, he knew that Lance wasn't going to let Blue's interference go without confronting him about it. Tomorrow, next week, or a month from now, Lance would never forget, but Blue didn't care. He would do it again, although he was not going to spend his time policing Lance's delinquencies. In fact, he hoped to never see the scoundrel again. Of course, he knew that it was wishful thinking.

Blue lost sight of the girl as she got sucked into a black hole in the audience in front of the main stage. He wasn't sure how he felt about that, but he was glad that she was safe. He would've liked a "thank you" from the girl, but then he thought that, perhaps, the girl was too embarrassed for what she was about to do. Blue didn't know her circumstances. Maybe her family was destitute, and she needed the money to help put food on the table. Maybe she lived by herself and needed money for her subsistence. It was not an unusual circumstance in this part of the world. If he had let the situation unfold, Lance and the Bandana Man would have got their money, the customer got his satisfaction, and the girl would have gotten to eat.

*Damn me.*

He convinced himself that they were all wrong. It was a crime. It was an ugly scene in this otherwise beautiful island country.

---

Turning his attention to the stage, Blue was delighted to see that the Vaimasina group was readying for their next dance. He was glad he hadn't missed their performance.

He pushed his way forward so that he could get a better look at Aumua. She started off in a sitting position in the front row. Blue smiled at how lovely Aumua looked on the bright afternoon. The thought of him breaking up the sordid event twenty minutes ago started to slowly ease from his mind. He thought, *that's what love does. Love despises the past. Love keeps one yearning and anticipating the future. When it doesn't, love is dead.*

Watching Aumua begin her moves, Blue forgot about Lance and his shameful shenanigans. It was out of his mind. Aumua was the only thing he now thought about. Love was truly alive.

Performing in the many cultural exhibitions and competitions wasn't the only thing the villagers of Vaimasina were doing during the festival week. They also had a presence at the market and the grounds of the Samoa Cultural Village, selling produce, traditional trinkets, and most famously *Koko Samoa*. Nobody made better hot chocolate than the Vaimasina booth, which was quite evident by how long the lines were every day.

When she wasn't performing, Aumua was in charge of the cocoa sales and made sure that they didn't run out of the much in demand *Koko Samoa*. She insisted that her group of helpers from the village had several hot tea kettles sitting on an open fire and ready to be used. This helped keep the line moving, which ensured greater sales.

Blue would often visit the stand. Since the night that he and Aumua kissed, he hadn't really had the chance to get close to her. She was up early and returned late to her aunt's house. So he would stand in line and wait his turn for a cup. Sometimes, it would take several minutes until he got to the stand. But he knew that seeing Aumua was worth the wait. As he approached the stand, Aumua would smile and personally make him a cup by pouring the hot water mixed with chopped cocoa paste. She would then add some sugar, and because it was for him, she would taste it first to make sure it was just right. Blue thought the way she made him his *Koko Samoa* was quite sexy. The flavor was dark and intense like Aumua's eyes, and he loved the richness of the taste. He particularly enjoyed the way Aumua licked her lips when he chewed on the earthy, bitter grinds that clustered at the bottom of the cup, the *pegu koko*, which tasted like natural cocoa.

He so badly wanted to kiss her again.

On one occasion when Blue approached the Vaimasina *Koko Samoa* line, he noticed the choir exhibition piano player standing in line for a cup. The piano player was a slender man in his late thirties with sinewy fingers. He had shifty eyes and a bit of a nervy twitch. He was in line by himself and became impatient whenever he felt that the line wasn't moving along at his speed. Blue remembered how impressed he was by the way the man played and wondered where he learned his art. Being a fellow piano player, Blue was compelled to talk to the impatient fellow.

"*Talofa,*" Blue greeted the piano player. The piano player nervously looked at Blue and nodded. The man acted as if he had never talked to a Caucasian before. "You play piano very nicely," Blue added in Samoan.

"Thanks," the man answered in English.

The piano player turned his attention to the line, visually counting how many people were in front of him.

"I'm looking for a piano turner. Do you know one?"

The piano player looked at Blue and sized him up as if he were some kind of competition.

"*Ioe,* me."

Blue couldn't believe how lucky he was. Most piano players don't have the skills for tuning a piano.

"And your name is?"

"Saitele."

"I'm Ronin."

Saitele fidgeted. He really was in no mood for chitchat. But Ronin's name sounded familiar.

"You the *palagi* from Vaimasina that dances with *Teine Sa*?"

*Shit.*

Blue couldn't believe that his incident with the seductive spirits reached across the island of Upolu to other villages.

"I, uh, can anyone truly dance with the *Teine Sa*, Saitele?"

"My uncle fell in love with one and disappeared. My sister won't brush her hair at night," the piano player said rather perfunctorily.

Blue was kind of relieved that Saitele seemed to empathize with him despite his abrupt tone. There was no need to continue the conversation about the *Teine Sa*, as they both understood that the supernatural phantoms were just something that sometimes one has to deal with. Blue sensed that he could return to his original topic conversation.

"How much do you charge to tune a piano?"

"Two hundred *tala*."

"Our church needs their piano tuned badly. Would you come out to do it?"

"Vaimasina? No."

Saitele was now at the front of the line.

"Why?"

"Too far. Church has no money."

"I'll pay you."

Saitele scrutinized Blue again.

"No."

"Can you recommend someone else?"

"No. I'm the only one."

"Two hundred and fifty *talas*."

"No."

"Three hundred... and a meal."

The pot was quickly sweetened for the piano player. Money was nice, but food was always nicer. Vaimasina village had always had a reputation for its bountiful *umus* in conjunction with the famous *Koko Samoa*. There was no way Saitele was going to turn down the offer.

"Okay, I will be there."

It was Saitele's turn to order his *Koko Samoa*.

"When?"

"I will be there."

Blue left it at that. He watched the man eagerly pay for two cups of hot chocolate, which he took to the shade of a tree to enjoy. As Blue walked away, he saw the man return to the line.

On the night before Blue would return to the village, he went to the venerable Aggie Grey's Hotel to watch Misi Sao sing and dance. The colonial style hotel was founded by the entrepreneur Aggie Grey in 1933 and was used extensively by American servicemen during World War II. James A. Michener's book, *South Pacific,* created much of the lure and legend that surrounded the hotel. In the 1950s and 1960s there were nights when distinguished movie stars such as Marlon Brando, Dorothy Lamour, Gary Cooper, Cheryl Ladd, and William Holden couldn't resist staying in the august hotel near the waterfront. Over the years, the hotel has been dismantled, rebuilt, developed, expanded, and modernized, as further accommodations and guest facilities were required. However, it never lost its colonial and historical charm.

Taking a seat at a cozy table for two, Blue could feel the anticipation from a continually growing crowd (mainly tourists) that was ready to be entertained. Earlier in the week, Blue learned that Misi had won the Miss *Fa'afafine* Pageant that took place a day before the Teuila Festival began. Misi's talent for singing and dancing was, indeed, what sealed the victory. The *fa'afafine* from Vaimasina wanted to use the crown to urge other young *fa'afafines* to be proud of who they were. But, perhaps, just as important, Misi hoped to help combat increasing cases of domestic violence against women, children and the *fa'afafine* community. Blue believed that Misi's fame and passion could be a sturdy advocate in the fight against discrimination of people in Samoa due to a person's gender, sexual orientation, disability, or socioeconomic status within the community.

Before the lights dimmed, Blue took advantage of the restaurant menu and ordered himself a meal consisting of a hamburger with fries. He hadn't really eaten any Western food since before his arrival to Samoa and was practically salivating at the thought of devouring an all-American repast. On his first full day in Apia, he noticed a McDonald's in the town center and couldn't wait to stuff his face with a Big Mac. Unfortunately, because of the festival, there was always a long line of people, and he didn't want to wait.

When his dinner arrived, he had never felt so hungry in

his life. He inhaled the burger and fries as if he had been lost at sea for the past month. He completed the meal within a minute or two.

Shortly after stuffing his mouth with the last of the fries, the show began.

As Misi came on the small stage, the extravagant outfit that the *fa'afafine* was wearing completely stunned Blue. He didn't even notice that pieces of fries fell out of his agape mouth at the sight of the entertainer.

Misi donned a white feather dress that sparkled under the lights of the stage. The white, silver, and blue makeup upon her face exquisitely highlighted the silver stars, which were painted on both cheeks. The performer's arm extension showed the white-feathered wings of a bird, and diamond-studded, three-inch heeled shoes made the *fa'afafine* reach well over six feet tall. Arguably, the most striking feature of Misi was the headdress that stretched more than two feet high and wide, and was full of white, silver and blue plumage. White and blue feather boas draped around the performer's neck and down to her knees.

*A peacock just called, and it wants its feathers back.*

Misi's stage presence was unforgettable, and no one could help but keep his or her eyes on the ostentatious human bird that easily preyed on the audience's senses.

The cheering and whistling started with the *fa'afafine*'s first number whose confident and composed introduction included a part *siva*, part Western dance to the beat of drums. The rest of the performance was an eclectic mix of dance numbers and songs from Broadway musicals such as, *The King and I*, *The Phantom of the Opera* and *South Pacific*. Misi controlled the stage and the floor of the audience. The versions from these classic show tunes had no boundaries and teased the audience who reveled in them and cheered for more. Indeed, the *fa'afafine's* effervescent, raunchy rendering of the song, "I'm Gonna Wash that Man Right Outta My Hair," would have made Mitzi Gaynor blush.

Blue enjoyed the Broadway tunes despite the fact that they were oddly covered by Misi. When he played piano at the resort, many guests would request a Broadway song. Although he rarely had music for the requests, he had no problem picking out the notes by ear and made it sound as if he had always known how to play the song. Fortunately, he heard a lot of Broadway hits because of his mother who loved to sing the songs or blast them through the house on their CD player. Listening to Misibrought back some of these fond memories, and he couldn't help but smile when he remembered how his mother would wake him up in the morning singing, "One Day More," from *Les Miserables*, and even his Aunt Ophelia would join in. Once awake, Blue would also add his singing voice, and together, the three of them would harmonize the unforgettable and dramatic act ender. It was an invigorating way to start the day.

Misi loved to engage with the audience and preferred performing from table to table rather than remaining on stage. The *fa'afafine* provocatively twirled around poles, danced on tables, and swirled on chairs. The audience cheered and goaded the performer, and Misi couldn't resist an inane and impulsive interaction with those at each table. The Vaimasina villager winked, blew kisses, shook and spanked the booty, drank from the audience's beverages, played with silverware and fans, teased women's hair, and grinded men and women, while all along singing in full voice. This was not a G-rated show.

Blue on the other hand, thought the performance was brilliantly cheesy. He was titillated by the showmanship that Misi exhibited from table to table. He was so enthralled with the performance that was different at each table, so that he didn't realize that the *fa'afafine* was making the way towards him. He laughed at the antics, awed at the sexuality, and cringed at the forced dancing with audience members. When Misi was just a table away, Blue suddenly grasped the situation that he would be engaged next, and this terrified him. He thought it was all fun and games until he got involved, and then it would just be embarrassing.

He quickly stood, hoping to sneak away before anyone would notice.

After a couple of steps, a spotlight caught him and trapped him in its bright ray. There was a pause in the show.

"Oh, no, no, no, no you don't my hot American cowboy," Misi teasingly said.

Blue slowly turned around. The entire audience had their eyes glued to him.

*Damn me.*

Misi pretended to twirl a lasso over her head and then imaginatively threw it at Blue. The *fa'afafine* began to pull Blue back towards the table.

"Come back here, cowboy."

Blue went along with the gag and returned to his table as if he was caught in a lasso.

"Let me cool you." Misi huffed and snorted like a bull.

*Oh, shit.*

The *fa'afafine* began to flap the giant wings and

pretended to fly to Blue's table. Then she sat on the table crossing her legs several times.

"Don't worry, I won't bite... very hard."

The audience laughed, loving every second. Blue was thinking that if Lance Lafau had broken his legs the day before, he wouldn't be in this predicament.

"I have a song just for you. One from the South Pacific," Misi coyly said. "One from my heart."

The audience cheered. Many spectators gathered around Blue's table.

Blue looked at Misi's garish face full of makeup. He couldn't believe that after all the singing, dancing, and movement that there wasn't a drop of sweat on the performer's face.

Misi smiled at Blue, winked, and began singing, "I'm in Love with a Wonderful Guy," from *South Pacific*. Blue knew the song. In fact, he felt a little nerdy for knowing the song. He was comforted, however, by the fact that it was a short song.

But not in Misi's world.

The three-minute song turned into a surreal twelve-minute romp around the entire audience and stage. It was full of sexual innuendos and subjective mischievous intentions. Misi whisked Blue away from his table, and he had to endure every minute of the tune by accompanying the *fa'afafine*, who towered over him by several inches, in dance and parade. The number of times he fell, bounced into people, and crashed into tables was countless. And each time he collapsed, Misi was there to pick him up and hug him with the comforting wings.

It was a nightmare for Blue, but the audience ate it up.

Misi finally ended the song with a masterful twirling and twining dance move while singing the repeated lyrics, "I'm in love, I'm in love, I'm in love..." Blue spun with the *fa'afafine*, which felt like a carnival ride. When they completely stopped, Blue's vision kept spinning as Misi finished the song with a swelling and dramatic flourish:

"I'm in love with a wonderful guyyyyyyyy!"

The audience roared.

Misi soared.

Blue was floored.

Misi helped Blue stand and kissed him on both sides of his face, leaving two sensual blue lip prints on his cheeks.

It was a standing ovation for the *fa'afafine*, although most of the fans were already standing by the end of the song. Misi was crying while sincerely appreciating the unceasing applause of the crowd. After saying, "thank you," a million times and blowing kisses, the performer spread the wings and flew away into the night.

As Blue stumbled back to his table, audience members congratulated and patted him on his back as he passed them. He crashed in the seat exhausted and leaned on back of the seat. He was sweating profusely and desperately tried to slate his thirst with the melted ice of his drink.

*What the hell was that all about?*

A waiter brought Blue several bottles of Vailima beer that some audience members had bought him. Blue downed one of the bottles. His stomach felt a little queasy, and he wasn't sure if it was because of the hamburger, the dancing, the beer, or a combination of all three. He belched and gagged, tasting the onions from his burger. As he watched the audience disperse from the area, he wondered how many people were from Vaimasina and how quickly Aumua was going to hear about the American *palagi* who made a fool out of himself. Blue slugged another beer.

"You're a good sport, Ronin," Misi said, approaching Blue. The *fa'afafine* had quickly changed into more casual wear and wore jean shorts with a white T-shirt with a 1980s slogan, "Choose Life," from the musical group, Wham. The startling makeup had also been removed.

"One thing I learned was how outta shape I am."

Misi laughed and sat down. Blue pushed a bottle of beer towards the indefatigable entertainer.

"When's the last time you danced like that?"

"I wasn't dancing. I was, uh, flopping."

"I think we make a good team. How about you coming on the road with me?"

Blue choked and chortled. "I'm gonna throw up."

"The show's not that bad, darling."

"No. I really don't feel so good."

Misi got a good look at Blue's sick face.

"Oh, darling, you look as green as the Wicked Witch of the West."

Misi then called out to a waiter in Samoan and within seconds the waiter had brought Blue a can of 7Up.

"It's time to try defying gravity," Misi sang, but Blue was in no mood for more Broadway musicals.

"Please... no more."

Misi moved right next to Blue.

"Here, lean your head on my bosom," Misi said, grabbing Blue's head and placing it on the breasts. "A bosom always makes a man feel better."

Misi kissed the top of his head. Blue didn't fight it.

However, he did wonder how many people were watching him lean his head on the breasts of a *fa'afafine*, and how he was going to explain this to Aumua.

"Doesn't that feel better?"

"Yeah," Blue answered, closing his eyes. He wasn't lying. There was something remarkably and magically comforting about laying his head on a bosom. Perhaps it was because he hadn't slept with a pillow in months.

"Darling, you've been looking rather anemic," Misi commented. "It's village life. It can wreck a Westerner's spirit and health. I think you should leave and move here."

"I have a job to do," Blue said in muffled tone. He did ask himself what that job really was.

"You can live in Apia and take the bus to Vaimasina and perform with me at night."

"I'm not a performer."

"Everyone's a performer, darling, if you want to make money and love. Just some are better than others at it."

Blue lifted his head off Misi's bosom and took sip of the 7Up followed by a swig of the beer.

"I like the village."

Misi's entourage of friends that included a couple of other *fa'afafines* approached the table. They had no time to waste talking to a *palagi* and pulled Misi off the chair.

"We're going to hit the Tusitala Tanoa bar to start. Care to join us?" Misi asked Blue.

Blue gulped the last bottle of beer followed by the last drop of the 7Up and groggily stood.

"No, thanks. I couldn't keep up with you."

"Hardly anyone can, darling."

Blue left first but stopped when Misi addressed him one last time.

"The village is just a bunch of cannibals, darling. They'll slowly eat you alive."

Blue smiled pathetically. He asked himself if he was surprised that the *fa'afafine* talked in metaphors, but his stomach hurt too much, and he was kind of buzzed to even try to comprehend what Misi had just said to him. He left the group and made his way to the street.

It was slow going on his way back to Aumua's aunt's house that was only about a ten-minute walk from the hotel. He stumbled on the uneven pavement in the dimly lit neighborhood. Although he hoped that the night air would cool him off, perhaps it was the beer that seemed to make him sweat even more. The anticipation of vomiting didn't help matters either, and it wasn't long before he had to keel over and barf in some bushes. Blue vomited a couple of more times, and when he finally stopped, swore never to eat Western food again. He then sat down to rest before moving on to the house and oddly thought about the cannibals of Vaimasina.

Blue looked up into the sky. It was a clear night, and because of the waning moon, the sparkling stars were out in force and seemed to multiply with a burst. He loved the starry nights in the village where there was hardly any light to hamper the viewing. He would often gaze and wait for a shooting star to wish on. Some nights he would have to wait a long time, stretching the muscles of his neck, while other nights a star (or two) would quickly fall into his lap. He reveled in the idea that a falling star had the gift of prophesy. And if it didn't, well, it certainly didn't dampen his spirit as he felt he had nothing to lose in the first place.

After stargazing for a while, Blue thought it was time that he should restart his walk to the house. Because he was typically a light drinker, he was still feeling the effects from the beer that he had consumed at the hotel. He wiped the sweat from his forehead and felt a little dehydrated. He also had a feeling that he didn't smell that great as a concoction of sweat, body odor, and vomit seemed to hover above him. He couldn't wait to get to the house to drink a bottle of water and take a shower.

About fifty yards into his continued journey, a pickup truck with a giant Samoan flag attached to the back of the cab pulled up next to him, scaring the bejesus out of Blue. Three men quickly jumped out of the truck with the determined intention of accosting the volunteer. Blue recognized that it was Lance Lafau, Bandana Man, and another Samoan man who was as large as a giant.

"I didn't know you like women with large dicks," Lance hissed with venom.

Blue didn't remember seeing Lance at the show. He wondered if Lance was referring to Misi and couldn't believe the vulgar way he referred to his own cousin. But before Blue could say anything, a jab cut across his cheek and into his nose. The coldcock crack from the fist knocked Blue to the ground.

"You smell like a fuckin' pig in shit," Lance added.

The three men kicked Blue in the ribs a few times before hopping back in the truck.

"Go home, *palagi!*"

The truck speeding away was the last thing that Blue heard for several minutes.

It was the sound of the insects of the night that rhythmically chirped and squeaked that gave Blue the realization that he was still alive. He lay on the ground and stared up at the sky. His nose throbbed and his sides burned. He could feel a stream of blood flowing down from his nose to his neck, and he wondered if his nose was broken. In fact, breathing through his nose produced a wheezing noise like a broken flute.

Blue would remain on the ground for some time. He knew that trying to stand was going to hurt. For the moment, he didn't mind lying on the ground. The stars above shimmied and shimmered for him. A second later a star shot across the sky and fell. Blue smiled. A dozen wishes came to mind, and he tried to decide which wish he needed the most.

When Blue finally stumbled into the *fale* at Aumua's aunt's house, he collapsed on a mat and couldn't wait to return to Vaimasina. He slept fitfully throughout the night with weird dreams of catching falling stars, drinking *Koko Samoa* with Lance, and trying to avoid being kissed by a blue-lipped Misi. He awoke every time he heard people come and go, and he hoped Aumua wouldn't see him in his current state. However, a restful night was mostly denied by the fact that he had to constantly change positions to ease the pain in his nose and side.

The sound of birds clattering and chattering awoke Blue the next morning. He heard that the Vaimasina bus would be returning to the village in the late morning and wanted to make sure he was on it. He rose straight up from his mat like a vampire from his coffin and looked around the *fale*. Normally, there were seven or eight other people using the *fale* during the festival week, but everyone had left, including Aumua, for either the day's events or work. Worrying that he might miss the bus, he quickly grabbed his bag. Blue took off his shirt and noticed that there was dried blood on it, which reminded him of his nose. It was sore to the touch. He then looked at his stomach area, and although black and blue, he assessed that the ribs weren't cracked or broken.

Arriving at the bus station, Blue was relieved to see that the distinctive Vaimasina bus was still there. Climbing the bus's steep steps was a little painful, but he managed to get to the top. Looking at the people of the half-full bus, he nodded and said, "*Talofa*," and sat down in one of the seats closest to the front of the bus. It didn't take long for him to fall asleep, and when he did, he dreamt of playing volleyball with the *Teine Sa* and Father Krimple. He awoke an hour later as the engine revved and the door of the bus closed, and he was a bit peeved that the bus hadn't moved since he got on. But once the door closed and the music started, he knew that the reggae version of Abba's "Dancing Queen" meant it was time to go and would provide the soundtrack to leaving the town of Apia. Blue wondered how many times Misi had danced to this song.

Blue was awake as the bus made its way east hugging the coast. The turquoise sea looked inviting, and he wished the bus would stop for ten minutes so that he could take a quick bath in the crystal clear and clean water. Eventually, the bus would veer south and then east again into the rugged, fertile interior, and it wouldn't be long before it arrived at the village. For this trip, the blasting music would keep him awake for the entire trip.

The village was quiet upon arrival as most of the villagers remained in Apia. As Blue hobbled off the bus and slowly made his way to his *fale*, his dogs were the only ones to greet his return. He saw them burling enthusiastically toward him about fifty yards away, tongues dangling out of the sides of their mouths like pink cucumbers.

*Damn me. This is gonna hurt.*

And he braced himself for the impact.

One by one, each dog jumped up onto his bruised stomach to say hello. Blue winced with each strike but was glad they couldn't reach his nose.

Blue was considering three options after arriving to his *fale*: the first was to take a cold shower, second was a splash in the moon-shape pool, or third could be a swim in the lagoon. He then remembered that he vowed never to go into the lagoon. Thus, he was down to just two options.

Approaching his *fale*, Blue noticed something didn't look right. As he got closer, he saw that all the blinds had been pulled up and it looked as if furniture had been placed around. Stepping into the *fale,* he was surprised to see a small wood table with a chair, a standing mirror, a nightstand with a new lamp on it, and a plastic rack to hang towels or clothes. A long extension cord with a power outlet had been rigged to provide electricity. Where the extension cord came from kind of baffled him. He tried to follow it outside his place until it wrapped around a house and disappeared. However, the best part of it all to Blue was that a three-inch piece of foam was placed underneath his mat that would surely make sleeping more comfortable.

Blue delayed his washing once again and quickly left his *fale* to try to figure out who added the furniture to his place. His dogs ardently followed him, sensing that there was an adventure afoot and perhaps food. Blue's first thought was to seek out Togi, who he found sitting on the steps of his father's *fale* openly smoking marijuana and vapidly staring at the alien-looking pandanus fruit. No doubt he was taking advantage of an empty village because he would never smoke in front of people.

"Bro, how was Apia?"

Blue slowly sat down next to Togi. The sitting motion was still very painful.

"It was… uh, uneventful," Blue lied. He wasn't in the mood to go into any detail about the week.

Togi passed Blue the joint and motioned for his friend to take a hit.

"Yeah, bro. I hate going there."

Blue never smoked a joint in his life and stared at it. He sniffed it and grimaced at the manmade cigarette role that smelled awful.

"But, bro, you look like I always look like when I come back from that place," Togi added. Blue tried to hand the joint back to Togi who denied it with a wave of his hand. "Take a hit. I can tell you're hurting. It will help your pain."

Blue sucked on the roll and coughed. He did it again and coughed again.

"Where'd you get this?" Blue asked.

"I have me a patch in the bush. Don't tell anyone."

Blue took another hit and didn't cough. Togi then grabbed it out of his hand.

"Was it you who put the stuff in my *fale*?"

"Yeah, bro. Father got it from Savea and made me put it in there. You just need a mini fridge to hold your beer," Togi said with a laugh.

"Where's your father?" Blue asked looking in the *fale*.

"Sitting with his cocoa."

A car pulled up a couple of houses from the *fale*. When the back door opened, Iris holding Keanu and Kobe stepped out. Walking towards the house, Iris was carrying not only Keanu, but she was holding a bundle of taro, a bag of vegetables, and cloth that she would probably make shirts out of.

When Togi saw his family, he quickly gave the joint to the volunteer. Blue didn't know what to do with it, so he smashed it against the *paepae* of the *fale*. A small stream of smoke drifted upward.

Kobe hugged his father and then jumped on Blue. After the hugs, the boy sat between the men and showed them a toy wooden bus with moving wheels. Unfortunately, Iris wasn't as excited to see the two men sitting together.

"You two keep out of trouble while I was in Apia?" Iris asked in Samoan.

"Yeah," Togi said, annoyed at being accused of something he didn't do.

"I just got here," Blue declared. "I was in Apia too. We were on the same bus going there."

"I can smell trouble. I smell it now."

Togi looked at Blue as Iris walked passed the men and into the *fale*.

"You sang beautifully by the way," Blue added, remembering that she was part of the Vaimasina choir.

Iris returned and smacked Togi on the back of the head. Kobe laughed.

"See? You couldn't have been bothered to come watch me sing?"

"I hear you sing every Sunday," Togi pleaded and stood up to follow his woman into the *fale*. Kobe went inside, still laughing at his father.

Blue slowly stood. It hurt to stand, and he kind of wished he still had that joint. Before he made the long trek to the cocoa plantation, Togi returned with Kobe on his back.

"Hey, I fixed the boat."

"*Calypso?*"

"Yeah, the boat that sunk on us."

"How'd you get it out of the water?" Blue had to ask.

"I pulled it out and fixed it."

Once again, Blue was impressed with the young man's strength.

"That's amazing."

"You want to go fishing?"

"No. Never again."

"I want to go fishing!" Kobe exclaimed in Samoan. "I want to go! I want to go!" Togi laughed and twirled his boy above his head like a propeller.

"All right. We go fishing."

Blue thought about heading to the cocoa plantation to thank the chief for the furniture. But the walk through the rough and uneven terrain seemed too daunting in his current state. Instead, he returned to his *fale*, finally showered, and slept through the rest of the day on his cushy new mat.

For the next couple of days, he took advantage of the quiet village and worked on his novel at his table, eating food that was made by Iris and brought to him by Togi. His friend would also bring several bottles of beer and an acoustic guitar, which usually meant that he would extend his stay. Blue liked listening to his friend play the guitar, especially after a few beers. Together, they would trade the instrument and sing classic, current pop, and Samoan songs late into the night until Iris came by to drag her man home. Naturally, she never left without giving Blue a disapproving scowl while handing him a shirt, or bread, or soap that she made for him. Although Blue graciously accepted the gifts, he often wondered who she thought was more of a bad influence: her man or him.

As the Teuila Festival came to a close, more and more people returned to Vaimasian. Blue could hear the excited greetings and subsequent chatter among those who attended the festival with those who didn't. Blue would later learn that the festival was a big success for the village not only monetarily, but it also produced positive individual and group outcomes in the various competitions.

Rain, sometimes in torrents, marred most of Sunday, and there would be no doubt that the Vaimasina bus would be delayed coming from Apia with the last of the festival villagers. Throughout the day, Blue was anticipating a chance to see Aumua, but as the weather worsened, he wondered if the bus even left Apia. Driving through the craggy mountainous areas was tricky, especially with flash floods occurring in the most unpredictable and innocuous spots of the road.

To take his mind off Aumua's pending arrival, Blue kept

safe and dry in his *fale* with his hounds. Although he was a little sore from his encounter with Lance Lafao and his cronies, he was glad none of his bones were broken. He worked on his novel until the hard rain and thunder knocked out the electricity. Fortunately, Togi would eventually show up at the *fale* with candles, and Blue was able to continue his work utilizing the charged battery of his computer. Blue actually enjoyed writing by candlelight. He thought it was romantic and Victorian.

"Mary Shelley just called, and she wants her candles back," Blue quipped to himself, but he thought that it didn't really sound that funny out loud.

By nightfall, he had given up on the idea that Aumua would return to the village. The bus most likely stayed in Apia until the next day when the weather and the roads would be better.

Later in the evening while working on his computer, Blue heard a scratching on his blinds. Initially, he thought it was probably just a rat making mischief as they usually do when it rains. A few minutes later the scratching sound happened again, and he stopped what he was doing to listen more carefully so that he could pinpoint the exact location. When it happened a third time, he was ready. He stood, slowly walked towards the part of the blinds where the scratching came from and pulled them apart. Nobody was there. He only saw the glint of lightning that briefly gave a glimpse of the rain slamming into the village homes and *fales.*

As Blue turned around to head back to his desk, he stopped when he heard the scratching again. He listened for a second or two. Thunder growled like a hungry stomach and momentarily interrupted the scratching noise. But then it started again. Frustrated, he impatiently went to the blinds and pulled the cord that lifted the entire section up to reveal Aumua standing in the rain. Blue let out a yelp of surprise that briefly awoke the dogs.

Aumua rushed inside and kissed him as if she had been thinking about this moment for days. Blue let go of the cord and the blinds fell back to the floor. The candles flickered with the sudden movement of the air.

"Aumua," Blue said after a break in the kiss and pulled her further in the *fale*. "I didn't think the bus would drive on a day like today."

"Bus stay in Apia, but I got a ride. I had to leave."

"Why?"

"To see you."

"You didn't have to come back in this weather."

"No. I wanted to come to you. You scared me."

There was a genuine worry in Aumua's tone that alerted Blue. He felt flattered that she would brave such a storm to come to him.

"I'm fine, Aumua."

"On your last night in Apia, I returned late to my auntie's house. You were already asleep, so I did not wake you. But you sleep strange that night. You tossed and turned and moaned. Maeva said you sleep like the devil was inside you."

*Leave it to Maeva to overdramatize my sleeping.*

"I got hurt, Aumua," Blue admitted. Although he was thinking that he got beat up by the son of the devil, he knew better than to blurt that out. "Look at my nose. I just had a fall, and it was hard to sleep that night."

Aumua scrutinized Blue's nose. She then leaned in with her nose, pressed it against Blue's nose, and took a deep breath. Blue had read about this traditional act of intimacy, which was once a common greeting practice throughout all of Polynesia. In Samoa it was called *feasogi*, or *'sogi*. Most Samoans had forgotten this tradition except those in the villages that were determined to reinstate certain *Fa'a Samoa* customs into their daily lives.

Blue found the act quite comforting and intimate. He didn't know at the time that the way Aumua performed the *'sogi* on him meant that she thought of herself as equal rank to him. Of course, Blue never believed in ranks or class distinctions and always wanted to be treated like everyone else. However, it was Aumua who was making a statement that Blue was part of her village, and she could love him as she liked.

"If you did have the devil in you, I would kick your ass to get him out," Aumua stated playfully and put Blue in a headlock.

Blue tried to free himself, but the more he wriggled, the more she tightened her grip. Finally, she let him go and then tried to pin him to the ground. Blue liked her frisky spirit, even though it kind of hurt. He could tell she spent most of her childhood wrestling with her brother and friends. It was just another endearing quality that Blue recognized and was attracted to. The contact and movement, however, caused Blue's side to hurt, forcing him to give up the fight and fall on his mat, pulling Aumua on top of him. The mosquito net draped around them, ensuring that no pesky bug would interrupt their passionate moment.

The dogs, too, awoke and cocked their heads wondering

if a dogpile was on. But after analyzing the situation, they seemed to know better than to get in the middle of the two lovers' frolic.

Aumua looked into Blue's pale blue eyes, and it seemed as if she was looking into his soul.

"Your eyes are heavy," Aumua said. "Heavy with desire."

"I know I want you."

"When was the last time you were loved?"

Blue thought about the question and wondered what exactly she meant.

"Uh... my mother loved me."

Aumua smiled. She was glad to hear that Blue recognized his mother's love for him. She examined his eyes again and looked deeper.

"And Harper?"

Although Blue still loved the way Aumua pronounced Harper's name, hearing it turned him off for a second or two.

*Damn me.*

Blue always felt that his girlfriend or fiancé was a great friend who never sat still and was constantly searching for different ways to have fun. But she was never really interested in having sex. Blue got the feeling that she was kind of grossed out by the whole act. In fact, they rarely slept together. The one time they had sex, Blue believed that it was only for her to compare her experience and have a few laughs with her annoying friends. It didn't take long for him to realize that Harper was more interested in teasing and tantalizing all her male friends, especially Blue, without crossing any sordid sexual line that many individuals his age experienced. It was frustrating for him, to say the least.

Plus, she had an irritating way of talking about random topics during sex, which was either gossip about her friends, family, or her dog. Blue thought their romance just felt wrong. It always felt wrong with Harper.

"Harper truly only loves stereotypical ideas of romance."

"I do not understand."

"She, uh, doesn't love me. She loves the idea that she loves me and the idea of dating."

"But she still loves?"

"Just herself."

Aumua giggled. She had never encountered a narcissistic person before. The belief that a person could not love another was foreign to her.

She looked into his eyes again.

"I see stars falling in your eyes."

"Is that a good thing?"

"It is...a beautiful thing. I like it."

For the first time in his life, Blue felt as if he was in the right place with the right girl. Never had he ever imagined that he would be locked body-to-body with a girl on the other side of the world—a girl who had the ability to grab his seething somber soul and embrace it like a doll. And it just felt right.

With both of his hands, Blue brushed her thick hair out of her face and pulled her towards him to kiss. And it just felt right.

A jolt of thunder cracked and quickly faded as if it was pushed aside by rainfall. The atmosphere inside the *fale* intensified, then became thick and stagnated with heightened sensual anticipation.

Their kissing inevitably led to the exciting and

exhilarating embarrassment of foreplay; their hands explored the wondrous differences of their bodies. After all the months of being with her in the jungle and wanting to touch her, he relished the moment to become entwined with her body like two mating snakes. His touch of her brown skin was nothing he had ever experienced, and it excited him.

For the rest of the night, the hard rain crashing upon the tin roof drowned out the sounds of their lovemaking, as their pulsating, sweaty bodies sprang and recoiled to the rhythm of the rain.

And it just felt right.

16

Mele Blue performed the *Finale: Allegro energico* of the Bruch violin concerto much as she lived her short life. Indeed, this third movement sounded like a folk dance, a gypsy romp that Mele executed and exploited with a virtuosic display of technical bravado, quirkiness, and sass. It was a perfect way to end a very charismatic piece. The notes didn't just bounce off the walls of the Stern Auditorium at Carnegie Hall, but rather they passionately and poetically danced with the members of the audience. The movement energized and spoke to Mele because that was how she had always treated people—by metaphorically drawing others into her and having a dance together.

Mele lived to share her life. The spirit of *Fa'a Samoa*, which she learned since she was born, was much more than doing things in a traditional manner such as cooking and tattooing. Similar to the Hawaiian's concept of *aloha*, *Fa'a Samoa* could also be translated to love, connection, and respect. Mele enjoyed giving herself entirely without expecting anything in return. Whether it was through music, her Samoan culture, her smile, or her positive personality, she simply opened herself up to people as if they were part of her own family. Her mind and heart were constantly in sync, and it was revealed every time she saw someone familiar or met someone new.

And now Mele was sharing her talent. To her, it was a sense of community service, or a sense of offering. Mele gave unconditionally. But living *Fa'a Samoa* only worked when there was reciprocity. It was a daily test of actions and consequences. Mele understood from a young age that if you give, you will also receive. She was taught to create, give, and receive positive actions and energy. The audience returned Mele's love, her passionate talent, and she could feel it down to her vigorously shifting fingers.

Sitting in Row M, Seat 112, Blue admired his daughter's verve and her ability to invite the audience inside her innermost thoughts, exemplified by her playing style. He believed that only a few had this gift. He certainly did not. He was too shy and perhaps, a little too selfish to reveal any intimate feelings while he performed on the piano. But Mele felt comfortable with this because she was constantly shown how important it was to learn the responsibility of giving back. In fact, Blue would remember those years before they came to the United States how much time the elder villagers would spend with the children imparting *Fa'a Samoa* on them. He saw firsthand what Margaret Mead meant when she observed, "Children must be taught how to think, not what to think." At the time, he truly believed the refreshing and liberating parts of this attitude, or philosophy, but he would later struggle with its concept as he tried to Americanize his daughter, despite being exposed to the incessant competitive drive of success, money, and an avaricious attitude spurned by a pop culture that promised it all, Mele naively (or purposely) kept her *Fa'a Samoa* ethos because it was well ingrained in her. Hundreds of years of tradition had been rooted in her, and she was proud to possess it and demonstrate it.

Blue began to question himself if he had taken away the culture that Mele had learned in Samoa. He felt guilty about it, and it made the pain around his eye throb a little more. But he was adamant that moving to the United States was best for his daughter. She could shine here. The past seven years had been turbulent for him and disappointing to say the least. Mele was the one bright spot—the one exception because she was exceptional. Blue knew that Mele was approaching her teen years. The pressures that teenage American girls endured to be pretty, graceful, talented, and successful were well documented, and he wondered how Mele would handle these confusing and stormy years. For now, however, her talent had driven her beyond even his expectations.

The only other person Blue could think of that had the gift like his daughter to inspire others was, of course, Scarlett. However, there was a difference. Despite dominating every competition, Scarlett played music to succeed, and Mele played music to share. Blue liked the fact that playing music was fun for his daughter, but for his friend it was a necessity and obsession to play every note perfectly. Mele took the time required, cared about others, and even made small gifts such as bracelets or headbands for her fellow competitors, while Scarlett entered a room like a giant with a club to crush the other participants. To Scarlett, it was a cutthroat and desperate business with only one goal in mind: to be the best and win.

As Mele beguiled and charmed the audience through the third movement that hit all the emotions, Blue smirked at the thought of the seriousness in which Scarlett managed her music. He recalled one afternoon in his junior year of high school when Scarlett came to his house to practice. It was the only time she ever came to his house with her cello... and Blue forgot about the practice session.

When Blue got home from school that day, he went to his room to change into a work outfit for playing piano at a nearby resort later that evening. He took his time undressing while listening to the song "Train in Vain" by The Clash. He danced, sang along, and strummed his acoustic guitar to the song. A few minutes later and unbeknown to Blue, Scarlett appeared in the doorway, holding her cello case.

To this day, as Blue sat in Row M, Seat 112, he had no idea how long Scarlett stood in the doorway and watched him pretend to be a rock star. If he had turned around, he would have seen a rare smile on Scarlett's face. If he had turned around, he would have seen her covering her mouth with her hand trying to hold her laughter. But he didn't turn around. Instead, he continued to tease his make-believe audience. When he took off his shirt, twirled it in the air, and then threw it to his imaginary fans, Scarlett's amusement quickly turned lovestruck, like an infatuated groupie at the sight of his bare chest.

If Blue had turned around, he would have seen Scarlett lose her inhibitions.

For a split second, she had forgotten about her cello. For a split second, she had become a normal teenage girl. For a split second, her eyes dilated, her hands got sweaty, and her legs quivered. For a split second, her heart fluttered. She was attracted to the opposite sex for the first time in her life. For a split second, her mind and body craved something that went further than practice and performance.

If Blue had turned around, he would have seen Scarlet as a girl full of humility and infatuation. But he didn't.

As Blue took off his jeans and began to twirl them in the air, his tighty-whitey underwear outlined all the cracks and bulges. Scarlett let out a gasp. Blue finally turned around.

"Shit, Scarlett!" Blue exclaimed, covering his bare chest. This was much worse than being caught with his barn door open. The whole farm was exposed.

"Sorry, sorry!" Scarlett pleaded while covering her eyes.

"What the hell are you doing here?!" Blue asked, trying to put his pants back on.

"I came to practice."

"In my room?"

"I'm sorry. Your babysitter showed me your room," Scarlett said. She was referring to Aunt Ophelia's friend and longtime neighbor, Vivi Pipe, who used to watch Blue when he was a child while his mother was working out of the county and his aunt was on an international assignment.

"I'm a little old to have a babysitter."

"I don't know. I just followed her to your room."

"She knows there's no piano in here!"

"Your room is messy and it kinda stinks in here."

"It looks and smells like a normal teenager's room."

"Why did you cover your chest?"

"What?"

"I mean your boy thingys were bouncing like …"

"Would you please go to the living room?!" Blue pleaded as he put on a shirt.

Scarlett picked up her cello case. "I'm sorry," she said before exiting the room. She was still trying hard to keep her laugh to herself.

In the living room, Scarlett set up her cello and tuned it. As she waited for Blue to come into the room, she was captivated by the odd, eclectic art pieces strewn throughout. She giggled and blushed at the nude figures in the paintings and the exposed female breasts and male genitalia of the statues. It was a much different room than the sterile environment in her home.

Several minutes later, Blue entered the room a little peeved and sat down at the piano. His back was to his friend. He started rehearsing Franz Schubert's *Arpeggione Sonata*. Once he started playing, Scarlett wasted no time playing along. After all, this was the reason why she was there.

After several measures, Blue suddenly slowed the pace of the piece until he came to a stop. It took another measure or so before Scarlett realized that he stopped playing. She raised her bow and looked at Blue.

"What were my boy, uh, thingys bouncing like?"

"Huh?"

"You stopped after you said that my boy toys were bouncing, like?"

"Oh, I don't know—like a jellyfish," Scarlett said with a snicker.

"What?"

"That's what came to mind."

Blue snorted and chuckled.

"You're so weird, Scar."

"I am not."

"Jellyfish? You talk like a homeschooled kid."

"I am a homeschooled kid."

Blue finally turned around and looked at her.

"You know, if you went to my high school, they'd eat you alive."

"Who?"

"Other kids. The cool kids."

"Why?"

"They don't like weirdoes."

"I'm not weird."

"You're different. And different is uncool to them."

"You like me."

"Yeah."

"Are you not cool then?"

"I..." Blue thought about it. "No. I'm not cool."

"So they don't like you either."

"No. Dude, now you're bringing me down."

Blue turned around and picked up where he left off with the Schubert piece. Scarlett continued playing as well. After a few measures, it was Scarlett's turn to stop.

"Why do you like me?"

"What?"

"Why do you like me?"

"Because I like that you're different. You're talented."

"The kids at your school aren't talented?"

"Not like you."

"You should've been homeschooled."

Blue laughed. He started playing again. Scarlett joined in with the piece. Moments later, Blue abruptly stopped.

"Really- a jellyfish?"

"I don't know about those things."

"Obviously."

Blue began playing and Scarlett quickly accompanied him. Soon it was Scarlett who stopped playing.

"This isn't right. It's not right," Scarlett commented.

"What isn't right?"

"This is environment. I feel like I'm playing in a bordello," Scarlett said standing up.

"What?"

"It's uncomfortable."

"Do you even know what bordello is?"

"Yes. It's a place of disrepute."

"You mean the artwork bothers you?"

"Is this art?"

"It's a collection."

"It doesn't feel right," Scarlett said as she began packing her cello. "We'll continue at my house. Mother said that the Arpeggione Sonata might be a good piece for college auditions."

"College auditions? That's, like, over a year away."

"The sooner we start, the sooner we'll be prepared."

"You mean the sooner we start, the sooner we kill ourselves."

"I'll see you at eight p.m."

"I can't."

"Why?"

"I gotta work."

"Playing Disney songs is work?"

"Don't knock it, Scar. People love the Disney songs, and they tip better when they hear one."

"See you at eight."

"I won't be there."

"You'll be there because you're different and talented, and it's where you're supposed to be."

As Scarlett left the room, Blue sighed.

"I guess we're both weird."

---

Sitting in Row M, M for Mele, Seat 112, Blue snickered at the thought of the anecdote with Scarlett. It seemed that all of the remembrances of Scarlett and him were typically odd. He chuckled, recalling that he did show up at Scarlett's house later that night to practice. Although he was late, he got the impression that Scarlett would've waited until midnight.

Mele completed the concerto with intricate finger movement enhanced by the orchestra. When the ending came to its dramatic show-stopping end, the audience gasped in astonishment and quickly applauded the twelve-year-old prodigy. It wasn't long before the entire crowd was standing and continuing with their ovation. From time to time the word, "bravo" was interjected within the clapping hands.

Although Mele had played the piece countless times, Blue knew that it would be futile to ask her later how she felt about the performance. Mele was always proud of herself, and she simply performed every piece as if it were the last time she would ever play it. Each concerto, sonata, and caprice was like a friend to her. She treated every musical composition as if it was a living companion—a best friend that she got to know quite well. She cherished the trust they placed in her with their secrets, desires, and vulnerabilities. Mele felt that it was her responsibility to play the pieces with perfection to gain and maintain a meaningful and sustainable trust.

The old lady next to Blue stood and took out a Kleenex from the sleeve of her sweater to wipe the tears from her eyes. She helped her husband to stand and applaud.

"You must be so proud," the old lady said to Blue in a voice that seemed to be louder than the cheers of the auditorium. Even the woman in front of Blue turned around and gave him an appreciative smile.

Blue tried to thank the old lady with a wink of the eye, but any facial expression he made reminded him of this wounds.

Blue watched his daughter and the conductor take their bows, shake hands with each other, and congratulate the orchestra. He knew that if Mele had the time and space, she would've hugged every member of the orchestra.

*Heck, she'd hug the entire audience if she could.*

As the audience began to settle down and take their seat, Blue caught a whiff of the scent of gardenia flowers. He knew it wasn't the woman with the heavy perfume in front of him, thus he looked at the young women to his right. All three were swiping their phones with their index finger. Without looking up from her phone, the woman sitting in the middle asked her companions if they thought that Mele's feet were cold since the auditorium was freezing. Naturally, Blue winced at the question. After living in the tropics for so many years, he would never take air-conditioning and cool air for granted again. Indeed, he came to appreciate the cold winter months after spending the past year in New York City.

Before everyone in the audience took their seat, Blue found the source of the gardenia scent. Sitting a couple of rows behind him was Mele's private teacher from the Mannes School of Music's Pre-College Program, Donna Ledante. The five-foot force of the violin profession with intricately braided hair was adorned with a couple of leis of gardenia and purple hibiscus flowers—the colors of Vaimasina village. There was no doubt that Mele had made the leis and presented them to Donna before the concert just as she did for the orchestra who were excited to wear them, as long as they didn't interfere with their playing.

Donna Ledante was born on the island of Martinique in the Caribbean. Her father was a *béké*, a descendant of the original French settlers. Although *békés* constituted a small percentage of the island's population, they often felt like the local elite or royalty that should have certain privileges, much to the resentment and envy of the larger population of African Creole. After years of schooling in Paris, he returned to the island and took a mundane job with the Ministry of Education where he met Donna's mother, a Creole, who was teaching in one of the primary schools in the capital city of Fort de France. The two had a long courtship, mostly because of Donna's father's family's dislike of the relationship and their attempts to prohibit the couple from seeing each other. One of the ways they did this was by sending Donna's father to Paris for schooling. The couple, however, persevered as love often does, and were eventually married. Within a year of their marriage, Donna's mother became pregnant with their one and only child.

The Ledantes were music lovers and often sang in the church choir and played music with their neighbors or Donna's mother's family. When Donna was four years old, she saw a violin in a store window and asked her mother what it was. Her mother, who always encouraged music to her daughter, bought the instrument, and Donna's forty-year bond with the violin began. Finding a permanent teacher of the string instrument proved to be tough on the island, but thankfully there were many visiting musicians from France who came to Martinique on holiday. Donna's parents would often inveigle, sometimes charming these visitors with money and homecooked meals, to spend some time teaching their daughter. Thus, Donna had many teachers, who on occasion weren't even violin players, throughout her early musical learning years.

When Donna was eleven years old, her parents sought adventure and a new life away from the island. They moved to the Flatbush neighborhood of Brooklyn where her father took a job at Brooklyn College teaching classes on International Business, and her mother became a cook in one of the many Caribbean restaurants in the area. The family thrived and acquired many friends from the Caribbean and others who came from all walks of life. Although the family enjoyed living in the big city, they were often homesick and never missed a chance to visit family and friends when money and time allowed. Additionally, the return visits home gave Donna's father a chance to show his family that he was doing much better than working in a rote ministry position.

Donna continued her violin lessons, now with a more permanent teacher. Having a settled instructor, it only took a couple years to catch up on her theory and technique. Over time, the two created a bond that was more than just instructor and pupil. They became good friends, and Donna couldn't wait for her Tuesday evening lesson every week.

In Donna's freshman year of high school, her family's good fortune changed rather drastically. Her father lost his job at the college, and due to visa issues, couldn't find another one of equal or more importance. As he took to drinking, Donna's mother worked as many hours as she could get at the restaurant. She tried to get her husband to work at the restaurant as well, but he thought the job was beneath him and believed that drinking was more dignified. Despite the efforts of Donna's mother, the finances of the family began to rapidly dwindle. The return visits to Martinique ceased.

Each night, as Donna's parents fought over finances, sometimes these arguments turned violent, and Donna's mother was often beaten. Donna would block out her parents' fights the only way she knew how: by playing her violin. She always believed that even a screechy, out-of-tune violin sounded sweeter than arguing voices. She vowed that she would never raise her voice in anger to anyone for the rest of her life.

Donna's violin lessons were also compromised by her father's inability to find a new job. Her mother tried to pay for the lessons, but the deeper they grew in debt, the harder it became to have money for such extracurricular activities. Fortunately, Donna's teacher, who no doubt saw the potential in her student, would often accept late payments and provide a few free lessons. This was act of compassion would live with Donna for the rest of her life.

As the prospect of the Ledantes returning to Martinique to live grew more and more inevitable. Donna's father dove deeper into drinking and just floated lifeless like a worm in a tequila bottle. Not even neighborhood friends could free him from his depression. They even offered jobs, but he quickly dismissed them.

Almost a year after Donna's father lost his job at the college, his body was found in the East River. It was one of those sultry New York summer evenings when the news of his death swept through Flatbush. The Caribbean community never liked to learn of the loss of one of their own, even if the deceased person's attitude and behavior had changed so radically. Many people tried to deduce how he died. Some thought he owed money to the Mafia, while others believed he committed suicide. Most people, however, including Donna's mother, knew that it was simply an accidental death where he drowned while in a drunken stupor.

With the death of Donna's father, it was believed by many that Donna and her mother would return to Martinique. But they didn't. The next year was rough for the two as they tried to make ends meet and at the same time tried to make sense of the death of Donna's father. How did it go so wrong so fast? They moved in with some friends who were also from the Caribbean. Donna's mother continued with her job as a cook and added working at another restaurant. Money was still tight, and they practically lived paycheck to paycheck.

Eventually, Donna started returning regularly with her private music teacher. The violin also provided a much-needed distraction from the memory of her father. She finished high school and studied violin performance at Brooklyn College for a year before transferring to Julliard. While at Julliard, she was honored to perform all over Manhattan, including Carnegie Hall and the Lincoln Center. She continued with higher education at Julliard and the Mannes School of Music.

After a twenty-year stint in various violin roles, including concertmaster with the New York Philharmonic, Donna decided it was time to give back all that she knew about performing with the violin and teach students in higher education across Manhattan and Brooklyn. Her teaching technique and pedagogue became quite popular, and it wasn't long before students sought her as their private teacher. The number of students that she had to turn down over the years was staggering. But those who did get formal training from her would go on to professional careers.

It was at the International Violin Competition in Las Vegas when Donna first heard Mele play. At the time, Donna had added teaching in the Pre-College Program for the Mannes School of Music to her already busy schedule. The program was mostly for students from age five to seventeen who showed a proclivity towards playing an instrument. Nevertheless, on a previous holiday in Sin City, she had agreed to be a judge at the competition. Donna was one that never liked taking vacations, and at first, she didn't want to go Las Vegas and leave her students even for a short time. And after hearing the first few participants perform rather perfunctorily, she second-guessed herself with accepting to be a judge. She checked herself, however, and remembered that these kids were playing their hearts out. But when ten-year-old Mele walked on stage in her bare feet, an orange hibiscus behind her ear that matched her *pulesati*, and bracelets of seashells, played the first few measures of Antonio Vivaldi's "The Four Seasons," *Winter*, Allegro non molto, Donna's mouth dropped, her eyes widened, and her heart skipped beats and fell to her stomach. Never before had she ever seen anyone attack the piece like that with such aplomb, yet arrogance. Donna wondered if Mele was taught this (highly unlikely) or if this was the way the young violinist interpreted the piece. Regardless, Donna was speechless and pondered the thought of what this girl could do with a cadenza. When Mele finished playing her second piece, Franz Schubert's, *The Bee*, and her third piece, the first movement of Felix Mendelssohn's "Violin Concerto Op.64," Donna felt, once again, that it was an exquisite performance that would last in her memory for some time.

Mele would easily win the competition, as all the judges enthusiastically voted for the Samoan girl.

After the competition, Donna wanted to desperately meet Mele but was caught chit-chatting with the other judges and the competition organizers. All were magnanimously thanking the esteemed violinist and teacher for taking time from her busy schedule to grace them as a judge. Each time that Donna was almost in the clear, someone would approach her and talk about the art of teaching youth—all of which Donna found banal.

As Donna glanced at the contestants taking pictures on the stage, she tried to find Mele among the crowd. She noticed that many of the competition's participants were also wearing handmade bracelets. Donna thought how strange it was that the winner was not on stage taking pictures like the others, some of which didn't even place. Little did the professional violinist know that Mele always and enthusiastically headed straight to the back of the auditorium to find her father and show him how well she performed. Sometimes, she even forgot to bring her violin along with her.

Thinking that Mele had left the building, Donna finally (and, perhaps, a little rudely) excused herself from the others and went straight for the exit.

Rushing outside of the auditorium, Donna was instantly stunned by the brightness of the sun. A gust of warm wind slapped her in the face like a crossed lover.She quickly adjusted her vision to the light and saw Mele with a violin case slung across her back and carrying the first-place trophy, walking with an adult Caucasian man in the parking lot. She also noticed that the island girl was wearing sandals, a smart move considering the heat of the pavement. As the two walked further away, they blurred from a heatwave made from baking car oil that rose from the ground of the parking lot. Donna moved rapidly towards the two, hoping to catch them before they reached their car, and all along she tried to speculate who the man was— perhaps, he was the girl's private teacher.

Out of nowhere, a black Mustang pulled up in front of Mele and her father. The driver laid on the horn. The windows were down, and to Donna it looked as if there were a couple of large thugs in the car. One of the men in the car yelled in a language that Donna was not familiar with. Mele responded in the same language, and a great cheer came from the brutes in the car.

"Dudes, we're gonna have to put a seatbelt on this trophy," Blue shouted proudly after grabbing the trophy from his daughter and raising it in the air.

"Aiieee!"

"Let's hit the casinos," the man in the back said.

"You don't have any money," Blue answered.

"We're gonna use your money, bro."

"Shit. You'll just lose it. Then, how we are gonna pay for gas for this jalopy to get home?"

"Cuz, we'll win it," the driver said.

"Yeah, we gonna get rich!" the back seat man said, and the two high-fived each other.

"You two boneheads couldn't win a game of Go Fish," Blue jibed.

The pause at the Mustang gave Donna time to reach them.

"Excuse me," Donna said and cleared her voice. "Excuse me."

Blue and Mele turned around.

"Yes," Donna added.

"Hey! You were one of the judges," Mele said with excitement.

"Yes. Hi. My name be Donna Ledante. I was very impressed with the way you performed."

"She wants to take your trophy back," the backseat man said jokingly.

"Hush! Don't be rude," Mele shouted back in Samoan.

"I thought you played well beyond your young age, and I just wanted to thank you. Yes."

Mele was fascinated with Donna's Caribbean accent.

"I missed a note in the Vivaldi piece."

"You missed a few, but I didn't tell the other judges."

Mele giggled.

"I just thought the notes I used sounded better." Mele giggled again.

That just confirmed to Donna that the girl could be exceptional. She quickly pondered what the girl could do with a Paganini piece.

"Did you make your bracelet?" Donna asked.

"Oh! I made them for all the violinists. Would you like this one?"

"No, you keep it. You made it. It's your art, expression—artistic expression. Yes?"

Mele shrugged her shoulders. "I usually share what I make," she said.

The driver of the car honked the horn again.

"Bro, we're melting in here," the back seat man said.

"Okay, May, we better go," Blue ordered. "We got a long drive home."

"Yes, I was wondering if you would be interested in somethin'?" Donna asked rashly while digging into her purse. "I'm also, or mainly a..." She then checked herself. "Are you Mele's violin instructor?" she asked Blue.

Mele laughed.

"Huh? No. I'm her dad."

"Oh, my. I apologize. Your daughter be very talented."

"I know. She likes to remind us."

Mele started to playfully hit her father. "I'm not like that!"

Donna found what she was looking for in her purse, which was a business card.

"Yes. This be my card. Take a moment. I teach in the pre-college program at the Mannes School. We'd love to have Mele join us this fall."

Blue took the card and examined it. Mele eagerly tried to look at the card as if it was something she had never seen before, like a block of gold.

Donna was never one to recruit students. In fact, most music schools in the country rarely take the time to engage with youth recitals, orchestras, and competitions. Typically, the student must go to the music school to prove his or her merit through a series of auditions to be accepted into a program. But there were, rarely, exceptions.

"She's only ten," Blue said, not trusting the card, or Donna Ledante.

"The program be for ages five to before they enter college. It's mainly a weekend program."

"You're in New York City," Blue added with just a slight tone of disgust.

"New York City," Mele said with excitement. She had heard of the place before in school, and she had seen glossy, colorful pictures of the city in books. "Where's that?"

"It's far from the Pacific Ocean, Mele,"

Blue let his daughter keep the card, a sign that he didn't need to bother with any more discussion about the program.

"Thank you. We'll look into it more when we get home," Blue lied.

"Yes, by all means. Please review our website. It will answer many of your questions, or question many of our answers. Yes. I believe your daughter would do extremely well with us."

Blue went to the car and got into the front seat. The two men got excited with anticipation that they were finally leaving.

Mele and Donna stood staring at each other in the hot parking lot. They could feel the cool air in their nostrils.

Although the two were from two disparate cultures, they were both island girls and there was a certain bond, an inquisitive interest in each other that instantly formed at that moment in a parking lot of a Las Vegas auditorium. Sometimes a person's life-changing moment could happen in the most inauspicious place. One person came from a Caribbean island while the other came from a Pacific island, and together they met by chance in the middle. Nonetheless, there was a connection that the two could feel.

"Did you make the braids in your hair?" Mele asked.

"I did, yes. My mother taught me how to make them when I was about your age."

Mele smiled. She understood. There was so much that her own mother had taught her in Samoa.

The car honked.

Mele waved with her fingers to Donna. She went to the car, but then quickly returned to Donna and shook her hand.

"*Toe feiloai*," Mele said in Samoan and then returned to the car.

Donna watched the Mustang speed away, practically before Mele's butt was even in the seat. She thought that the chance of them meeting each other again was slim, but at least she got to share this moment.

Once the car was out of sight, Donna opened her hand to reveal a bracelet that the Samoan girl had worn during the competition. Donna smiled and tied the bracelet on her wrist before heading back into the auditorium.

***

As everyone settled into their seats in the Stern Auditorium at Carnegie Hall, it looked as though the only two people left standing were Blue and Donna. They looked at each other, and Donna gave a nod of proud approval for her prodigy's performance. Donna had always thought that Blue was a little off and couldn't quite make out what his profession was. Over the past year and half, he just seemed to float in and out of his daughter's rehearsal. She grew more intrigued with the young man, especially once she learned that he was writing a novel, the plot of which sounded like the story of the movie, *Titanic*. But she never said that out loud and encouraged him to push himself and finish it. "Art doesn't want to just sit on a laptop, Ronin," she would say a few times to him. "It wants out to live and breathe."

There was one other occasion where Donna became impressed with Blue. On a day when the subway seemed to be knotted with delays, Donna was late arriving at her Mannes studio for her lesson with Mele. As she hurriedly approached the room, a sweet rendition of Charlie Chaplin's, *Smile,* was coming from her studio and forced her pace to a slow walk. Before entering the room, she paused at the door to listen to the duo for a second or two. She tried to conjecture which piano teacher was filling the time and playing along with Mele until she arrived.

The song was performed quite exquisitely so that it sounded as if the duo had played together more than once. It had an unpredictable, whimsical tone and attitude and Donna felt that could have been performed in front of an audience in any of New York's concert halls.

She decided to wait until the end before opening the door. When she did, she wasn't surprised to see Mele holding her violin, but she was a bit stunned to see Blue sitting at the piano.

Blue stood immediately from the piano and looked as if he just got his hands caught in the cookie jar.

"That was lovely," Donna said, putting her purse and satchel on top of the piano. "Ronin, take a moment. I didn't know that played piano."

"I don't play much anymore. I just try to keep up with her."

Donna thought what a wonderful metaphor that was but was afraid to wonder about its hidden truth.

"Would you two honor me and perform that tune again?"

"It's *tamā's* favorite," Mele said.

"Yes?"

"It was the first song we played together," Mele added.

"Yes. Astonishing. I could hear that you've obviously have played it a million times together."

"We don't even need music anymore."

"I love those first songs. They have such a place in our hearts, don't they? Yes. They be like a... like a first kiss, aren't they?"

Mele giggled.

It was the sound of the door closing that forced Donna to turn around, and she noticed that Blue wasn't in the room.

"Oh! I guess he had somewhere to be. Yes?" Donna said.

"He doesn't have anywhere to be."

"He left so quickly that a melody played on the piano by the wind of his leavin'.'"

"Should I get out the Bruch piece?"

"No. Let's continue with pieces that lie like ghosts in the back of our minds. Yes? That's where the music be today."

Donna paused, staring at the door. Perhaps Blue only stepped out for a minute to get some water or something. After a minute or two, it was apparent that he was not going to return.

---

It was Mele's voice from the stage that forced Blue and Donna to quickly take their seats in the Stern Auditorium.

"*Talofa* everyone. *Talofa lava*," Mele said into the microphone. "Sometimes my teacher, Ms. Donna Ledante, likes me to dig deep in my memory and play songs from my village that I learned from my mother and aunties. Ms. Donna thinks it's calming and therapeutic. They're not so calming and therapeutic playing here in front of all of you."

The audience laughed with Mele.

"Tonight, I'd like to play a couple of those songs—one now and one later. This one is kinda the unofficial anthem of Samoa, and it sounds pretty cool rearranged to include a full orchestra. I hope you like it."

Mele handed the microphone to the conductor, grabbed her violin, and enthusiastically brought it up to her chin. But then she remembered something that she was supposed to say. She dropped her violin to her side and went back to the conductor, asking him for the microphone. He turned it on for her. A muffled "awl," rose from the audience.

"Sorry. I forgot to tell you the name of the song. It's called, *Uso Samoa*. Uhm- 'We Are Samoa.' Thank you. *Samoa, e pele oe I si ou fatu*."

The audience cheered.

The old lady sitting next to Blue leaned towards him and stated, "She's so adorable."

Written in the 1970s, "We Are Samoa," had been covered many times. Although the song had aged, the revival with a full orchestra and Mele leading the way on violin gave the song a new and bright, yet nostalgic tone. In fact, being performed on these kinds of instruments gave the song a newer, classy edge that most Samoans would agree had been long overdue.

Blue shifted in his seat in search of a more comfortable position that didn't make his side hurt as much. Once he found the right spot, he was able to concentrate on the piece that Mele and the orchestra was performing. Blue knew the lyrics to "We Are Samoa," in Samoan and he tried to sing along underneath his breath. He particularly liked the phrase that voiced, "Oh! What happy feelings from such happy people. We Are Samoa," and he longed for that first year living in idyllic Vaimasina. Indeed, it was a happy time existing predominantly among harmoniously good-natured people. He never believed that a place like that existed.

Towards the end of the song, the young woman sitting

to Blue's right grabbed his hand. It was cold and wet like mushy ice, but he didn't pull his hand away. He couldn't recall the last time a woman held his hand. He thought that the young woman was either being fresh with him, or she was moved by the music from the stage. Whichever was the reason, he didn't care.

However, the hand felt strange to Blue. It got colder and squishier. He furtively looked at the hand, not wanting to make a big deal of it, and to his horror, he saw that the flesh was peeling right off the bone. It was a gruesome sight, and a sickening feeling overcame him. He felt as if he was in the middle of a grotesque urban legend. He quickly pulled his hand away at the same time the woman leaned her stinky, stringy head of seaweed on his shoulder.

Blue suddenly and shockingly recognized that it was Scarlett.

Blue quickly jolted out of his seat just as Mele and the orchestra finished playing. The audience applauded and many people joined Blue in giving a standing ovation. Blue looked around at others as they stood and then looked back at Scarlett who had disappeared. The young woman, however, was leering at Blue with a queer expression on her face as she slowly stood to join her girlfriends in the ovation.

Mele and the conductor took their bows and then showed their appreciation to one another, the orchestra, and the audience, as Blue sat back down in his seat. The beauty and innocence of "We Are Samoa" had now ended, and the conclusion of the song made him feel that he was a long way from that first year in Samoa.

He felt a long way from California.

He felt a long way from the audience in Carnegie Hall.

He felt a long way from Mele.

The intermission lights of the auditorium rose like the sun rose in Vaimasina—bright, full of optimism, and warmth for the coming day. Blue sat apprehensively in his seat. He worried about what the future held for him, Mele, and for him with Mele. He always admired those who solely lived in the present. Nevertheless, he truly believed that the future would be nothing like living in Samoa.

As the audience continued their cheer, Blue sat in Row M, M for Mele, Seat 112 and stared into the backs of the people standing in front of him. When Scarlett leaned her salty, sea-foaming head on Blue's shoulder again, he didn't jump or jolt from his seat. Instead, he stroked hair soggy hair and enjoyed the now because he had no idea how long the now would last.

17

———————

Blue felt a poke at his leg and a shake of his shoulder. He opened his eyes and shot up in his chair. He thought he heard the words, "Mr. *Lanu Moana,*" and looked around for frivolous students looking for some fun. However, all he saw was Aumua inquisitively staring at him. Blue stood up, trying to hide the fact that he was sleeping on the job.

"I, uh...was just wait-waiting for my students," Blue stammered with embarrassment.

"There aren't any students," Aumua responded with a quirky smile.

"Huh?"

"They all went home about an hour ago."

*Damn Me.*

Blue pathetically looked at Aumua.

*Did I really waste a day sleeping and almost getting crushed by a piano?*

Aumua smiled as if she heard his thoughts. She then picked up his backpack and shoved it into his chest.

"We have to go," she commanded.

"Where?"

"The forest," she said. "Father wants me to teach you Samoan."

Blue wasn't really in the mood to go for a walk in the steaming jungle. He envisioned himself returning to his *fale*, having a shower, changing his clothes, and working on his novel until it was time to head over to Fiame's home for dinner—wherever she lived. He didn't dare want to not show up. His absence would just open himself up to more questions the next time he saw her. Nevertheless, he was used to doing things he didn't feel like doing. His mother always made him start practicing piano or interrupted his alone time in his room to go to a show or a movie. He'd complain at first, but then would eventually enjoy the occasion.

Aumua led him on a very well-trodden path in the Samoan jungle just beyond the grassy field of the village. The late afternoon sun streamed sunrays through the tropical foliage in the hopes of completing its path to the earth. Some of the larger leaves leaked droplets from the storm earlier in the day. Birds chattered and clattered in the trees above, and every once in a while, one would swoop past the couple and reposition itself for an afternoon snack on a branch.

Aumua and Blue were quiet as they made their way along the path. Blue wondered where they were going and thought, perhaps, that she was leading him to some kind of romantic *fale* or building in the bush where she would teach him Samoan. At first, Blue marveled at the tropical foliage of the idyllic forest but became even more enamored by his host. He couldn't help noticing how Aumua seemed so at ease and cool in her natural habitat. Her long black hair was pinned up in a bun on the top of her head, and beads of sweat formed on the back of her neck. Blue was particularly enchanted that she was wearing yellow and white frangipani flowers behind her right ear. He wasn't sure if was her or the jungle, or both, that smelled fragrant and fresh.

The silence was killing Blue. He tried to think of something to say, or a joke to tell. He never learned how to flirt and often would blurt out a random *faux pas*. Sometimes he would even recognize it when it happened.

"Why can't you play cards in the jungle?" Blue asked her.

Aumua stopped next to a copse of banana plants and turned to him. Blue wasn't quite sure if she heard him, but he, nonetheless answered his own joke.

"Because there are too many cheetahs."

Blue smiled proudly at the old standard joke. Aumua only stared at him, then turned her attention to a bunch of bananas hanging from the plant.

"Tough crowd," Blue added as if speaking to himself.

*God, I'm such a moron. Cheetahs don't even live in Samoa.*

Blue wiped the sweat off his face with the bottom of his shirt.

Aumua reached for the right banana and separated it from the rest of the bunch. She held it up to Blue.

"*Fa'i,*" said Aumua.

"Banana," acknowledged Blue. Aumua shook her head.

"*Fa'i.*"

"*Fa'i,*" Blue responded.

Aumua smiled and then peeled the banana and took a couple of bites. Blue was instantly infatuated and tried to clear the dirty thoughts that flooded his mind.

*Oh God.*

"*'Ai,*" the village vixen stated.

"*'Ai,*" Blue repeated.

"Eat. *'Ai.*"

"*'Ai.*"

A butterfly fluttered by. Aumua pointed to it and said, "*pepe.*"

"*Pepe* is butterfly."

Aumua smiled and nodded. "*Pepe* also means baby."

The two continued this interactive learning game as they made their way through the bush. Blue learned the Samoan for every animal, bird, insect, tree, shrub, flower, and environmental conditions they encountered. For Aumua, who was closely tied to the land like many of the villagers, it was most important for her to teach from the land. The Samoan pleasantries and formalities, she believed, he would learn during the course of daily life within the village.

Blue never had an affinity for learning different languages. He took two years of high school Spanish and was fairly adequate. He also took one semester of German in college, which he barely passed and vowed never to return for another semester. He knew he was in trouble in that class when he invariably kept spelling the word, "*ja,*" with a "y"—ya. Even the word, "*sí,*" in Spanish was so much easier to remember.

However, Blue enjoyed learning Samoan. He thought words and phrases had a certain poetic rhythm that made the language easy to learn and speak. He would put much more effort into learning the language, not only because he wanted to impress Aumua, but he also wanted to engage with the villagers. Blue knew that they would rather communicate in their own language rather than to take the time to translate sentences in English in their mind. Besides, he knew he would be spending the next two years in the country and didn't want to be always treated like a *palagi*.

Aumua eventually led him to the natural, crescent moon-shaped pool of freshwater where the village received its namesake. The area mesmerized Blue. A small waterfall trickled down from the verdant mountains, and tropical foliage dangled over parts of the water and cast soothing shadows that constantly changed and shifted with the movement of the sun. A couple of large boulders made excellent diving boards. With the exception of the ripples that the waterfall created at its base, the water was crystal clear. The pool was teeming with fish, shrimp, and the occasional eel. A narrow stream rushed away into the jungle and found the sea a half mile from the village. The bucolic landscape looked like a scene out of a James Norman Hall novel.

Blue was transfixed by the pool's inviting call. He licked his lips as the scent of the waterfall cascading on a group of jagged rocks. He wanted to rip off his clothes and splash in the refreshing spring.

*Can I just skinny-dip now?*

Aumua realized that she had lost her student. She stopped with the lesson and quickly dove into the water, which broke Blue's trance. He watched her resurface, giggling and splashing water towards him. Blue thought about Aumua's ancestors who came to the pool over the generations to cool off, bathe, and catch a tasty snack. Aumua playfully began goading him in Samoan to jump into the water. It didn't take much to convince him to have a swim. He started taking off his shirt, forcing Aumua to turn around in the water.

"Keep your clothes on, please," demanded Aumua.

"Clothes on?"

There was a time before the missionaries arrived when the villagers swam and frolicked in the pool while naked. But these days they swam with their clothes on. Rarely do they even own a swimsuit and feel more comfortable jumping in the water fully dressed.

Blue did as commanded and dove into the crisp, invigorating water. Since he hadn't had a shower in several days, the pool felt extra cleansing.

It was a perfect way to end the hot day, and Blue thought about coming here every chance he got. He turned on his back and floated, his arms and legs spread like a starfish.He stared at the coconut trees swaying high and bending toward the water. The moon in its half stage appeared when the trees separated. Blue squirted water from his teeth and was quite relaxed in this tranquil and serene place until Aumua whimsically snuck up to him and dunked him underneath the water. Blue was amazed how the stern teacher had become playful, and how comfortable she quickly became in front of him. Blue resurfaced and retaliated by splashing water at her. A splash fight ensued like two kids in a suburban backyard pool until their arms got tired.

"There's a legend with this pool and how the first coconut tree came to Samoa," Aumua said proudly. "Of course, every village in Samoa will tell the same story and argue over who truly owns it."

"Legends and myths are largely made of truths—Tolkien," Blue quoted.

Aumua looked at him quizzically and continued.

"There was this beautiful girl named Sina, who had a pet eel that fell in love with her. This made Sina afraid, so she tried to run away, but the eel followed her. Sina thought she had escaped the eel. But one day when she was gathering water from the village pool, she was shocked to find the eel staring up at her."

"Whoa. If an eel looked at me, I'd run."

"Angrily, Sina said, *E pupula mai, ou mata ole alelo!*"

"Which means?"

"You stare at me with eyes like a demon!"

"Of course."

"The village chiefs came and killed the eel," continued Aumua. "Before dying, the eel asked Sina to bury its head. With remorse, Sina agreed to the eel's request. From the site of the eel's head burial, a coconut tree grew. When removing the husk from a coconut, there are three distinct round marks that appear like a face of the eel. Legend says every time Sina drinks from the coconut, she kissed the eel."

"Eeww," was Blue's only remark.

"I guess we're all like Sina."

Twilight in the tropics tiptoes in quietly, and darkness falls like a quick curtain. Aumua's senses knew it was time to leave the pool. For one reason, darkness in the bush was a time when mischievous spirits, or *aitus*, roamed freely, looking for mortal souls to scare, play with, or look for revenge toward those who disrespected them. But perhaps, more importantly, it was almost *Sa* time and the elders of the *aiga* always frowned upon those who were late to this nightly prayer.

"We must leave, Mr. Ronin."

"Now? But it's so nice," Blue pleaded, looking at the shadows of the palm trees cast by the moon.

"*Aitus!*"

Blue looked fervently in the water.

"Huh? What is that? Piranha or something?"

Aumua was now out of the water.

"Come! *Aitus!*" yelled the village girl, knowing that choosing ghosts as the reason to leave would be more dramatic and should make her naïve companion move more quickly.

The excitement in Aumua's tone was enough for Blue to hurry out of the water.

"We should not be here. *Aitus.*"

"What's an *aitu?*" asked Blue.

"Spirits."

Aumua began walking back to the village at a brisk pace. Blue followed her closely. His heavy clothes made it difficult to keep up with her, and a chill traveled down his spine.

As the night descended upon the couple, strange noises emitted from jungle's darkness all around them. This only hastened Aumua's steps. Blue believed that it was only birds or the wind whistling through the foliage. Regardless of what was making the noises, Blue didn't want to stick around in the bush. He had seen too many horror movies of creatures attacking innocent people in the forest. Aumua's apprehensive reaction was good enough for him to return to the village as quickly as possible.

By the time the two made it to the grassy field, the bells of the church began to ring, signifying the beginning of the *Sa*. Hearing the church bells, Aumua began to run to her house and was closely followed by Blue.

*Why am I always trying to keep up with everyone?*

Before Aumua dove into her home, Blue stopped her.

"Wait. I'm supposed to go to Fiame's."

"Fiame's *fale* is down that road on the right."

"Thank- *fa'afetai*," Blue said, hoping to impress his teacher.

"*Ou te tulimatai atu i taeao*," which she translated, "I look forward to tomorrow." She smiled, rinsed out water from her long hair, and hurriedly went inside her house.

18

The German composer Max Bruch's Violin Concerto No.1 in G minor, Op.26 was (and still is) one of his most beloved orchestral pieces. The piece possessed quite the passionate orchestral writing that was admired by violinists for its melodies. In the Romantic period of the mid-19th century and early 20th century, the piece was so popular that Bruch himself would become annoyed when he received invitation after invitation to perform it. In modern times, however, young amateurs learning the instrument to seasoned professionals loved the concerto and eagerly learned to perform one to all three of the piece's movements.

Mele Blue absolutely adored the first movement of the concerto—Vorspeil, allegro moderato. She had a habit of practicing it with verve, attacking the themes of the short movement with conviction and style way beyond her twelve years. Sometimes, much to Donna Ledante's chagrin, she played the movement too fast, which was a common tendency among young, overzealous performers. Tonight, however, would Mele have to keep up with the orchestra, or would the orchestra have to keep up with her, or would there be complete synergy between the two? The latter seemed to be winning at the moment.

Blue looked at the audience to his left and then to his right and couldn't help but notice that everyone was completely engaged with the barefoot violinist. He noticed how his daughter had such stage presence and always did even in her younger days competing. Mele's body movement with each note was full of passion and ardor, and Blue could remember how her first private instructor tried to get her to play standing still to no avail. Perhaps, it was Mele's upbringing when she learned the different *sivas* in Samoa and then later attaching these constant and poetic movement of hands, hips and feet, particularly the feet, to the European orchestral compositions that made it difficult for her to play the violin standing still.

*The hula meets Haydn.*

Blue chuckled to himself. Only the woman in front of him slightly turned her head when she heard his quick, yet discourteous outburst. Blue, nonetheless, kept to his thoughts and remembered when Mele was performing Antonio Vivaldi's *Summer,* from The Four Seasons at a competition and used the entire stage. He was told that during this performance, she closed her eyes during the delicate segments of the piece and came dangerously close to swaying herself off the stage. The judges sitting in the front room would throw their arms up ready to break her fall. The audience gasped every time she flirted with the edge of the stage.

On this evening, however, the audience was gasping for a different reason. They were amazed that a preteen girl in bare feet was performing a difficult piece with such passion and professionalism. They have seen their fair share of young prodigies grace the stages of Carnegie Hall. This wasn't just a violinist—this was Mele Blue. This was her stage and her party. And this was her announcement that she had come forth to share her talent with the world.

Sitting in Seat 112 of Row M, Blue enjoyed feeling the audience's admiration for his daughter's performance. For all of Mele's competitions and recitals, Blue never sat in the audience for fear of hearing her slip up. He usually waited outside, or backstage, or in the foyer of a theater while she performed. But even waiting in these off places, he knew when Mele was playing. He always recognized her style, tone, and desire. After the competition, she would seek out her father to show him the trophy or the medal that she had just won. Mele never slipped up or made a mistake, and Blue would try to remember this during the subsequent competitions. But it was futile. As soon the first violinist took the stage, he would leave and wait until his daughter eventually found him.

As Mele played the closing measures of the first movement, Blue glanced at the old couple next to him. Every note engrossed the old lady. She was moving her hand to the rhythm of the melody like a backseat conductor. Her husband, however, was settled into his chair and out cold, his chin resting peacefully on his chest. Over the past few years, his seat at Carnegie Hall had been one of the best places for him to take a nap.

When the first movement ended, a hushed awe and

admiration ensued over the audience. Seconds later, a group of first-time symphony goers began to clap, which triggered a rippling effect on other newbies to applaud, including the three young ladies to Blue's right. This instantly woke up the old man who probably wondered if the performance had ended. Blue could overhear words such as, "bravo" and "wow" coming from people sitting near him. He even heard one of the young ladies next to him ask her friends if Mele's feet were cold.

Naturally, Blue didn't make an effort to applaud, though he wanted to. His broken hand was hurting, but he also knew the etiquette of not clapping in between movements. He thought about foregoing this courteous restraint. After all, this was his Mele on the stage—his half-Samoan daughter looking as radiant as a polished pearl. She simply amazed. She had spent twelve years and traveled over seven thousand miles to entertain the people tonight. It was a long and often troublesome journey, and Blue wanted to cheer for her. He wanted to clap for her hard work and devotion. But he couldn't. He wasn't a green patron of the arts, and this wasn't a schoolroom recital. This was Mele Blue at Carnegie Hall.

*Save it for the end.*

He wondered if he should've bought her flowers for the close of tonight's performance. He had never bought her flowers before. He could never afford it. Mele would've loved flowers. She was a child from the land—practically born from the land. Like all Samoans, she was simply in tune with her environment, respecting what it provides and takes away. Blue liked to believe that his daughter's silky black hair was made from flower petals.

*Damn me.*

Mele didn't bow or even acknowledge the admiration from the audience. Instead, she started the second movement—the adagio, with much aplomb and concentration. It was a heartfelt and warm movement filled with beautiful melodies. It wouldn't take many measures before the old lady next to Blue began to tear up. Blue always believed that adagios, when beautifully played, were meant to make the listener cry. They could summon lost loved ones, provoke memories that a person does and doesn't even have, and momentarily numb any physical and mental pain. In fact, Blue was astonished that he temporarily couldn't feel the pulsating pain of his broken nose and the shiner around his eye.

Unsurprisingly, the old man didn't have a chance staying awake against the poignant strains of the violin. Blue wondered what the sleeping man was dreaming about. Adagios have a way of metaphysically transferring one to a desired time and place to fulfill a fantasy. Blue noticed the old man's head drop with a jerk and bounce back. A definite smile formed on his face.

*Wherever he is, he's not gonna wanna leave.*

Blue then noticed that the three young women were sitting stiff and still as stones. This was the first time the trio had stopped fidgeting in their seats. Undoubtedly, Blue thought, they were thinking of an unrequited or current lover. Perhaps, two of the three want to express their fond affection for the other. With a slight look, Blue surreptitiously anticipated to see if the middle woman would hold hands with either of her seatmates. Adagios create romance, and Blue found himself looking longer at the young women.

As Mele passionately navigated her way through the movement, Blue leaned closer to the young woman next to him. His eyes were firmly on the hands of the woman sitting in the middle. He knew that adagios had a way of bringing people together, and he wanted to hold her hand. It had been a long time since he held a woman's hand. Indeed, he believed he was being a little perverted, but he wanted to see romance unfold. He knew that lovers across the auditorium would be frozen arm in arm, hand in hand, head on head. Blue wanted Mele to create this romance, to bring people, lovers, together.

*Like the Pied Piper.*

Blue thought about that.

*Wait. That fairytale dude played some stupid flute or something.*

Blue's fantasy felt as if it was becoming a reality when he realized that the old lady grabbed his hand to hold. The hand was cold, and Blue thought he was holding crushed ice. He leaned back in his seat and looked at the old lady whose attention was solely given to Mele. He saw a single teardrop trickling down her cheek and decided that he would not pull his hand away despite having a broken finger from the fracas of a couple days earlier. Instead, he squeezed her hand harder with the hopes of, perhaps, warming her up a little.

Blue turned his focus to his daughter on stage and was proud to see how she was impeccably performing the movement. He could remember sitting in on Mele's private lesson one rainy day a couple of weeks ago with her private teacher, Donna Ledante, in the pre-college program at the Mannes School of Music. Mele was practicing the adagio when Donna stopped her and asked her what she was thinking about while she played.

"My mother," Mele answered.

"Yes. Take a moment. What about her?" Donna asked in a Caribbean accent.

"It reminds me how I left her."

After seven years, it was the first time that Blue ever heard his daughter blame herself for leaving Aumua.

"Don't you think your mother can feel that you're always with her?" Donna asked.

"Oh, yes. But not like an *aitu*."

"A what?"

"A ghost. Sometimes I could feel her hugging me."

"A mother's hug be a wonderful feelin'. I'm fifty-one years old and I can still feel my mother's hug."

"Really?"

"Yes. And to interpret the music as a mother's hug is beautiful, Mele. Yes? It be human, emotion, devotion."

"Well, it's like, when I play this movement, I feel like each note flies to my mother and swirls around her. And each note keeps swirling around her until all the notes of the movement join them and wrap around her like a hug. It's like my way to tell her that I love her and that I'm with her."

Donna smiled, impressed by the young prodigy's intuitiveness. Donna looked at Blue, who shared a quick glance back.

"Yes. Thank you for sharin', Mele," Donna said, a bit humbled. "I have no doubt that's what happens. Yes."

Blue stared at Mele on stage and thought that if anyone

could transcend musical notes to a distant land, it would be Mele. He envisioned the notes that she was playing rising in the air and traveling across the country and the ocean to her mother. Blue could see Aumua trying to catch each note and never letting go. Aumua would be the kind of mother who would wrap the notes around her like a sarong and wear it with such delight and pride throughout the village. Everyone would ask Aumua for permission to wear the sarong just to feel, sense, and smell Mele again.

The melodious, yet melancholy melodies of the adagio began to haunt Blue. The rich tones that Mele was producing from the violin reminded him of his only friend, Scarlett Wang, who liked playing profound and complicated mellow pieces on the cello. Blue was always amused by her total concentration on a piece and her total devotion to practicing the cello. He enjoyed the challenge of making her laugh, which he achieved on rare occasions, and only when Scarlett was in the mood.

Unfortunately, Mele's playing didn't help Blue reminisce about the good times he had with Scarlett growing up. He didn't remember the days they frolicked at the cove, or played in the backyard, or practiced music together until she or her parents kicked him out of her house for misbehaving and losing concentration from the music. Instead, Blue could only remember seeing the dead Scarlett on that stormy night at his *fale* in the early days of being in Samoa. He could recall Scarlett's whitish-green face and blood-red eyes forlornly staring at him through the slats of the blinds. The moment scared the hell out of him. It still does.

Blue tried to remember something positive, something wonderful, or something funny from his time with Scarlett.

But he couldn't. The music wouldn't allow him to have any fond memories. It was her ghoulish face, her death mask that he only thought about.

*Damn me, and damn you, Mele.*

Blue believed that he should've let Scarlett into his *fale* that night because that was what she wanted. He left her out in the rain—out in death. But he now thought that she wanted to be with him. He felt guilty and sad about that night. He turned away from her and didn't look. It was just like her death at Sabatini's Beach when he wasn't paying attention. She was trying to reach out to him, and he ignored her. Blue was afraid of Scarlett after that stormy night in his *fale*.

He tried to stop thinking about Scarlett.

But the music—the way Mele played only heightened his shame and his guilt.

*Adagios are so damn unforgiving.*

# ACKNOWLEDGMENTS

I'm very grateful to have the support in creating a project of this magnitude. I can't express my deepest gratitude and appreciation enough for publisher, Frank Eastland, and the team at Publish Authority for their genuine dedication and hard work bringing the written words to book format. Not to sound cliché, but it truly takes "a village" to produce a publication. I also must add a very heartfelt and profound recognition to Janie Mills for her diligent and constructive editing work on the book. Her professional scrutiny helped the story be told even better. A special thanks has to be given to Melissa Fisher and Reaghan Rebstock, respectively. They devote many hours throughout the year promoting and making my books accessible to the public.

Additionally, I would be remiss if I didn't acknowledge my friend and colleague Simi Tanielu in Samoa. I cherished our time talking about the Samoan culture over a cup of *Koko Samoa* that Simi's mother prepared for us from the coco trees in her backyard.

Another individual that I'd like to call out is Jared Chou for his passionate research on Ragtime piano players.

A sincere appreciation definitely needs to be given to my wife, Shannon, for her patience and love of me for taking over the kitchen table and working late into the evening on occasion.

I also have to recognize my daughter, Devin, whose continued, enthusiastic exploration of violin performance has been an inspiration to the story.

I also must convey an honest acknowledgement for the time I spent writing the novel in the many lonely motel and hotel rooms in Fiji, Kiribati, Samoa, and Thailand, as well as American cities from California to New York.

And, finally, I have to give a barky thanks to my biggest fans- my dogs: Daphne, Dutch, and Finny. When I worked outside, they sat devotedly by my side eagerly wondering what was going to happen on the next page... okay, more likely, they were just wondering when suppertime would roll around..

# ABOUT THE AUTHOR

Brandon Oswald is a native Southern Californian who has never lived far from the ocean; he became fascinated with stories of adventure in the South Seas at an early age. His interest in the culture and history of the Pacific Islands was heightened by a volunteer trip to Rarotonga, Cook Islands in 2002. There, he had the privilege of organizing and cataloging the material of several different kinds of libraries throughout the island, including facilities at a college, a primary school, and a public library. Brandon obtained his Master's degree in Archives and Records Management at the University of Dundee, Scotland, where he developed skills in preserving records of enduring value. His experiences inspired him to create the nonprofit organization, Island Culture Archival Support (ICAS), where he currently serves as the Executive Director and Archivist. ICAS provides voluntary archival assistance to cultural heritage organizations in the Pacific Islands. Brandon has volunteered at various archives, libraries, and museums in the Pacific Islands, helping these organizations preserve their records, heritage and history. He has served all over the region, including Kiribati and Palau in Micronesia, Fiji, Solomon Islands, and Vanuatu in Melanesia, and the Cook Islands and Samoa in Polynesia.

Additionally, Brandon is the author of the books *Mr. Moonlight of the South Seas: The Extraordinary Life of Robert Dean Frisbie,* and *The Darkland: A Melanesian Experience.* He has had several articles published in archival newsletters and has had the honor of publishing several papers regarding cultural preservation in the Pacific Islands for major international conferences. These papers include *Partnership in Paradise: The Importance of Collaboration for Handling Traditional Cultural Expression Material in the Pacific Islands, Keeping the Canoe Afloat: Project Sustainability in Pacific Islands Cultural Heritage Organizations* and *The "Aloha" Archives: A Nonprofit Organization's View of Collaboration, Peace and Harmony in Cultural Heritage Organizations in the Pacific Islands.*

# GLOSSARY

## SAMOAN TO ENGLISH

*aiga*: family

*aitu*: ghost

*ali'i*: high chief

*alofa*: love

*'ava*: beverage made from the Piper methysticum plant

*Fa'a Samoa*: the Samoan way of doing things

*fa'afafine*: in the manner of a woman, a third gender

*fa'apapa*: sweet coconut bread

*faafetai (lava)*: thank you (very much)

*fale*: house

*fale tele*: meeting house or big house

*ioe*: yes

*lavalava*: a sarong-like garment, a wrap

*leai*: no

*malie*: shark

*malu*: traditional female tattoo

*matai*: chief

*moana*: ocean

*Ou te alofa ia te oe*: I love you

*oka i'a*: raw fish marinated in lemon juice and coconut milk

*paepae*: stone foundation of a fale

*palusami*: coconut milk baked in taro leaves

*panikeke*: Samoan pancake

*palagi*: European, white man

*puletasi*: traditional item of clothing worn by Samoan women and girls

*sa*: daily curfew at dusk for 30 minutes for prayer

*sapasui-* Samoan chop suey

*sau loa*: Come on

*siapo*: traditional fabric, art

*siva*: Samoan dance

*soifua manaia*: Good luck

*tala*: Western Samoa's currency

*talo*: taro

*talofa (lava)*: hello

*tamá*: father

*tanoa*: wooden bowl used for mixing 'ava

*tatau*: tattoo

*Teine Sa*: spirit women

*tina*: mother

*toe feiloai*: see you again

*tofa*: goodbye

*toonai*: Sunday morning meal, brunch

*tulafale*: orator chief

*'ula*: necklace

*ulu*: breadfruit

*umu*: earth oven

# THANK YOU FOR READING

If you enjoyed *M for Mele*, Book 1 of *The Barefoot Serenade* trilogy, we invite you to share your thoughts and reactions online and with friends and family.

Publish Authority

www.ingramcontent.com/pod-product-compliance
Lightning Source LLC
Chambersburg PA
CBHW070618300726
48975CB00006B/1859